Los Angelt

New Prison Reform Could Not Come ~~~~ ~~~~

Taylor Price, March 31, 2037

Prisoners were said to be the lost children of our society. They went unseen, unheard, having to rely on the parents in the system for all their needs—clothes, food, and medicine. Yet unlike real parents, those people were not concerned about the well-being of those in their care, but rather on the ease of their role, the wage at the end of the month and whatever "extras" they could glean from the prisoners themselves.

Prison guards literally held all the keys in the world of the inmate and could decide on what, if any, privileges they received. A barter system existed where those who paid the most had the greatest freedom; where the drug barons, corporate fraudsters, and the wealthy lived a life of luxury while those charged with lesser crimes, but were poor, suffered the most.

This reporter was not only given evidence of this corrupt hierarchy, but also of the "money for lives" deals that were rife within the justice system. A system where roommate changes that led to murders, accidental deaths and even wholesale torture could be bought from guards on a sliding scale. This was reported in the exposé that shook the foundations of the system seven years ago.

The year that followed saw the then Chief Justice, Jack Greenslade, try to get a handle on the situation by dismissing 272 prison guards across the country, which had little impact for the 4998 prisoners who died in custody the following year.

The Prisoner Lives Matter (PLM) campaign that erupted across the nation threatened to bring the country to a standstill with mass walkouts, disrupted road and rail networks, and the refusal of people to cooperate with any law enforcement agency. This led to an unprecedented U-turn by the President, who signed into effect the first of a series of laws that would completely change the way the prison service operated.

1

With the introduction of the first guard-less prison here in California, there came more uproar. Firstly, in who the contracts for these prisons went to—friends and business interests of sitting congressmen—and then at the impersonal treatment of the prisoners inside. One thing is for sure, with zero murders in these prisons in the past five years, they are here to stay. They just didn't come soon enough for the tens of thousands who'd died before.

However, the disparity between the youth provision and the adult service is as stark as that of the U.S. and any third-world country. The facility of the former include online courses, daily exercise, online counseling, and a fast, efficient delivery system. In contrast, the adults do not have easy access to courses or electronic devices save for a preapproved tablet that can be purchased from the facilities itself. There is little counseling or reformative work and those who need it are on a very long waiting list. The exercise allowance is minimal at best, with yard space available every other day, and the number of "lost" letters and packages would put even the most inefficient and corrupt mail service to shame.

Despite the dramatic fall in death rates, nonfatal injuries have more than doubled, and suicide attempts have skyrocketed, the vast majority of which are from the recently transferred youth offenders who, having had almost bearable conditions before, get moved into a living hell. It is only due to the swift and decisive actions of suicide-prevention artificial intelligence (AI) software, which monitors behavior and intention, that death rate does not spiral out of control.

An anonymous spokesperson for the adult prison service in California has blamed the disparity on the sheer number of adult inmates and the tight budgets these facilities must work under. "We have solved the problem of inmate murders and prison guard control, but we still have a way to go to get it perfect."

With the budgets of these large corporations coming under scrutiny after the lavish spending of their CEOs and shareholder payouts, there may be some changes to come, but considering the links and friends in Congress, those changes won't come anywhere near soon enough.

Part 1

Chapter 1 - Miles

Miles sat there staring at the eyes that reflected back from the rearview mirror. The adrenaline of the situation he'd put himself in was ramping up to capacity, yet his hands remained steady on the wheel. After seasons of racing, he was used to the sensation. If he closed his eyes now, he knew he'd be able to recall the noise from the track, the motors running at full speed, the cheer of the crowd—that was where he felt at ease.

He looked over at the entrance to the bank. The popper had just disappeared inside which gave him 120 seconds of peace before all hell broke loose. This was the calm before the storm, the red lights on the race grid counting down to launch. Yet the eyes looking back at him appeared different from what he was used to. There was no helmet, no fire-retardant balaclava covering everything except for a slit for his eyes. He was not Miles the racing driver, he was Miles the runner, the getaway driver.

As he continued to look at them, they began to morph into the eyes of his father. What would he think if he knew where his son was? Miles didn't need to guess; he knew that he'd be ashamed of him, of that there was no doubt. Yet the stab of pain that knowledge caused did little to negate his need for the thrill, the necessity for speed.

It had been a niggle at first, a pull toward the dangerous that had provided success on the track. Taking risks his opponents, who were far older, would not, wanting to see nothing but the needle as far right as it could go. The checkered flags were a byproduct, a welcome benefit, but it was the speed that was the real objective. That desire had quickly built into a demand and when the racing season was over, it had nowhere else to go but fester and torment his mind and body.

He readjusted the mirror back into place and took a deep breathe. *Just this once*, he told himself. *I'll just do it this once.*

Inside the bank, the popper lifted the gun to his waist and slowly slid the stick drive across the counter. The teller behind froze, her eyes staring at the opening of the shiny metal object that was turning into view. Her eyes instinctively moved down to the panic button below the counter that she knew would instantly drop a curtain of solid steel between her and it. She paused and looked up into the eyes of the man holding the gun. He simply shook his head. The stories she had heard of tellers being shot before the barrier fell filled her mind, causing her body to tremble. She had only been gossiping with Julie the other day about how, although the money gets saved and the perpetrator arrested, it did little for the one who copped the bullet.

She hesitated, not sure which way her fingers should go. She knew she should press the button, but the fear and adrenaline had caused a momentary break from her training. If she didn't press it, then her job would be over. She would be fired and the career she had only just started would be over. It would be difficult to get another with a black mark like that against her name. She looked into the eyes of the man holding the gun and wondered if he could do it, if he could pull the trigger. His stare told her everything she needed to know.

She picked up the stick and glanced to her side—no help was coming—and slid it into her computer.

Almost instantly the screen buzzed and flickered with activity. Accounts flashed up and then disappeared, the numbers in them drained to zero. While it was busy working, she looked over again at the smooth metal O that faced her and imagined the deadly metal projectile erupting from its core to strike her dead. She looked higher, nervous at those eyes, but noticed they were busy scanning the room, checking to see if he had been found out.

This was her chance, the opportunity to save her career and the bank's money. She reached down as fast as she could to hit the button…but it wasn't there. She looked down in panic and saw that she was two inches off. She slid her finger along to find it, just as the man's glare returned to her.

The second that followed crawled by like an hour. The man glancing down at where her hand was, the loud click as the curtain's safety catch unhooked, the change from surprise to anger on his face, the squeeze of the trigger, the rumble of slats dropping from the ceiling, the deafening shot and slam as the barriers crashed on top of the counter sounding almost as one.

Confusion echoed from the people in the branch as the man turned and ran. He leapt down the steps and through the door before the end of the second that followed.

Miles heard the shot from where he was. He'd been counting the seconds between the traffic lights in the distance when it rang out. His first thought was, *Shit, he's going to come out early*, and that was quickly followed by, *Fuck, he's killed someone*.

The precise time of entry and exit of the building had been worked out to coincide with the traffic lights and route that would be their escape. Coming out early meant he would have to improvise, even slow down at points if necessary. That would make for a poor getaway.

The doors burst open, and Miles's heart leapt as the popper bundled into the passenger seat.

"Go, go!"

Miles floored it, the electric motors spooling up fast and thrusting them back into their seats.

"What happened?" Miles asked as he just caught the lights at the first junction.

His companion didn't answer; he was too busy pulling out his laptop and logging in.

"Did you shoot somebody?"

"Just keep your eyes on the fucking road!"

A sharp chicane around a stopped car just in time to make the green light beyond.

"Please, please, please...don't have pulled it out," the popper begged.

Miles's heart was racing through his chest as he sped along. Robbing banks was one thing, but murder! He turned a sharp right along a one-way street to avoid the lights on 5th. The cars parked along the narrow road whipped by like helicopter blades.

"Yes! The fucking bitch left it in!" the popper shouted with glee.

Miles looked across at the screen that displayed a long series of numbers in an offshore account somewhere.

He turned back just in time to see the red light ahead and a mother and pram walk out into the street. He slammed on his brakes and swerved, missing them by inches. They slid sideways into the midday traffic beyond, pinballing from car to truck, and smashed to a bloody halt.

Muffled sounds of shouts and screams filtered through the haze of Miles's consciousness as he raised his eyes to look in the mirror. The last thing he saw that day was the look of horror on the woman's face, gripping the pram in terror, but safe.

Chapter 2 – Mike & Mary

The trial that followed was particularly short and emotional. Despite being only fifteen years old with no previous convictions, Miles Howard was sentenced to fifteen years in prison for aggravated robbery and attempted murder. It didn't matter that he was only the runner; he was an accomplice and, therefore, may as well have committed the act himself.

The only thing that kept the sentence from being twenty-five years, the same as the popper's who had pulled the trigger, was the testimony of the young woman Miles had saved. She told of how he had seen her and skidded to miss them, how she had seen his eyes in the mirror before he passed out. She had heard from the paramedics later that he had mumbled about her and the baby in his delirious state, long after the crash.

This found some sympathy, but not much. He was taken away and remanded at the California Automated Juvenile Detention Center that had recently been completed just outside Littlerock.

His parents, Mike and Mary Howard, wept in the courthouse. Mike had been holding it together since they had rushed to the hospital on that fateful day, not knowing if they were visiting their injured son or his corpse . But now, Mike couldn't hold back the flood of emotions that burst out. The press was there in force, which made the battle to get out through the building a challenge. *Fucking mongrels,* thought Mike. *Only after a story. They don't give a damn about the people involved or the actual consequence of the words they write.* He hated every one of them.

That evening, he sat out on the steps of the porch with a beer and tried to figure out where it had all gone wrong. As far as he could tell, he had done everything he was supposed to. From the time he met Mary in high school, he had loved her completely, and the year after graduation, when a child was on the way, he had started his own garage with inheritance money that came from the passing of Mary's parents. It meant that he could provide for his new family.

Mary took classes at night to learn accounting and would start her career the year after, taking care of local businesses in the neighborhood. They were a solid, determined team.

The expected baby was not to be, however, and after years of trying, they had all but given up hope. Then without warning, Mary began to get ill. They had feared the worst, the Big C that had taken her mother, and Mary went for tests immediately. When these came back clear, a friendly young nurse just happened to run a pregnancy test, and there it was.

Miles was a wonderful child, full of energy and giggles. Always wanting to be thrown in the air or spun around the playground. Mike had built him his first electric go-kart when he was just six, but oh, he just took to it as if born to be in that seat.

He remembered when he first took him to the transport museum, the first day he heard a combustion engine other than the pieces of crap that still clogged up the streets. The v12 turbo-charged engine inside a case was used for demonstrations twice a day. They'd actually start it up and let it roar for a minute. The experience was supposed to highlight the dangers of carbon dioxide and the evils of the engine, but to Miles, it was the most beautiful sound he had ever heard, and he took every opportunity to go back and listen. After that, father and son decided to rebuild an old classic together, Korinna, to be able to hear that sound whenever they wanted. They would spend hours together under the hood, Miles handing him wrenches and drills like he knew what was needed before being asked. Korinna was theirs, and the joy they got from driving around on Sundays as a family was immeasurable. She hadn't been turned over since the day Miles was in the hospital and now sat covered beside the house.

Of course, everything was electric now. No fossil-fuel engine had been manufactured in a long time and the trade-in offers that the government backed saw the vast majority swapped out for cleaner versions. But there were still some who kept the old engines running with black market and basement made fuel, but these typically fell into two categories. People with money who maintained classic cars and collections; and people who just wanted to stick their middle finger up to the man. He had received countless offers for Korinna but had never considered letting her go. She was a part of his son, a part that he could still keep close.

Mike recalled how proud he was when Miles started competing with the kart he'd built, winning trophy after trophy until he was approached by a Formula E4 team and made history by being the youngest driver ever in the series, racing on his fourteenth birthday. The progression to Formula E3 was almost guaranteed when he reached sixteen—he would have been set for life. But that wasn't to be.

How the hell could Miles do something as stupid as being a runner? He hadn't even known who the popper was! Not a friend from school, but someone much older. Mike sniggered, *fucking popper*. What a ridiculous name for them. Geeks who wrote code and stole millions by simply *popping* the stick into the bank's computer. Bank robbery had sure changed since he was a kid. The pandemics and the global recession led to paper money being seen as dangerous by consumers, and with the bank's greed at trying to save by not printing the stuff, real paper and coin money had been discontinued. That meant the need for large gangs with bags and bombs had all but vanished. It was in the realms of the computer nerds now, with codes being the only brute force required.

The widespread domination of driverless vehicles had also meant the ability to actually drive, and at speed, was a commodity, especially for poppers. Mike could see why Miles would be attractive to them, but he didn't know why the hell his son had agreed to do it in the first place. He had his whole life and career ahead of him!

Mike continued to beat himself up over the details until Mary came outside to join him.

"Hey, honey," she said, sitting down next to him, her warm hand on his cold back.

He glanced up momentarily before returning his gaze to the floor.

"It's getting late, maybe we should turn in for the day. It's been a long one."

Mike didn't move.

She sat down next to him, the pair unable to comprehend the events of the past few weeks and the outcome of the day. How quickly their little family had been blown apart.

Mike finally broke the silence, "Maybe it's my fault?"

Mary looked at him.

"Don't you ever say that. You did nothing to make this happen."

"If I hadn't built that bloody kart, never took him racing, then we wouldn't be in this mess."

"You can't go blaming yourself for what he's done. You were amazing to encourage him in his passion. What he decided to do with it was his choice and his alone."

They both knew that was true, but they also wished that damn kart had never been a part of their lives. It was now dismantled and piled next to the recycling bin. However, if Miles had taken after his mother, had been an accountant instead of a driver, he still might have become a runner. It was his choice. You just couldn't win.

Mary stood up and reached out her hand. With a sigh, Mike took it and stood up, his body stiff and old. Their fingers wrapped naturally around each other's as she led the way inside their quiet and empty house.

Chapter 3 - Ed

"Ed! Get your ass out of bed. You're gonna be late!" Jane yelled as she moved past the stairs and into the kitchen where the rest of the family was having breakfast.

Ed was already awake and sitting on the edge of his bed, staring at the floor. The faces of the band members in the heavy-rock posters around his room watched the same battle of wills unfold as they had done countless times before, unable to help him from their frozen poses. His emotional mind was screaming at him to stay in bed, telling him that he would only be heading into school for another beating. That the bullying would be as bad as ever and that it hurt too much to go through again. Better off just curling up under the nice warm duvet and letting the day pass you by.

There was an opposition to this, of sorts. A voice that had been growing weaker over the last year or so, until it was barely audible anymore. It whispered to him to keep going, to get up and stay focused on the lessons and subjects, that it might not be that bad today. It knew of the persistent torment that had been his life, that had worn him away to just the hardened shell he had been slowly crawling inside of. It tried to counter this with feelings of positivity and memories of past happiness, almost a distant memory. Even though it didn't make a compelling case, it still managed to pull him up and force him to head downstairs. He walked into the kitchen to join everybody else and slumped down in his chair.

"You're getting later and later," his mom said from one end of the table.

He just grunted a reply, feigning tiredness and teenage angst, and began to eat the cold toast from the center of the table.

"You've done all your homework, girls?" Jane asked her daughters, who were still stuffing their faces. They both nodded, spooning another round of oatmeal into their mouths. They both seemed as chirpy and annoying as ever.

"You'd better be careful! Anymore, and you're gonna pop!" their dad joked from the other end of the table.

12

They both giggled and shoved more in.

"How are you doing this morning, son?" he continued, looking over at Ed with sympathetic eyes.

"I'm okay," Ed replied with effort.

Jane stared across at Peter and made a face, nodding in Ed's direction, prompting the question.

"So, I was thinking, I'm not lecturing this weekend, so thought about hiking up to the Point, if you fancy coming along. Just us men."

More words that took more effort. "I don't know. I have homework to catch up on."

"I know, but half a day in the open air would do you good. I'll pack those barbeque sausages you love and even cook up my famous pasta dish to go with them."

Ed looked up at his father's expectant face and then across to his mother's and sisters', who all seemed to be waiting for his answer, the table on pause. He knew they were just trying to help. He didn't have the energy to refuse.

"Sure."

"Great!"

The table hit play, and everyone resumed their activities.

Peter said, "I'll get our stuff ready, and we'll head out early on Saturday."

With the main business of the morning taken care of, Jane checked her watch.

"Come on, Ed, we've got to get a move on."

She got up and kissed her daughters and husband, then headed for the door. Ed scraped his chair back and followed, picking up his bag as he went.

"Bye, son. Have a great day."

In the car next to his mother, he stared at the early spring morning that was dawning. He glanced up at his bedroom window and wished he had listened to the louder voice that had urged him to stay. He didn't know why he hadn't.

The drive to school was relatively short. His mother parked in the staff parking lot, and they both got out.

"Don't forget I have a meeting tomorrow night, so you'll have to take the bus home."

Ed grunted in the affirmative. The buildup of emotion seemed to congregate around his throat and make communication difficult. It blocked the doors to the outside world and made him focus on the internal instead. Music was the only thing that broke through; it wound its way around the gaps in his defenses, snuck through the holes in the barricades.

As they walked to the entrance, he reached into his pocket and drew out his headphones and drilled them in deep to block out as much of the surrounding noise as he could. His mom kissed his head, and he saw her mouth the words, *I love you. Have a good day.'* The heavy drumming that had erupted in his ears had swallowed her voice.

As she headed off to her classroom, Ed walked down to his locker. When he got close, he could see it was already open, his books spilled onto the floor. He stood over them and looked inside. On the shelf was a folded piece of paper like a birthday card, but instead of a warm greeting on the front, there was a buck-toothed donkey with a tall, pointed hat, the word *Dunce* written down the front of it.

Ed grabbed it, squeezing it tight between his fist, trying to stop his peripheral vision taking in the pointing and laughing that was going on all around him. He knelt down to pick up his stuff and returned it to its place. He grabbed what he needed and closed it.

As much as he tried, he couldn't help but see the faces of his peers jutting their teeth out and going cross-eyed at him, mocking him. In his ears, Slipknot's "Psychosocial" opening guitar and drumbeat dropped. *Another day. Just keep it together, keep it together,* but the emotional turmoil was raging inside. Why couldn't they just leave him alone? They had had their fun; it was now time to move on.

He walked around the corner and into his English class. He was the first one there as usual, the rest of the bottom set class tended to arrive late if at all. His mother taught the middle set, and it was agreed that it wouldn't be good for him to be in her class. So, they initially moved him to the upper set, but he found the work too hard, and he didn't last long before being moved down to the bottom. The work was much easier, too easy, but the change had prompted even more attention than usual from the kids around him. The son of a teacher being so stupid they had to put him with the dumbasses.

As he walked along the tables, he felt a rush of air as the door opened behind him and then, before he got to his desk, a shove on the shoulder. He stopped and turned around.

It was Hunter and his posse of idiots. He made a gesture for Ed to remove his earbuds, which he did, slowly.

"So, how's it going there, Eeyore?" Hunter sneered, and the kids behind him laughed.

Ed went to return his earbuds when Hunter grabbed his hand. "Don't be rude. I'm talking to you."

Ed felt his emotions well up, fear and anger swirling in his stomach, the rational voice being drowned out. *Hold it together.*

"Wow! If my parents were teachers, they'd be so disappointed in me. Maybe it just shows how shit yours are at their jobs. Just look at the state of you."

Ed shrugged off Hunter's hand and replaced the earbuds. He turned to walk away.

"Don't you fucking walk away from me!" Hunter yelled, grabbing his shoulder. And then it happened. The dam broke. The year of torment and abuse finally found its limit, the final straw had been placed. Every piece of anger, hatred, resentment, and fury broke loose and, in an instant, swept from his brain to his stomach and into his fist.

He spun around and released it all, every part of him that had suddenly been crammed into his tightly curled fingers, compacting them like steel. He swung it out, wanting to release it like an athlete releasing a ball, to get rid of it more than to strike anyone. He had had enough of it and wanted to hurl it as far away as possible.

Then the fist connected. A loud snap splintered out as he made contact with Hunter's cheek, feeling bone smash into fragments under the skin, his jaw becoming detached from its moorings. His face whipped to the side as he stumbled backward.

Ed's eyes regained focus in time to see Hunter's feet catch on the table leg as he tried to turn and break his fall. The desk behind came into view, the side of Hunter's head crashing into the corner and forcing his left ear to slap against his left shoulder at an unnatural angle. Ed wasn't sure if the snap that echoed around the room came from Hunter's neck or the table that split apart underneath him, and before he could figure it out, Hunter was lying on the floor, still.

For the first time in his life, the volume of the world had been switched to mute without the aid of his headphones. He could still see the images before him in a kind of out-of-focus way, but the sounds were gone. He couldn't hear the shouts from the boys, the running and tripping over tables, trying to get help. The call for teachers and their yells for backup to contain the mob of kids that began to gather, their phones out to record the awful spectacle.

What did come into focus for Ed, though, was his mother's face as she rushed through the door, the look of horror as she took in the scene. He saw her running over to him, wrapping her arms around him. The rest was a black hole.

Chapter 4 – Peter & Jane

Despite the testimony of several students regarding the bullying, the school suspended Ed while the trial took place. Not wanting to exacerbate things further, or for their reputation to be tarnished, the higher-ups erred on the side of caution and did nothing. They didn't want to be seen as too hard on him after the bullying came out, but they didn't want to be seen as too weak either due to the nature of what he had done. In the end, they waited until the court ruled and then they expelled him.

The third-degree felony and the ten years that would be his life now meant that school would be a distant memory by the time he got out, so the expulsion was a pointless act by the school to appease a certain demographic of its population. Jane lost her position at the school. Well, more forced out by parents and a governing body who seemed more interested in keeping the waters smooth than stopping any faculty member from drowning.

This meant they had to live off Peter's lecturer's salary. They almost had to sell their home to pay for Ed's lawyer, but a drive from some supportive parents allowed them to keep hold of it, for now. With their savings drained and their family decimated, they were in no fit state and barely hung on throughout the court case. When the verdict was read out loud, the collective heart of the family broke into so many pieces it was difficult to see how they would ever be stuck back together.

Peter spent his mornings and evenings staring into the bedroom corner at the bags he had packed for their hike, praying to anyone who was listening for the chance to go back to that day, to stop pretending everything was okay, and to talk openly and honestly with his son.

Jane struggled with the same thoughts, that she should have known something serious was wrong with him, that the chatter in the school and the comments she caught from other students should have raised alarm bells. But they hadn't; she'd just let it go. It had been easier to brush it off, and now they were all paying the cost. The feeling that she had let down her whole family; that her son was to lose ten years of his life because of her, was unbearable.

The collective guilt started to eat away at them until, one morning at the breakfast table, the first words of change were finally spoken.

"We have to do something," Peter said, staring down at his cereal that was turning to mush.

The girls looked up, wary at what that meant.

"What can we do?" Jane asked, keeping her eyes low.

Peter stopped stirring the milk in his bowl and stared across at his wife for what felt like the first time in months.

"Something. We have to do something. We have to talk about it—if not to ourselves, then to someone else. We can't keep it all in, and we can't seem to let it go."

Big fat tears began to spill onto the table from Jane's cheeks. Her head fell lower to hide her shame. Peter's hand traveled across the gulf of the table and found hers and held it tight. She squeezed it as if it were the only lifeline that could save her from drowning under the weight of it all. The girls took their cue, and without a word, they both leant across the table and covered their parents' hands in their own. The family, what was left of it, would not give in so easily. They were together and possibly closer than they have been in a very long time.

Eventually, Jane looked up, red eyed. "Okay, let's get some help."

Peter smiled gently at her, and for the first time, they thought there may be a way through this.

Chapter 5 - William

William lay in bed, thinking about Rebecca. He had awoken to the thoughts of the previous evening, to the image and smell of her that lingered in the warm parts of his mind. He could still taste her candied lips and bubblegum tongue on his that was so sweet. He smiled and turned over, realizing his body was reacting to the thoughts. His desires had become noticeable lately, especially when discussing girls with his friends. He was perhaps a late bloomer in that regard. His pals had all kissed girls before, and of course, he had to go along with the story that he had as well. And now he actually had. Now he knew what all the fuss was about.

He closed his eyes and allowed himself to imagine what would come next, second base, third, and more. As he began getting excited, he heard a noise from downstairs. He paused, looking at the door but realized it would probably be Rosa, their maid. His mother would still be sleeping her hangover off in the next room.

***

Beverley Anderson lay in her bed alone. The high thread count on her Egyptian cotton sheets did nothing to abate the pounding in her head. She should have been used to hangovers by now, but there she was, nursing another one. She had been lunching with the ladies with champagne, then finishing off bottles of wine alone at home for as long as she wanted to remember.

An image of the chemical compounds in both drinks floated around her mind as if they were toying with her. Reminding her of who she used to be and who she was now in one simple joke.

She rolled over and cracked an eye open far enough to see the clock next to the bed: 7:55. Now, if only she could remember what day it was. She lay there listening for sounds of William, who would be up by now, getting ready for school if it were a weekday. She heard nothing to start with; then, slowly, the sound of a car pulling on the gravel drive outside began to grow. Was David back early?

The sound felt different though, heavier, like there could have been more than one vehicle. She tried to recall if she had any workmen scheduled or had arranged anything with friends, but her mind was a thumping blank.

Then came the knock on the door, loud and serious.

She slid out of bed, her mind returning as the adrenaline started to circulate. She went to the large expanse of window that looked down over the sweeping driveway and saw two police vehicles parked by the front door, one a sedan and the other a large SUV.

Checking that her robe was tied up and pulled around straight, she headed for the balcony that overlooked the front door. She could see Rosa walking across the lobby to answer. The man showed her his badge and a sheet of paper. Rosa turned to stare up at Mrs. Anderson with a look of horror on her face.

Beverley rushed down, using both hands on the banister to ensure she didn't fall.

"Is it David? Is David okay?" she shouted as she reached the final step.

Several of the men had already begun to walk into the house. When she later looked back at this moment, she would remember how rude she thought that was, not wait to be invited in.

"No, ma'am, we're not here about that. We're here about William."

William? Wasn't he in his room? Scattered images of the night before popped up and then burst as she tried to recall seeing him until, at last, one of them provided her with an answer. She had seen him in his room talking on the phone when she'd gone to bed.

"No, but he's here," Beverley began, pointing up the stairs.

"Yes, ma'am." The officer gestured in the same direction, and the two large men walked past them and headed up.

"What are you doing? You can't just barge in and go up!"

"Yes, we can, ma'am. Here's a warrant for the arrest of William Anderson for fraud and embezzlement charges that have been filed against him by the employees of Murlow and Young."

Beverley began to laugh at him. "What do you mean fraud and embezzlement? He's only sixteen years old!"

"I'm sorry ma'am, but he is registered as the owner of the company and, therefore, the one liable for the charges."

Her mind began to whirl at what was going on. From behind her a familiar voice cried out.

"Mom!"

Her natural instincts took over, and she was just about to run to him, but the officer held her back, his hand on her wrist.

"I wouldn't do that; it could be seen as obstruction of justice."

She pulled her hand away, furious.

"We'll see what my husband has to say about this!"

She lifted her wrist and tapped a button on her watch. Seconds later, it was ringing with David's face on the front.

"Bev, what are you doing? Do you know what time it is here?"

"The police are here, and they're arresting William!"

David's voice was suddenly awake. "Arresting him, for what?"

She held out her wrist toward the officer with a look that told him he should explain.

The officer cleared his throat before leaning forward to speak into the watch.

"Good morning, sir. This is Detective Brant from the California Bureau of Investigation. I have a warrant for the arrest of William Anderson under the charges of fraud and embezzlement from the employees of Murlow and Young."

There was a brief pause on the other end, and then the word, "Shit."

Beverley glared at her wrist. "What do you mean *shit*? You know something about this?"

"It was a company I had put under William's name to hold until we decided what to do with it. It was a tax issue. We'd bought the company last year, and it was in holding."

"You put your son's name on a company!" She thought about who she was talking to and what he was capable of. "Have you put my name on any of your companies?"

"Listen, we'll talk about it when I get there. I'm calling Frank now; he'll meet you at the station. Just go with it for now, and it'll all be cleared up soon. I'm on my way."

The line went dead.

"Mom!"

Her handcuffed, hair-tousled son was being led across the lobby toward the door, his eyes pleading with her to help him.

She rushed for him, but the detective stepped forward, blocking her.

"Ma'am, considering the situation, we'll wait for you to get dressed so you can follow us. That's the best I can offer at the moment."

She looked at the detective, who seemed to be showing some kind of sympathy toward her, or maybe he was just worried about what she might say about him to his superiors.

She nodded and spoke past him to her son, "It's okay, honey. I'll follow behind. Frank will meet us there, and your dad is on his way."

She ran toward the stairs, her hangover cleared, the only thought in her head now was how she was going to kill her husband.

Chapter 6 – Beverley & David

On the eve of the hearing, Beverley sat in her luxurious house with a large glass of gin and stared into the open fire that had begun to die. She swirled the clear liquid around her glass and tried to comprehend everything that had happened. Not just the arrest of her son or the impossible lying and scheming of her husband, but how she herself had ended up here, in this mess of a life.

She thought back to the days when she was a top chemical engineer with her own company, full of bright ideas and energy with a passion to make a difference. She recalled the breakout incubator lab where she first worked on a material that could save lives, their small team more like family. The camaraderie, the excitement they shared, the ambition of it all. They were going to change the world. Their pulse material would be used to create hearts, muscles, and fibers that could save millions and improve the lives of so many more around the world.

Their idealism was breathtaking and the funds for development they received equally so. But with every new leap forward, the research and development stalled, and it became difficult to overcome the challenges that emerged. The year after year that followed saw investors getting anxious and angry at the lack of progress. There was one, though, who saw the potential of the technology. One who, when the vultures came to tear it apart, had purchased the whole company, lock, stock, and barrel.

David Anderson.

She couldn't believe that after all she had accomplished, she would be rescued by someone so opposite to her. So brash, materialistic, and yet so charming and generous. She tried as best as she could to not fall for his advances, but he was the kind of guy who knew what he wanted and always made sure he got it. They were married within a year, and William followed closely behind.

She tried not to see what had become of the company she sold to him, the switch of development to military and aerospace designs. She lost track of her work family and threw herself into raising her son. What else was there to do? She met new friends, friends who shopped, gossiped, and drank. She went along with it; numbing the pain well enough. But now, sitting here, she realized she had drifted too far, fallen down the rabbit hole too deep. She didn't have a clue what her husband was up to or the consequences of it. She had only just learned that she was a named owner of three similar companies that were *'in holding'*, waiting to be split up and sold off.

She would no longer sign anything without full knowledge of what it was and how it could affect her. On the solid wood coffee table in front of her were three folders with a breakdown of these companies she apparently owned. The thought had occurred to her a few days ago that she could use these companies as leverage, maybe even as a way to build herself back up and do something useful instead of drowning herself in alcohol and self-pity.

Two of the companies were mid-level telecommunications companies, each with a series of local TV networks and radio stations. Due to the close eye the Federal Communications Commission had on the gathering of media outlets, her name had been used instead of David's, presumably because he already owned several others already and didn't want his monopoly detected.

The third company was an engineering lab that worked on projects for the military, NASA, and the like. This one she was interested in, at least this was until she realized it was run by one of her former colleagues, one she had let down when she'd sold out. So, that too was tainted.

The fire cracked and brought her attention back to the here and now. Frank had done all he could to show that the fraud and embezzlement of the staff's pension fund was done by the former managing director. But with that man had disappeared with all the money, leaving no evidence or tracks to follow. The responsibility fell naturally to the owner of the business, whether they were sixteen or not. Frank had said that after several talks with the prosecutor and judge, and with the guarantee that the funds would be paid back from David, the likely outcome would be a five-year sentence. Five years to a boy of sixteen was everything.

It was high school, homecoming, college even, his first date, his first kiss, all gone or pushed back to who knew when.

She had been reading about the new California Juvenile Automated Detention Center, about how it offered the latest in design and safety. The boys would be kept separate with well-timed and coordinated meals, activities, and learning. In each room there would be toilet facilities, a computer to access support, counseling, and a variety of online courses. No matter how state-of-the-art it appeared, Beverley couldn't get the cold, stark, impersonal feeling of the place out of her mind. She could picture automated gates and doors, buzzers, and electronic announcements, faces through screens rather than in person. But what was the alternative? At least she knew he would be safe, although in the old system, she would have been able to buy his safety and all the luxuries he could want. He could have good food, computer games to play, and access to the outside would. Now he would be treated like any other. All the money they had and they couldn't do anything to make his life better in there. That just wasn't right. What the hell was the point of it all if you couldn't use it on the ones you loved?

She brought the glass to her lips and finished off what was left. She put it on the table and reclined into the comfort of the high-back leather chair. The warmth from the fire on her skin and the heat from the alcohol began to drain her consciousness, and it wasn't long before she was asleep. Not a comforting, restful sleep, but one filled with cold steel, barren rooms, and metallic monsters. The shadows of the fire danced across her closed eyelids and projected images of fear that swept over her face and the face of her son, her poor son.

Chapter 7 – Donnie

Donnie looked down at his cell phone perched to the right of the steering wheel. His heart skipped a beat when he saw the name flash up and then fell when he realized where he was. He contemplated leaving it to go to voicemail, but he needed to hear her voice too much.

"Hey, Lucy."

"Hey, baby, what are you up to?"

"Oh, nothing. Just delivering some stuff for my dad."

"Cool. You still coming around later, before I go to work?"

A fire ignited in Donnie's stomach at the thought of his Lucy at work.

"I'll be there," the anger in his voice noticeable.

"Don't be angry, baby. You know we need the money to get away. I wouldn't be doing this if we didn't need it."

His knuckles turned white as he gripped the wheel tighter, afraid to answer in case his emotions seeped through the microphone.

"Listen, baby, I've got to go," he managed, "but I'll be over later."

There was a pause before she answered, "Okay, I'll be waiting."

He hung up and slowly allowed his hands to loosen enough to turn on the radio. He needed some tunes to stay calm. He was close to the border and needed to look as natural as possible.

He took his mind away to the dream that he and Lucy had begun to create. The idea of getting away, of starting again, drew them together and had grown into a need. She'd had a rough childhood, abusive and alcoholic parents, a series of assaults from her stepfather, all of which led her to work for his father at the strip club, a place he now hated.

From their late night talks, he had come to realize that his parents were no less abusive. They didn't beat him, and although they drank, he wouldn't consider them alcoholics. They were just criminals, plain and simple, who had brought him up to follow in their footsteps.

He lowered his window to allow the air to circulate and cool his face. He had to get more money, he had to get Lucy away from the club, and he had to find another way of living that didn't involve keeping under the police radar and living in the shadows. This trip would help. With the border back into the US just ahead, all he had to do was just stay calm.

**

The double row of police vehicles and unmarked cars flanked the road about two-and-a-half miles across the border, three cars on each side. Instead of the main border crossing from Mexicali or Tijuana, they were holed up across from the smaller Nueva Tijuana in between. Detective Brant had already eaten at the iHop that was within walking distance of the checkpoint and was now one of the lead cars parked and waiting. The suspect would be back within the hour, and he needed to be well fed in case the sting went tits up.

He knew from previous tails and from the informant they had arrested last week that once the boy had crossed the border, he would take the 125 north for speed. It was a toll road, so had fewer cars than 905, and its route was more direct. They were stationed just past the toll booths and had arranged for all vehicles to pass through it. This allowed for correct identification and a nice slow capture. It would have been easier to arrest him before he made it through the barrier, but Uncle Sam wanted his toll, so it was decided they would sit and wait until the kid had crossed.

As Brant sat there, waiting for the signal to come through the radio from the guard in the booth, he thought back to all the kids he had arrested over his years. It was a rarity at the beginning and usually involved petty crimes. There were some gang issues still, but these had mostly been wiped out through the targeted youth programs that had sprung up across the country. These were great at providing meaningful activities for kids to focus on, even building family-like units for those who were lacking their own.

There were still kids, however, who chose to follow a different path, especially if they were born into it. The teen they were waiting for now probably had little choice but to go into the family business. Both parents were major players in the Los Angeles drug and vice world, each one controlling a different part since their split. He felt sorry in a way for the children who were brought up in that environment. It would have taken something miraculous to pull them away from the dark side.

The actual number of child arrests he couldn't quite put a figure on, but he knew they had gone up considerably. He wondered if the new automated juvenile facilities had anything to do with it. Before them, the shitshow that was the prison service was so goddam awful—that in itself was a deterrent which gave kids a real hard choice to make. Get banged up in a place that beat you, starved you, and would probably kill you *or* don't rob that store for a couple hundred bucks? But now inside these new facilities, you had your own spaces, rooms, computer courses. Hell, it was a lot better than most of these kids had on the outside, youth programs or not.

The adult versions of prison were markedly different, however. With the sheer number of prisoners, the budget couldn't stretch to match their juvenile counterparts. Rooms were half the size, outside breaks were half as long, and the range of activities fluctuated between reading and masturbation, with the latter discouraged by the AI camera in the rooms. There had been a few deaths over the years, mostly due to glitches in the system, but what do you expect when you give a multibillion-dollar contract to a friend who spends mere millions on running the thing?

There was talk of high-level poppers who had tried to hack the system, but since there was a lack of input opportunities, it proved difficult for them to gain any real footing. The facilities were self-contained with no electronic communication with the outside world. That, and the fact that a line of code in the wrong place could just as easily end up crushing them between the heavy automatic doors or stop food delivery until they starved made it wise to not even try.

The radio crackled into life, "He's in the line, fifth car back."

Brant sat up and shuffled his butt back into his seat. The meal earlier had made him feel warm and content, but now he needed to be awake and alert.

"Three cars to go."

He started the engine along with the other vehicles, and it reminded him of the start of the Le Mans car race he had seen on a history channel.

"Okay, he's coming through now."

The nondescript brown car pulled away from the booth, and before he managed to get out of second gear, Brant and the other lead car switched on its lights and raced forward, blocking off the road. The brown car came to a sudden halt, inches before it hit them, as the two rear cars flew in behind, creating a tight box. The vehicles in the middle drove in at a steadier pace to squeeze the sides and keep the doors from opening, trapping the occupant .

From where he sat, Brant could see the shocked and angry face of the seventeen-year-old boy behind the wheel. He looked frantically around for a possible way out, but the realization quickly dawned on him that he was going nowhere, apart from in the back of one of those cop cars in handcuffs.

Chapter 8 – Desi & Marcus

Desi sat at her desk in the back of her bar. She had bought and renamed Desi's Hideout Saloon only six months ago but had already settled into the place. It had made good economic sense for several reasons. First, it was a place that had a heavy turnover of clientele, which meant laundering any funds coming from other sources was easy enough. Then there was the crackdown on the selling of drugs in all establishments that served alcohol. This saloon, therefore, provided her a space that was controlled and managed, so she didn't have to worry so much about her dealers getting caught. And finally, she had a sentimental attachment to the place. This was the bar in which her father had been stabbed to death when she was a child, over an affair with a gang leader's girl. He was never that bright and could rot in hell for all she cared. The first night she had taken over the place, she stood in the spot where it happened and poured a whole bottle of Jack Daniel's on the floor—just to piss him off, if ever he was looking down.

She was finishing up counting the previous night's takings when there was a knock at the office door. It opened, and a face poked through.

"What's up?" she said.

"Um, I've got Marcus out here wanting to speak to you." His Irish lilt gave some melody to the words but made them no more appealing.

She stopped what she was doing and stared at him. "What's that piece of shit doing here? I told him never to step foot in this place."

"I know, but he said it's important."

She put the last of the cash in the safe at her feet and said, "Okay, let's see what he wants."

The door closed and, a few seconds later, opened up again without the courtesy knock. In walked Marcus, looking anxious, his head slung low.

"You've a nerve coming in here," she started.

"Yeah, I know, and I wouldn't unless I had to. I thought it best that you heard it straight from me instead of anyone else."

She sniggered, "What, you got that bitch prostitute pregnant or something?"

He looked up now, locking eyes with her. "Firstly, she is not a bitch or a prostitute. She was just a mistake, which I fully accepted was my doing. I'm not going over it again."

"Damn right it was your doing."

"She meant nothing to me, and no, she's not pregnant."

"Well, she meant enough that you would shit all over our marriage for to be with her."

"Look, Desi, I'm not here to argue."

"Why are you here?"

He looked back at his feet again. "Donnie's been arrested."

"What?" She was on her feet now, "What for?"

Marcus swallowed hard and shuffled his feet before answering. "He was caught bringing in a stash of drugs from Mexico this afternoon."

"Are you fucking kidding me? Drugs? Why the fuck was he bringing drugs…?" She was enraged, and her breathing and heart rate both jumped into high gear. "That's my domain. We agreed when we split up that I took the drugs and you took the whores. So why the fuck is he getting drugs for you?"

He looked at her, seeing her nostrils flare and her eyes redden with all the fury of a bull that's just been speared, ready to charge at the culprit. He chose his words carefully so as not to show any red flags.

"An old contact reached out, offered them to me at a rate I couldn't refuse. I just wanted to get them in hand. I had no plans to do anything with them. I wasn't trying to step on your toes. I'm sorry; I know it was wrong."

Her anger hadn't tipped over the line, but it hadn't backed down any either.

"Fucking right you were wrong. And now look at where it's landed you. Well, not you… No, you stay nice and clean. But our son!"

"He volunteered to do it! Look, I'll figure it out. I've got Bob with him now, and I'll pay whatever bail they set. He'll be fine."

"Fine! You have no idea if he'll be fine, so don't pretend that you do." She started pacing the floor, , the old wooden boards creaking beneath her boots.

Without looking at him, she asked, "How did they know he was bringing the stuff across the border?"

"Apparently, one of the boys who was selling the drugs got pinched last week and ratted all he knew. It didn't take much to piece together."

She stopped pacing. "You had people selling drugs out there already?"

He realized his mistake, and his face flushed. He scanned the ceiling for an adequate answer but found nothing but cracks and stains.

She walked up to him and slapped him hard across the face. His own anger began to boil as his ear rang and vision blurred, but before he naturally retaliated, he heard an internal voice telling him that he probably deserved that one.

"You get him out," she said, pointing at him. "Or so help me I will take this second betrayal as seriously as I should."

Marcus looked down at his bloody fingers that had been feeling the inside of his cheek. He glared at her. "I will get him out."

"And?"

"And I won't get any more drugs to sell."

"You chose to start selling woman, even with girls the same age as your daughter, so don't go playing the hardship card on me. If I find that it's not stopped, then there will be consequences."

"Don't go threatening me, Desi. I'm not one of your lap dogs that'll bend over for you."

"No? You used to bend every which way I told you to."

"Those days are gone."

"They are, so don't expect any preferential treatment or be surprised when I treat you like any other rival who tries to mess with my shit."

He nodded and headed for the door. As he opened it to leave, she called after him, "And...thanks for coming to tell me in person."

"Sure," he said, giving a sly smile as he closed the door.

She walked over to the phone and called Bob. He had been their lawyer for years, so she knew his number by heart. He picked up on the first ring.

"Hi, Desi."

"Hi, Bob. How's he doing?"

"He's doing okay, considering. He knows to keep his mouth shut."

"What are we looking at?"

Bob sighed, "Well, considering that he's only seventeen and it's his first offence, then it wouldn't normally be bad—a fine and suspended sentence maybe…"

"But?"

"But they have a witness who is willing to testify to reduce their own sentence, so if that happens, then we're looking at jail time for Donnie."

"Shit. How long?"

"If I can get it under five, I'd be lucky."

"Fuck. What can I do?"

"Well, the most obvious thing is to persuade the witness not to testify."

"Okay, I'll see what I can do."

"Desi."

"Yeah?"

"Don't do anything too stupid. It could also worsen the situation."

"So, you want me to persuade them with just foul language?"

"I'm only giving you advice here. If the kid or parents are hard-asses, and they use any threats or injuries in the case, then the sentence could easily go to ten years or more."

Desi hung up the phone without another word and contemplated her options. There were a few tricks she could try to help her son out, even though he'd decided to go with his father after the split. She was mother, after all. She had fewer options for what to do about Marcus. He was still her husband, and although he was a complete fucking idiot at times, she still had feelings for him.

She opened up a fresh bottle of Jack from a stash of boxes piled in the corner and sat down. As she poured herself a tall one, she could almost feel her father looking down at her and laughing.

Chapter 9 – Chris

It was difficult to tell whether it was the handcuffs that hurt more or the humiliation of being led off campus in front of all his peers and stuffed into the back of a police cruiser.

The look on their faces, the pointing, the laughter all replayed through Chris's mind as they drove him away to the station. He had almost forgotten what humiliation had tasted like. He had lived with the comments and looks of disgust from having two fathers for most of his life and couldn't believe that in this day and age there was still a stigma. Now his attempt at being the big man all came crashing down around him.

As he stared out of the window at the houses and cars passing, he realized that the cost he was about to pay for the approval of his peers would be more than it was worth.

He remained quiet for the journey but compliant with every instruction he was given. When they reached their destination, they helped him out of the car and led him through to be processed. Prints, DNA, photos, retinal scan, the works. Once complete, they placed him in an interview room. His parents were being contacted, but in the meantime, a CBI detective wanted a word.

Chris sat alone in the room for a while, stewing, staring at his reflection in the one-way mirror that ran along the back wall. He imagined the phone call his parents would be getting and their reaction, the shit that he would face when they got here.

The door opened.

The detective walked in with a thin manila folder and a hot coffee. After placing both on the desk, he sat across from Chris. He casually took a sip of the coffee, his eyes not leaving Chris for a moment. After his thirst was apparently quenched, he looked down at the folder and went to open it up but stopped. Instead, he just tapped on the top for a few seconds.

"Christopher Price. Born August 5th. Son of Taylor Price the journalist, and Jeremy Price the author. Twin sister Madeleine. Senior at Canyon Crest Academy.'"

He paused.

Chris presumed that was more for effect than waiting for him to respond in some way. He stayed silent.

The detective continued. "We've had an eye on you for a while young man," he said, tapping the folder once again. "You had quite the haul of drugs on you this morning. More than we expected and certainly more than any *personal use* excuse you could come up with. So, before I ask any questions, there's something I want to tell you. You don't have to speak to me at all without your parents or lawyer being present. You can remain silent if you like. But it may be easier some things before they get here, and if you do, we can be as accommodating and pleasant as possible and offer the best outcome. Do you understand?"

Chris nodded.

"Okay, first off, with the amount of gear in your bag and the fact that you were arrested on school grounds, we could easily be looking at prison time in the double figures."

Chris's heart suddenly felt claustrophobic, caged behind its bony jail, his eyes wide in fear. Still, he remained silent.

"So, my first question is this, why did you have so much stuff on you?"

He started to answer, but his throat was so dry he just coughed. The detective pushed across the remains of his coffee, and Chris drank it down without a second thought before he tried again to speak.

"I had just picked up a new stash that morning, and instead of bringing it home first, I just went to school. I figured I would take it home after."

The detective smiled. "So, teenage laziness was the culprit!"

Chris blushed at the probable truth in that.

"We're off to a good start. Next, how long would a stash like that last these days?"

Chris thought that was an odd question but tried to work out the average to give an answer. "Around three to four weeks, give or take."

"I see." The detective raised his eyebrows. "That's quite a bit of selling you've got going on. So, you get a new delivery of goods every month?"

"Yeah, about that."

36

"And how long has this been happening?"

"Around six months."

"Very good. You're doing great. Now, who provides these goods for you to sell?"

Chris's stomach lurched. He was afraid of that question more than any other. When he had started six months ago, he was told in no uncertain terms that if he got pinched, he was to keep his mouth shut and take what was coming—it would be a whole lot better than the consequences his dealer would dole out if he didn't. He wrestled with this in his mind now, feeling the stress in his neck and shoulders. He had already answered questions, but they didn't mean much. That particular question, however, meant everything.

"Chris, Chris," the detective said, pulling him back into the room. "It's not a trick question. It has a simple answer, and one that would do you a lot of good by answering."

He opened his mouth to speak but closed it again. He did this several times, his mouth fighting for possession over his brain.

"I can't tell you," was all he allowed to pass.

The door opened, and an officer looked in. "His parents are here."

The detective sighed. "Last chance, son."

Chris just shook his head; his time was up. His dads were here.

"Okay." The detective stood up with another sigh and left the room, locking it behind him. He walked through the station to a waiting area where two men stood, looking anxious. "Mr. and Mr. Price?"

"Yes," they said, moving over to the desk.

"Come this way, if you would." The detective opened the door through to the back and followed as they passed, directing them to the interview room next to the one their son was currently sat in.

"Where's Chris?" Taylor asked as they sat down.

"He's close by and safe. Don't worry about that."

"I'll decide what to worry about, thank you, Detective…"

"Brant."

"… Detective Brant."

Jeremy placed a hand on Taylor's in the hope it relaxed him enough to find out what was going on before he went off on one of his rants.

"Mr. and Mr. Price, Christopher was arrested this morning at his school with a considerable amount of drugs in his possession."

"Drugs? Chris doesn't do drugs!"

"He may not *do* them, but he sure as hell sells them."

"That's impossible. I want to see him right away," Taylor said.

"Yes, I'll take you to see him in a moment. Before that, I wanted to let you know where you stand in all of this, so you know what's at stake."

"Go on," Jeremy said.

"The amount of drugs and the location of Chris's arrest could mean prison time… ten to fifteen years."

There was an audible gasp opposite him. But before they were allowed to respond he continued.

"Now, I know Christopher is just a small-time seller in a much larger network. It's those people that I really want. If you can persuade him to give me the names of these people and any other information that would help, then that sentence will be reduced considerably."

"Are you bribing us?"

"No, Mr. Price. I'm saying the judge will look very favorably on the fact that your son made a mistake and has helped make amends by assisting us get to the people really involved."

Taylor and Jeremy looked at each other, their eyes conversing without the need for words.

"What will his sentence be reduced to if he cooperates?" Taylor asked.

Brant sucked through his teeth, "Oh, I would think it wouldn't be more than a few years, at most."

Taylor thought about this for a second. "And where would he be located?"

Brant leaned forward. "He would probably stay at the automated juvenile detention center just outside Littlerock."

"Until he's eighteen. Then what?"

Brant leaned back again. "Then he'll be transferred to the nearest adult facility for the rest of his sentence."

"Uh-uh, no way. I have written articles about those places; I know all about them. There's no way I want my son going somewhere like that."

"Mr. Price, your son *will* be going to a place like that. The only thing you have a small bit of control over is for how long."

The frustration and anguish were palpable and made the air thick and heavy. Hearts were thumping and breaking at the same time.

Jeremy said, "Okay, let's see him."

Brant stood up and took them into the room next door. As soon as they entered, Jeremy ran over and hugged his son. Taylor was close behind.

"I'm sorry, Dad," Chris said, his eyes filling with tears.

Brant let the reunion happen for a few seconds and then interrupted. "Gentlemen, if you please." He motioned to the chairs in the corner. "Pull those chairs around the table here."

They did just that, then sat down, Jeremy still holding his son's hand.

"I've explained to your fathers the situation and the likely outcome of your arrest. They have something to say to you about the questions I'd like answered."

Taylor began to speak, but Jeremy took over. "Look son, I know it's a difficult situation, and those you did this for are not good people. I know they would have threatened you or us to keep quiet, but the only way this works out is if we are completely open and honest with the police. We can't give in to the fear. We are stronger than that."

Chris looked between his fathers, a stony look of determination on Taylor's face and the concerned strength on Jeremy's.

From them, Chris found his courage. "Okay, what do you want to know?"

"Who do you get the drugs from, Chris?" Brant asked.

"There's a guy, about my age, name's Donnie Fuller. He's the one who got me into it and gets me all my gear. He goes across the border each month to pick up a new supply, nothing huge, but enough for several of us to sell each month."

Brant smiled. He knew Donnie and the family well. "Tell me about this border crossing."

Chapter 10

The soft double beeps of the morning alarm began to bounce off the white stone walls that refused to let them escape. Instead, it forced them to bounce around the enclosure until they had run out of energy and there was nothing left but an echo. Miles was already awake. The noise had been his accompaniment every morning for the last two years, so his body clock was prepared for them. He counted the usual series of five pairs as the daylight LEDs began to grow. It would take five minutes for them to go from dawn to a full day's brightness, which was an attempt to simulate natural conditions, but the unnatural rate of illumination made it stand out even more as a falsehood.

He lay there in his bunk and allowed his eyes to open into the gloom. He had been dreaming of racing his go-kart as a kid, getting faster and faster, far in the lead, or so he thought. He kept coming up to the back of the pack to lap them, only to realize he was, in fact, last, forcing him to maneuver up the track once again. His parents were looking on from the side, but instead of them smiling at his pace, they looked sullen and just shook their heads at him every time he passed.

It was a common dream, and one that left him with a hole in his stomach where once there was a fire, the empty charred remains of a dream. As the lights began to reach their full strength, another set of double beeps sounded to signal the start of the day. Miles slid to the ladder at the end of his bunk and climbed down. Underneath was his desk and stool that faced a computer screen on the wall. When he reached the bottom, he instinctively turned toward the toilet bowl in the far corner. The coldness of the hard floor shot through his feet and straight to his bladder.

He washed up in the sink above the toilet, the wastewater flowing down to fill up the cistern beneath, no waste. From the opposite wall he grabbed his tracksuit bottoms and a t-shirt from the shelf and quickly got changed, pulling his socks on to warm his toes. He remembered when he'd first arrived, how surprised he was that he didn't have to wear an orange jumpsuit, but it didn't take him long to realize why. They were on their own, separated from everyone else by walls and cages, so it made no difference what you wore. Space was extremely limited though, so whatever you had, had to be versatile and compact.

Suddenly the lights flashed in his room and a single double beep sounded. He sighed and walked over to the door at the front of his room. Next to it there was a small metallic block that stuck out from the wall with a thin roller on the top. Miles raised his hand and rolled one of his fingers across it. A single satisfied beep sounded, and all was well.

The morning roll call was a pretty simple DNA test to check that you were still there. He had tried to trick it after the first week, in an attempt to steal some extra time in bed. He had put a dollop of spit on the roller the night before, but it didn't work. It had to be rolled to be activated, so he had no choice but to get up. Then he had the pleasure of having to wipe off the stale spit for it to work.

He looked down underneath the front door. There was a four-inch step below that housed the sliding door of the delivery service. Thin, cuboid robots scooted along tracks underneath the floors outside, delivering food, parcels, and letters and removing waste and empties. It was pretty efficient for anything a few inches tall. He assumed everything was scanned and checked before delivered to make sure he didn't receive anything he wasn't allowed and communications were within the rules.

As he stared at the sliding door, he could hear the machines whizzing by outside, but nothing stopped for him.

He sighed and sat on the stool under his bed. It was uncomfortable with no back or padding to it. He swiveled it around and hit the *wake* button on the keyboard that was built into the desk.

The screen in front flickered alive with a soft welcoming voice, "*Good morning, Miles.*"

"Radio," he replied, which opened the facility's station to let music stream through the speakers on either side of the monitor. It was a welcome break from the deathly silence. The Spotify account was locked and controlled by the facility with only a single playlist of music available. You could request new songs to be added if they didn't break the rules (no swearing, no sexual content, no mention of gang affiliation). That left a pretty short list.

The other playlist was for podcasts and had a similar set of criteria. They had to be educational, ideally linked to a course that you were studying. They had to be useful and not derogatory or anti anything and could only come from an affiliated site. Some people had set up their own podcast to send messages to the inmates, but this was quickly discovered, and a subsequent set of policies and firewalls were put in place to prevent it happening again.

The facility was an electronic island with no link to the outside world except through their systems. It wasn't surprising people tried to come up with ingenious ways to bypass the communication censors.

He was on the second floor, so had about two hours until the exercise yard was lifted to his level. It was a pretty cool system of cages that lifted like a skirt around the whole building, allowing the individual yards to be brought to them, instead of them having to go down to it.

He clicked open the English course that he'd started last week and continued where he had left off. He had never read *The Adventures of Huckleberry Finn* before and was enjoying it, although he felt the exaggeration of morality throughout was a bit stinging. But that seemed to be the regular program in here, all Mary Poppins and Disney goodness that left a bittersweet taste in your mouth.

It wasn't long before the thin cover below his door slid back, and his breakfast was delivered. A yellow mush of eggs atop a single slice of bread. As he picked it up, he could feel what was left its warmth draining through his fingers. He raised it to his nose and could swear he smelled the oil or grease from the machine waiters wafting around it. He didn't mind the smell so much, it reminded him of fast engines and smooth wheels, but he'd much prefer it not to be in his food. He dropped the plate on the desk and tucked in.

Time moved differently in here. There were so few indicators of its passage that it played tricks on you if you weren't careful.

The mind scrambled for clues and tried to adjust itself accordingly, so much so that hours could pass by in mere seconds. In his first month here, he had been reading in his bed for what seemed like hours, and when he had finished the book, he was prepared to get ready for the evening beeps and lights out. When he jumped down and started to get ready for bed, he lifted the latch to the window in the back door of his room and was shocked to see blazing sunlight streaming in. At first, he thought he had read through the night and it was the next morning already, but when he woke up his computer, it read the same date as when he had started and showed the time of late afternoon.

It took a long time for his body and mind to adjust to the passage of a day, and it began to assign packets of time to activities to help keep track. His computer courses generally took two hours before he felt tired. The clock at the bottom helped keep track. Reading, exercise all seemed to take around an hour. He could write a letter in just half an hour now; there were no electronic communications allowed, so he had to go back to the stone age and learn how to send messages the old-fashioned way. The prison's computer system was an isolated loop, cut off from the rest of the world. With everything automated, the system had to secure against viruses and bugs as the deliberate attempts at sabotage.

He couldn't believe that people used to write letters like in longhand and then have to wait days or even weeks for a reply. The frustration must have been unbelievable! It was all so slow back then.

After he'd finished a module, he checked the time. Almost there. He went over to the back door and pulled on his trainers. He would be allowed out into the yard soon, so wanted to be ready to make the most of every second. He sat on the toilet seat, tying his shoelaces, when he heard the smooth rumble coming through the building like a train riding up the walls outside. He stood and waited.

There was a loud clunk of something locking into place, and the rumbling stopped. A second later, a green light appeared next to the door. Miles happily slapped the light with the palm of his hand. The back door slid open, and a wave of warm fresh air blew over him. It made his senses tingle—who knew joy could be found in the most basic of things? He stepped out onto a short runway surrounded by a strong metal cage. The runway led into a small rectangular yard a few feet beyond. Either side of him were runways from his neighbors' doors—these were slightly longer and went past his. This meant that the individual exercise yards could be staggered, closer, farther, closer, farther, like a tessellated pattern to fit them all in as tightly as possible to save space.

The prison was six stories high, and every level had two hours of access to the yards each day, although the time wasn't equally spaced. Those on the ground floor would be first. Then after an hour, the yards would be lifted to the next level and so on. When they reached the top, it spent two hours there before making its descent again for everyone else's second hour. Miles was often jealous of the top floor for having that much time in one chunk. He would sometimes be too tired or bored to go back out for his second hour, especially if the temperature had dropped by the evening.

As he walked into his yard this morning, he saw others begin to emerge as if from hibernation, poking their heads out to test the weather. From the cell next to him on the left came Malik, a fourteen-year-old who was in for breaking-and-entering and theft. His family had made a living out of it and used Malik as their entry guy. He was so small and thin he could easily squeeze through any window, or even a pet door. He waved at Miles as he came out and passed by.

"Hey, Miles."

"Hey, Malik."

"How're you doing?"

"Yeah, I'm okay. You?"

"I'd be good if my food didn't taste like it's been warmed up in the hood of an old truck."

They both laughed, and Miles's thoughts drifted to engines and speed.

"No Donnie again today?" Malik pointed across to the other side of Miles.

Miles looked over at the closed door to his right. Donnie had only been here a month but rarely came out, especially on the first session. He preferred to wallow in his room, all mean and moody. He was not adjusting to it well. Miles could tell he had a bad attitude from the start. He had tried to make friends with Donnie, but that apparently wasn't something Donnie had wanted. Miles kinda felt sorry for him; he was obviously a badass in the world outside, but in here, there was no one he could be badass to except himself.

"I guess not!" replied Miles. He picked up the ball that was in the corner and started bouncing it around. He looked up at the basketball net at the end and threw the ball toward it, but before it got close, it hit the roof of the cage and fell short. He could hear Malik laughing from across the way.

"Wishful thinking," he called across.

Yeah, thought Miles. *Wishful thinking.*

Chapter 11

Ed sat there and stared at the counselor on the screen.

"How are you doing this morning?"

"I'm okay," he lied.

"That's good. How are the courses going? You managing to get through any of them?"

"I'm getting there."

The face opposite him looked down at something on his desk. "It looks like you've started seven different topics this past week but haven't got past the first module in any of them."

Ed shrugged. "Didn't much like them."

The face sighed. "I know it can be tough to stay focused in there, but it's important to get an education and qualifications for when you get out."

Ed's eyes narrowed. "I've got another nine years to worry about that!"

"Well, it's closer to eight actually. You're coming up on your second year soon, and access to these courses may not be so readily available for much longer."

Ed didn't much care. His mind was stuck in the past, so his future had no influence over today.

"Ed, do you understand what I'm saying?"

"Yeah, sure."

There was a hesitation, something the counselor wanted to say but couldn't. "Okay, so… shall we set a goal to complete just one topic by this time next week?"

Ed didn't respond.

"Any topic."

"Yeah, sure."

The counselor seemed exasperated with Ed's lack of motivation. He had been working with Ed for well over a year and with little progress, really. But Ed just wasn't into improving himself. It was so hard to deal with the trauma of the event that brought you to a place like this while being enclosed in it, trapped in a cell of its memory. It caused the trauma to remain locked up as well, stuck inside the prison of your own mind. No freedom for the brain to try new things. With only set activities and routines that didn't change, how could you expect any change in the pain? There was no reason to achieve positive outcomes or to try to excel, only day after day of monotony with the end so far out of sight it became meaningless. No interaction with others to form meaningful bonds, only solitude designed to break you down and draw you away from any form of society. In psychological terms, it was labeled as *collateral consequences*, but it should really be called a *lifetime of punishment*—the chance of successfully reintegrating to life outside was next to zero.

The counselor tried a different tack. "How's the diary going? Have you been doing the exercise? What positive things have you noticed and are thankful for each day?"

Ed thought about the ridiculousness of the question and stared down at the diary in front of him.

"Ed?"

He moved his hand up to pick it up and couldn't help but let his eyes wander over to the scar and disfigured knuckle on the back of his hand. He rubbed it with the other, and the event that had caused the misshape and landed him in here came flooding back. The anger began to well up inside, tearing his eyes. The release of that emotion was still palpable. The unforgettable sound of bone crashing against bone. The fall, the screams. The look on his mother's face.

"Ed! Focus on me and not the past... Ed."

Without looking up, Ed switched off the monitor and stood, the stool hitting the lunch and breakfast trays that were on the floor behind him, untouched. He climbed up into his bunk and wrapped the blanket around him, not daring to close his eyes for fear of a more vivid reenactment of the nightmare. He just lay there and stared out at the wall opposite him, a wall that was empty, featureless, that had no meaning except to simply be there, and he tried with all his might to just be that wall.

Chapter 12

The delivery door slid back, and a parcel almost the same size and shape of the opening was shoved inside. William turned from the computer with excitement and leapt from the stool. He picked up the package and put it on his desk, using his pen to pierce the tape that bound it.

The first thing he could see was a card in a gorgeously thick envelope. He opened it up and held the green tab as he pulled it out. The picture on the cover began to move. An image of a man standing on top of a mountain looking triumphant, the camera panning around him, a flag flapping behind him. A banner across the top spelled out the words: *One year down.*

He stared at the moving image as it reset several times, wondering what it would feel like to be as free as that. He opened the card and began reading his mother's handwriting, telling him how proud she was of him, how strong he was, and how she couldn't wait for him to be home again. He missed her, and as strange as it sounded, he felt closer to her now than he had before. Perhaps it was the thought of losing something that made it all the more precious.

The card was signed from both his parents, although he knew his dad would have had little to do with it. He stood it on his desk and pulled more of the wrapping from the parcel. There were a few more adhesive cork squares to go on the wall behind his desk; the ones there now held photos and letters. There was a new set of clothes, trousers, and a thick t-shirt, a pile of notebooks for his courses, and replacement ink cartridges for his pen. Then he saw the deep-purple glimmer underneath. This was what he had been waiting for. He pulled the corner and slid out a thick slab of chocolate. Food was not normally allowed to be sent except for special occasions, and he would wait with great anticipation for this treat.

As he pulled it out, though, his eyes fell on the clean pack of bound paper that it sat on. He looked closer and recognized it as an official document from his father or, more likely, his lawyer. He decided not to focus on that for now and pushed it to one side. Then slowly, as if he were a safe cracker, he began to peel open the wrapper so delicately that the glued edges parted as smooth as hot butter.

He unfolded the brown slab as if he were removing a blanket from a lover. He stared at it lying there, his mouth salivating, savoring the waft of cocoa that rose to his nose and filtered around his tingling tongue. He counted the 136 square portions, 17 by 8.

When he had first received one of these in the mail, he vowed to make it last and to have just one square per day, but it didn't take more than two days for it to be gone. These days he had a much better system that he was able to maintain. He would allow a whole row of eight squares on the first day as a treat. Then each day that followed he would allow four squares. That still gave him over two months of chocolatey goodness. With his birthday coming up and Christmas shortly after, he knew he wouldn't have to wait long for more.

He rubbed his hands on his trousers to dry them, then carefully lifted the end of the bar. With tender fingers, he cleanly snapped off the first row. Putting this atop the notebooks, he refolded the wrapper and slid the bar into the back corner of his desk. His attention returned to the strip that was waiting for him, lying there seductively, wanting him to just eat it all.

His palms felt sweaty as he just watched it for a while. He knew it was ridiculous, but he couldn't help himself. The anticipation of having what you desired right in front of you—and holding back—was a small, yet powerful sensation. He felt his arousal grow as he leaned forward to get a deeper smell, his tongue emerging to pick up the tiny particles of chocolate that floated in the air above it.

He lifted off the stool for a second, just enough to pull down his trousers and pants. In his mind he could see the half-remembered image of Rebecca, her glistening lips, her eyes staring, her bra straps showing. His hand was making steady strokes as he imagined her close to him, her lips and sweet breath palpable. The kiss had now turned into something other than his memory, a mixture of imagination and desire. Their mouths coming together deep and hard, tongues fencing inside as he felt himself bubbling up. The image of white wet knickers beneath short skirts tipped him over, and as he picked up the slice of chocolate and bit into it, he exploded.

Chapter 13

The bright daylight of the ceiling didn't penetrate far into the cave-like duvet. The bunched-up fibers inside the sewn channels appeared like streams of gray clouds overhead, blotting out the day while the warm, humid air trapped inside felt heavy, as if a storm was brewing. Donnie had crawled back inside after breakfast, lunch, and dinner in hopes of speeding the day along. It was having no effect, and if anything kept it running a little behind, it was the thoughts that littered his mind, dragging out each second.

He took a deep breath and pushed away the cover, blinking as the light hit his eyes. He climbed over the side of the bed, ignoring the ladder, and jumped down. On his desk were two trays of empty plates from the food delivered that day. Grabbing them up, he hit the waste button on the wall, and seconds later, he heard the whizzing of a delivery drone pull up outside. The thin door on the floor slid open, and he fed the trays inside. The machine swallowed them up, closed the door, and sped off.

With his desk cleared, he sat down on the stool and woke the computer. "Good afternoon, Donnie," the calm voice spilled out of the speakers. He ignored it and went past all the unopened programs, to the music. He had been adding songs to a queue he had created from the tracks that were the least lame. He hit the *play* button. What he wouldn't give for the freedom to select what he actually wanted to hear.

He then opened the text document he had been typing away at for the last few days. He had tried to write the letter straight onto paper, but without spellcheck, it looked all wrong. He pulled out a pad of paper and picked up a pen. No matter which way he tried to hold it, however, it never felt comfortable in his hand. He stared at the screen for a few minutes before he began to copy the words.

Lucy,

I miss you like crazy. I'm sorry I haven't written since being in here. It has been hard getting used to it and the month has just disappeared. I also didn't know what to say or if it would be safe to send anything. I can't believe that I won't see you until I get out, 5 years is a long time. I know you want to video-visit, but I'm not sure that's a good idea at the moment. People will know and if my Dad finds out there'll be trouble, especially if he found out what we were planning.

I'm sorry I didn't tell you about the job. We were so close to leaving this shit hole and starting a new life for ourselves that I just couldn't help but do it. Do you forgive me? Do you still have our money hidden safe? Don't tell anyone about it because they'll take it and we'd be fucked.

Are you still working? No don't tell me. It drives me crazy to think about you and those other men staring at you while I'm stuck in here. I wish I could do something to make it stop. This place is torture. I can't do anything or go anywhere. The room is so small. I get to go out twice a day to a small yard but it's no size at all. I can see the people next to me, but I don't want to talk to those assholes, I just want you. Do you still want me?

Don't forget our dream baby. Getting out of this city and leaving everything of our past behind us. We'll head to a nice small town with normal people. Get regular jobs. Get our own place with a yard for your chickens and a dog. We can be together, our own family. Don't lose sight of the dream, baby. That and you are the only things that keep me going. I'll do anything to make it come true. They have courses in here that might be good for me to do. You know, to get some qualifications before we start out. I'll do them if you promise that you'll try to find another job, a regular job. I can't take you working at my dad's place anymore.

I hope you write back soon and if you can, send me a photo of you. I love you. I miss you.

Donnie

As he folded the paper inside the envelope, he could hear the rumble of the yard lowering outside for its second pass. A sudden feeling of claustrophobia washed over him as he stood and walked over to the back door to hit the green button. As the door opened, he inhaled deeply; it felt like he had been holding his breath the whole time he had been inside.

He stepped out and walked up the long track to the yard at the end and lay down in the middle. He put his hands behind his head and looked up through the squares of the cage at the darkening sky beyond, but his eyes were focused inside, on the fading image of Lucy, his mind trying to hold on to the shape, the lines and edges of her face that were starting to slip away.

Chapter 14

Lying on his bed, propped up by a thin folded pillow, Chris read the final chapter of his father's latest book. The murderer had been revealed, and all the clues along the twisty-turny road had been highlighted and accounted for. Now the characters in the usually quiet, sleepy (but strangely murderous) New England town were coming to terms with the outcome and moving on with their lives.

He liked the way the path behind could be seen so clearly at the end, and he found it fun to flick back to the earlier chapters to read them again, now knowing where they led. He also felt strangely comforted by the familiar residents of the place he knew so well. He had grown up with them—all their histories, foibles, and sleuthing ways. It was a warm taste of a familiar surrounding that was so needed in this stark, minimalist room.

He closed the cover and let the book fall to his chest. He had found that since being here, all the false bravado and front he displayed at school had fallen away as quickly and easily as the skin from a ripe banana, leaving the soft, delicate parts exposed. He had looked for covers to wrap around himself, to feel safe inside of, and had found them in his father's books and articles. In these, he heard their voices and feel the familiar world of their words.

He wedged the book along the edge of the bed and picked up a newspaper from several days ago. It was already folded to his father's article: "New Prison Reform Couldn't Come Soon Enough."

He re-read it with a strange feeling of relief and dread in his stomach. Relief that he was in here at a time that saw the prisoners more protected than ever; that the facilities were the best available. However, with his eighteenth birthday less than four months away, he was terrified at what the transfer to the adult facility would be like. His imagination played with ideas of rundown buildings, slops of food, and a room even starker than the one he was in. As exposed as he felt, he was sure the move would strip off another layer to reveal the sensitive, nervous underbelly he still tried to keep hidden.

The lights flashed with a single soft beep. He pulled himself out of his fear-induced depression that had started to take over and shuffled to the foot of the bed, trying not to wrinkle the paper and books along the side. He climbed down the steps, went over to the front door, and rolled his finger across the small metal box next to it. A contented beep sounded in reply.

He turned and looked at the line of books across the back of his desk, their spines forming a picture of Nightly Falls that was created inside their folds. A place he knew well. A place he could escape to by simply opening the pages.

He climbed back into bed and buried himself under the duvet. He picked up the book and turned to the start of the last chapter again, feeling a need to return to a safer place. Out of the corner of his eye, the newspaper kept making its way into his awareness. The threat from the ink etched onto its pages seeped into his mind and brought with it the image of large men with their own ink-covered bodies. He rolled over to face the other side and tried to focus on the warm familiar surroundings of the book. The worry of where he was heading would still be there in the morning, so for now at least, he could find comfort in the familiar.

A series of five double beeps sounded, and he knew he had five minutes before the lights would slowly dim to blackness and he would be alone in the dark once again.

Part 2

Chapter 15

The newsroom was a cacophony of hurried conversations, ringing telephones and clattering keyboards that would drive most people dizzy. Taylor was at his desk and appeared to be in a trance, his eyes unfocused on the blank screen ahead of him, his ears oblivious to the noise. Ever since he had written that article the previous week, an idea had begun to form in his mind. It had started as a little niggle, a small tinkle of a bell that was being pulled by a thin strand from his subconsciousness; but it had grown until now it was a fully formed clapping toll of a cathedral tower.

The idea became so big it had taken on a life of its own, consuming his hours, growing on the energy he was feeding it. He hadn't shared it with his husband yet. There was no need to do that until he had the answer to a query he had put out to one of his contacts. Until he had that, he had nothing.

His eyes lowered to the telephone, waiting for that question to become an answer. While he sat there, his mind instinctively went to the other major thought that dominated his mind. He had seen pictures of the rooms in the Automated Juvenile Detention Center but found it hard to place his son, Chris, inside one of them. For starters, it was clean, bare, and tidy, something vastly opposite to his room at home, the room that was still waiting for him as he had left it. But more than that, it was a room for a criminal, for a menace to society to be incarcerated and kept away from the good people of California. His son didn't fit that description. His son was just a kid who'd made a mistake, who'd been led down the wrong path. Led by a piece of shit from a family of criminals who all deserved to be in that room. Not his son.

The phone rang, and without any hesitation, he snapped out his hand and pulled the receiver to his ear.

"Hello."

"Taylor? This is Jim."

"Yes, Jim. What have you got for me?"

"I've got the date and the names and…"

"And what?"

"You're not going to like it."

Taylor leaned forward, picked up a pen and hovered it over the blank pad before him. "Give it to me."

"He's being transferred on the 26th of November at 10am from the Juvenile Detention Center to the California City Automated Correctional Facility just north of Edward's Airforce Base. It's a single-sex, low- to medium-level 2 security site, so... not too bad."

Taylor pulled out another notepad from his bag and flipped the pages until he found the one he wanted. He scanned down the list of facilities he had researched until he got to the right one. He moved his finger across the page until it reached the column under the heading *Transfer Suicide Attempt Rate'* and stopped at 72%.

"Not great either," he replied into the phone.

"That's not the part you're not going to like. There are four other prisoners being transported along with him. They are Miles Howard, William Anderson, Edward Porter...and...Donnie Fuller."

At the last name, the pen froze above the page. Taylor turned his head and brought his mouth closer to the microphone. "You sure it's him?"

"It's him."

"Fuck."

"Yeah. I'll try and get more but thought that would be enough for now."

Taylor's mind was racing too much to reply.

"Don't forget the price for this."

"Yeah, sure," he said and hung up. He couldn't believe the sheer lunacy of the dice that God had thrown. Why did it have to be him—Donnie Fuller? Of all people, why him—the one person who had caused his son to be imprisoned in the first place, the one piece of shit who deserved to be? Then another question fully formed in Taylor's mind: how could he break Chris out of there, to be free?

Chapter 16

Taylor paused at the door, his hand reaching for the knob. He had spent the few hours after the call trying to put some of the pieces together and contemplated how the conversation with his husband would go. Nothing that came to mind was pretty.

He turned the handle and went inside. The generous wooden lobby was a space that always made him feel at ease. The walnut lines and curves, the smell of the forest helped ground him. Directly in front, to the right of the stairs, was a large open doorway that led into the kitchen, the heart of the house. To the left was the living room, warm and comforting. But it was to his right that he looked, at the door to Jeremy's study where he knew he would be hunched over his computer, drawing out devilishly satisfying schemes for his next book.

Taylor took a deep breath and went straight for the door, despite the rising panic that begged him to escape to the kitchen to pour a large drink. He opened it without paying attention to these voices and was warmed by the sight of Jeremy sitting exactly where he had pictured him.

Jeremy looked up with a smile that quickly turned into a frown as he caught the worried look on his husband's face.

"What's up?" he asked.

"Jer, come over here. I want to talk to you about something."

Taylor motioned to the sofa against the back wall. towardJeremy stood, nervous, and followed. They both sat down, angled toward each other, and waited. Taylor tried to find the starting thread that would allow the planned speech to flow, but at that moment, it was eluding him, dancing on the breeze of his mind as if it were teasing a kitten.

"So," he finally began, "how's the ideas for the new book coming along?"

Jeremy was surprised at the benevolent question. "It's fine. What's going on?"

"Okay," he sighed, deciding to just say what he needed to as best he could and basically wing it.

"After the article was published last week, I've been having thoughts about Chris."

"What about Chris?"

"About how we can help him, maybe even save his life."

Jeremy's frown deepened. "I don't know what you mean."

"You read my article; you've seen the data about what happens to kids after they transfer to the adult facilities. A large proportion die, or at least attempt to. Those who are saved are left in total depression, unable to have any control over their life, or death. Their mind withers even if their body remains."

"Yes, but that won't be our Chris. He's stronger than that."

"Is he? How were the last few letters from him? It's all getting to him, and I think the transfer will be too much for him to cope with."

Jeremy let the image of his son sink in—depressed and alone with something snapping inside him where the only way out he could see was suicide. He shook his head to erase the nightmarish picture.

"But what can we do?" he said "Chris is in there and *will* at some point be moved."

"November 26th at 10am."

Jeremy stared him. "How do you know?"

"I've had someone look into it."

"So, we have three months before he's gone." Jeremy looked down at the slippers on his feet.

"Not necessarily."

It took a few seconds for the words to register and when they did, he looked up. "What do you mean, *not necessarily?*"

"I have an idea about how to save him," Taylor said, "and I need you to help make it happen."

Jeremy leaned back slightly, worried about what might come out of his husband's mouth next.

"I want to break him out of prison."

"What! Are you insane? How the hell are you going to break him out of prison, let alone deal with what would happen afterwards?"

"I have a plan…well, I have the makings of a plan, but it will need a lot more work before its ready."

Jeremy's mind was racing—the secure automated unit which they couldn't even step into, the DNA checks, the impenetrable IT security system. The scale of the problem scrambled his mind. Taylor could see cogs inside his head starting to steam as they clunked and whirred. He reached into his bag and pulled out a notebook, slapping it on the coffee table in front of them.

"Here's what I've got so far."

He opened the notepad to a page of bullet points and scribbles and began pointing to the problems one by one.

"Where he is now is impossible to get to. There are no guards and no access for outsiders except in emergencies. Everything is automated including the exercise yard. The security is tight with so many doors and walls to get through that even if you did have the keys, it would take hours."

"Okay."

"The adult prison is even worse. More inmates, means larger facility, more doors and walls, less time outside, higher likelihood of being seen and caught."

"Okaaay."

"So, we have to get him in transit. Between facilities"

Jeremy allowed his mind to become focused on the problem as if it were a plot in one of his books. It was a coping mechanism that kept the idea in some form of fictional fantasy rather than the real world.

"So, he will be taken to the transport truck inside the youth facility, driven to the adult facility…"

"The California City Automated Correctional Facility B," interrupted Taylor.

"…Driven there and then taken to his new cell." Jeremy said. "So, you'd need to know if there will be guards used for the transfer, what security measures are in place, what and where DNA tests are administered, length of journey, route taken…and that's even before you get to actually stopping the thing and getting him out."

Taylor made notes as the questions came. "We have some information that will help…and some that may not."

"What do you mean?"

"I know DNA tests are carried out as they leave the cell, when they enter the truck, when they exit, and when they enter their new cell."

"Okay, that's useful."

"What's tricky is that he will be transferred with four other inmates."

"So, we have to either convince them to join us...or at the least, to not get in the way."

"It gets worse. One of the prisoners being transported is Donnie Fuller."

Jeremy slumped back into the sofa and stared at him. "You've got to be kidding me."

"I wish I was."

"There's no way I want that little punk out on the streets, especially after what his family tried to do to us to keep us quiet. He deserves to rot in prison as far as I'm concerned."

"I agree with you. However, there's no getting away from the fact that he'll be there."

"Then it can't be done...and even if it could, I want no part of it." Jeremy stood up and went back to his computer.

"Maybe we could talk about it later, when the shock has calmed some?"

Jeremy just waved his hand at his husband, who had started to head for the door. When Taylor had closed it behind him, Jeremy stopped pretending to focus on the screen and sat back. What the fuck was his husband getting him into and what the hell was he going to do about it? How could he even contemplate planning a breakout? *It's ridiculous*, he told himself, despite the sense of excitement he began to feel deep in his gut. The same feeling he got when the scheme of a new book began to blossom.

Chapter 17

Taylor didn't mention it later at dinner with Chris's twin sister, Maddie, at the table, even though it was obvious there was an elephant in the room. He didn't even say anything when they went to bed that night. Their routine was civil yet perfunctory that ended with Jeremy rolling over and turning his light out without even reading a page from one of the books next to his bed.

Taylor sat up with his legs warmed by the laptop perched on them, yet still feeling the icy chill from his side. He could understand the Jeremy's reaction. He had felt the same to begin with, too, but the danger their son was in was a much bigger than the feeling of fear that encircled them. The awareness of the injustice of taking Donnie out and the danger of even thinking of such a thing wasn't lost on him either. Still, he knew eventually Jeremy would see this was the only way to protect their son.

While Jeremy came to grips with the idea, there was no reason not to carry on gathering all the information needed. They didn't have long, and if they were really going to do this, they would need all the knowledge they could get.

Taylor started with the first name on the list, Miles Howard. He read the articles about the robbery, how he had been caught because he had crashed in order to save a woman and her baby. He got a sense that this was a good kid really, who had become mixed up with the wrong people, just like Chris. He read about his promising driving career and how it had all gone away after the trial. He had been in prison for over two years already, and Taylor wondered how he was coping with being in there for so long. His sentence of fifteen years was a long one, which meant he would be in the adult prison far longer than Chris-and so had much more of a need to get out.

He switched to the parents now, Mary and Mike Howard. There was a picture of them leaving the courthouse, and to Taylor, they looked like normal, decent folk. Mike owned a garage, and Mary was an accountant. He dug deeper and easily found their address from Mary's business details; she was self-employed and used her home as a base. Her telephone number was also listed.

Before he closed the computer for the night, he stared at the picture of Miles in his racing gear on the screen. A handsome, happy-go-lucky kid who had no idea what was in store for him come the end of November.

But not if Taylor could help it!

***

The next morning's routine was a little less frosty than the previous night. At breakfast, Maddie was talking away, oblivious that there may have been an issue.

At his desk in the newsroom, Taylor reviewed the details about the Howard family. They seemed like the perfect place to start, but something was holding him back. It could have been Jeremy's reaction to the idea, but he knew that Donnie Fuller had a lot to do with that. It could have been the wholesome feeling he got from the look of Miles's parents—maybe they were people unlikely to agree to a criminal act such as this. Maybe he was just a chickenshit who was scared of actually talking to them, to put it out there as an idea without a plan behind it. That was probably closer to the truth which made him angry at himself. He stood up, grabbed his jacket, and marched toward the elevator.

Less than an hour later, he pulled up outside the two-story plank-siding home. He could see Mike's garage at the end of the block. It had a nice cozy feel to the area. Not affluent at all, but certainly all-American. Taylor got out the vehicle and walked toward the wooden steps that led up to the porch, each one creaking as he stepped on it. He paused a moment before he rang the bell.

It took almost a minute before a woman could be seen through the window towardheading for the door. She opened it without particularly looking at who was behind it, a trust that was noticed by Taylor.

"Hi?" she said.

"Hi…Mary Howard?"

"That's me. How can I help you?"

"My name is Taylor Price, and I'm a journalist…"

Before he could say another word, Mary's eyes darted to her husband's garage. "No thank you," she said, and started to close the door.

"Please, Mrs. Howard, I'm here to help."

"That's what they all say. I would have thought you'd have had enough of it by now."

Taylor contemplated sticking his foot in the doorway as he had done many times before with difficult encounters, but he decided against it. He needed her trust, not her fear.

"Mrs. Howard…"

The door closed.

Undeterred, he shouted through the door, "Mrs. Howard, my son is in the same prison as Miles. I have information that will help him."

Through the curtain, he could see her outline pause.

"Mrs. Howard, this is something you're really going to want to know. Miles's life could depend on it."

She stayed frozen for a few seconds before turning around and opening the door again, this time not so wide.

"What information?"

"May I come inside? It's not something you'd want to discuss on the doorstep."

She looked again toward the garage and then stepped aside, inviting him in. She closed the door quickly behind him and led the way into the living room. It was small and quaint with a table in front of the sofa with piles of accounting paperwork neatly stacked upon it. Obviously where Mary did her work.

Taylor sat on the sofa while Mary sat opposite him, in what was probably Mike's chair.

"So, what information do you have about Miles?"

"Mrs. Howard…"

"Please, call me Mary."

"Mary, may I ask if you read the *Los Angeles Times* at all?"

She stared at him, unblinking. "Occasionally."

Taylor squirmed a little in the seat. He hated talking about his own work.

"I wrote an article last week about the state of the prison system, focused on the youth transfers and their…ability to cope with the change to adult prison."

Mary flushed a little at this but didn't remove her eyes from him.

"Yes, I read that. It chilled me to the bone."

That's good, thought Taylor. *I need to lay it on thicker.*

"Well, the situation with the prison system is dire and extremely detrimental to the young people who are in there. The suicide rate is astronomically high, and even though they catch most of the attempts, they don't catch all, and even if they do, the youth are often mentally scarred for life."

Mary's eyes started to tear as his words came out. She sniffed and wiped a corner of her eye.

"And what does this have to do with Miles exactly?"

"Miles is set to be transferred on the 26th of November."

Mary knew that it would happen, of course it would, but to have an exact date made it all too real. For the first time, she looked away from him, her eyes now beginning to stream. Taylor felt some guilt rise but knew this reaction was a good thing. He was just about to continue when the front door opened and in strode Mike.

The man took one look at his crying wife and his face turned to thunder.

"What the hell are you doing to my wife?" he bellowed, moving closer.

Taylor shuffled away on the seat, his hand coming up to placate the man coming toward him, but before it was needed, Mary's hand reached out and stopped him from advancing any farther.

She wiped her eyes with a handkerchief from her sleeve and took a breath. Looking up into her husband's eyes, she spoke. "This is Mr. Price, a journalist."

The word *journalist* made Mike bristle even more.

"Scumbag, wanting to get another story at the cost of our son, do you?"

He started moving forward again, but Mary held him back.

"His son is in the same prison as Miles. He came to tell us there is now a date for his transfer to the adult prison."

Mike's face softened slightly, but he was still angry. He knelt beside his wife and looked at her.

"When?"

"November 26th."

He looked down to do the calculation. "Three months."

They held each other's hands, and their foreheads touched. It was such a moment of love that Taylor almost forgot there was more to add and felt guilty about having to break up the scene.

He cleared his throat. "Actually, there's more."

They both turned their heads toward him but said nothing.

"Please," he said, gesturing for them to sit on the sofa together. He stood and sat where Mary had been.

They still held each other's hands as Taylor continued.

"As you know from my article last week, the likelihood that something terrible will happen to Miles after his transfer is very high indeed. That coupled with the length of time he has left to serve means there's a significant chance he'll be damaged beyond repair."

Mary's eyes began to well again, and Mike's anger looked like it was simmering just beneath the surface.

"My son, Chris, will also be transferred along with your son, and although his sentence is not as long, I'm still concerned the outcome for him will be the same."

"But what the hell can we do about it?" Mike bellowed. "They're in there and will be moved. We've gone through all the appeals, through all the options possible. There's no way we can stop it from happening."

Taylor paused a second for effect. "There is a way."

They both stared now in anticipation at the revelation that could save their son.

"We could break them out."

It took a second to register before Mike abruptly stood. "Right, you've had your fun. Now you can get out."

He moved toward Taylor, unhindered now, and forced him to his feet.

"But I'm serious…" Taylor tried to continue.

"Sure you are," replied Mike, walking him to the door. He was just about to open the latch when Mary spoke.

"Mike."

He stopped and turned around.

"I want to hear what he has to say."

Mike looked at his wife with surprise and then at Taylor with disgust. Taylor took his chance and made his way back into the room. toward

"There are five boys being transferred that day, including Miles and my son. At 10am, they will be loaded up and driven to the California City Automated Correctional Facility B, where they will be deposited for the rest of their term. My plan is to break them out while they're in transit, before they get to their destination."

"And how do you propose to do that, Mr. Price?" asked Mary.

"That…I don't know exactly yet, but I have informants working on getting us more information as we speak."

Mary looked at Mike who was looking back at her. There was some unspoken communication happening between their eyes that Taylor could feel but not hear.

"Thank you for coming over, Mr. Price. I think Mike and I would like to talk about what you have said here today."

"Of course. Here's my card if you need to contact me. It has my cell and email address." He handed it to Mary and walked past Mike to the door. "Although, if you email me, don't mention exactly what we've spoken about here today. Just let me know if it's something you would like to pursue further."

Mary nodded as she joined Mike by the door. Taylor saw himself out and looked back at them holding each other and the card as he closed the door. "Well, that could've gone better," he said to himself.

Chapter 18

The following few days were quiet. Taylor mentioned nothing more about his idea to Jeremy, and things seemed to be going back to normal between them. Jeremy seemed happy that Taylor hadn't raised the topic again, but Taylor's thoughts were consumed with the meeting he'd had with the Howards. He'd heard nothing from them since, nor the police, if they had decided to go that route, but he knew he had to tell Jeremy about it, just in case. That evening, Maddie was staying at a friend's house for dinner, so it was good a time as any.

They often cooked together in a way that would cause even the closest chef and sous-chef to be envious. They leaned across and moved around each other in such synchronicity that it was almost like a dance. These were the times when they felt the closest to each other, working in unison—except on this night, they were not their usual chatty selves.

When they finally sat down at the table to eat, Taylor found he wasn't able to pick up his cutlery, the weight of what he wanted to say bled into the cold metal and forced the fork and knife to remain on the table. Jeremy was already eating when he noticed the lack of movement opposite him.

"What's up?"

"I have something to tell you," Taylor began.

Jeremy put his own cutlery down and stared across at him.

"The other day I went to see the parents of Miles Howard."

A look of fear swept across Jeremy's face. "You did what?"

"I found out their information and visited. Told them about the transfer and my idea about what we could do about it."

Jeremy's cheeks flushed as confused anger started to rise. "Why the hell would you do that? I told you my feelings on it, so you had no right to go behind my back and actually talk to the other families. Christ, you've put us in so much jeopardy." The pause that followed allowed Jeremy to catch his breath *and* for his curiosity to rear its head. "What did they say?"

"They said they would think about it."

Jeremy looked down at the table before his next question. "When was this?"

Taylor squirmed a little. "Three days ago."

"Three days! And you're only just telling me now?"

"Well…."

"What if they go to the cops? What if they've already gone, and we're being watched?"

"Now, don't get over dramatic."

"Over dramatic! Are you serious?"

"Look, even if they go to the police, what can they say? That I told them about the scheduled transfer and that I want to break them out. Where's the proof? I haven't actually done anything yet."

"No, but it would put a bloody huge spotlight on us."

Taylor had to agree and nodded. "I'll call them tomorrow and speak to them again. Try to figure out what their thoughts are and what they might have done."

"Don't you dare. You've done enough damage."

As the silence settled between them, a buzzing began in Taylor's trouser pocket. He pulled it out and looked down at his phone, recognizing the number instantly. He turned the screen toward Jeremy and said, "It's them."

Jeremy's heart stopped along with his lungs.

Taylor hit the green button and put it on speakerphone. "Hello."

"Hello, Mr. Price?" came the soft voice of Mary Howard.

"Yes, Mrs. Howard. This is Taylor. How are you?"

The clunky question made the partners both wince as they stared at the speaker.

"I'm fine, thank you." There was a pause, a breath. "I'm not quite sure how to say this, Mr. Price, but Mike and I have been talking, a lot, about your visit and…"

All eyes were on the phone. Nothing moved as the seconds fell over the edge of a cliff.

"…and we would like to know more about what you said. I know that's not a definite answer, but we would need more information before we can say more."

Even though Jeremy and Taylor had been holding their breaths, they gave a collective gasp before Taylor answered.

"Yes, of course, Mrs. Howard."

"Mary, please."

"Of course, Mary. When I have more to share, I will do so."

"Okay."

"Okay, well…thank you so much for calling. I look forward to speaking again soon."

"Thank you. Goodbye."

"Goodbye."

The phone went blank as Taylor dropped it on the table. They looked into each other's eyes, the air beginning to normalize enough to speak.

"That doesn't mean you're off the hook," Jeremy said.

A smile began to form in the corners of Taylor's mouth. "No, but it's better than the alternative."

"I haven't agreed to anything here."

Taylor began to get excited now, his fingers tapping on the phone. "I know, but look at it. That's one down, three to go!"

"You're getting ahead of yourself. Even if—and it's a big if—even if all the families agree to be part of it, we don't even know what *it* is yet. What any of the plan might be, or if it might even be possible. Don't you think we had better get that straight first before you go off and speak to anyone else?"

Taylor's hint of a smile widened. "You said *we*."

"Well, I can't go letting you cock this up, can I?"

Taylor jumped up and ran around to his husband, kissing him on the cheek and hugging him tight.

"We can do this, right?"

"Hmmm, we'll see."

Chapter 19

For the next few days, Taylor pumped his informants for every scrap of intel he could get. Jeremy had cleared his wall and had begun to put up all the information they obtained. He gave Taylor new queries as they arose, for which they dutifully sought answers. By the end of the weekend, they had all the answers they wanted, but still no clear way of making it happen.

They both sat there and stared at the wall.

"Okay, hot shot, talk me through what we've got," said Taylor.

Jeremy stood up as if giving a lecture and began. "Okay, the truck will drive to the California Automated Juvenile Detention Center and park within a secure loading bay. There will be two drivers in the front who remain in the vehicle at all times, so there's no contact between them and the prisoners. The kids will be automatically checked out of their rooms and a single pathway opened to the loading bay. Here they'll enter one at a time, and the doors shut. The truck has full CCTV so the guards will be able to see and hear everything that's happening in the back. When they're all in, they will exit the facility and make their way to the California City Automated Correctional Facility B, where the reverse process will happen."

Taylor nodded in understanding.

"There are two possible routes the truck could take, both of which are pretty standard and have no deviation or obvious places for hijacking. It's all main roads and freeways and would take around seventy-four minutes end to end."

The routes were marked in red on a large wall map and looked fairly straight. Jeremy moved onto the booklet hanging next to it.

"The truck is a bomb-proof E708 series with fully automatic driving capability and manual override. The driving software has built-in evasion protocols, in case of trouble. Both guards will be armed and expected to use their weapons if required. There is actually a clause in their employment contract that results in instant dismissal if they fail to put their lives on the line to protect their cargo."

Taylor put his hand up like a school child. Jeremy nodded at him.

"What are the rear doors like on the thing?"

"The doors have automatic opening and closing; however, they're only able to open or close automatically when the vehicle is docked at a facility."

Taylor frowned, and Jeremy continued.

"DNA scans are taken upon leaving the cell, entry and exit of the truck, and entry into their new cell. That means that at most, we have would have thirty to forty minutes before we're found out. That's if we can stop the truck and open the back without the guards shooting us and the truck driving off on high alert."

"So, the things we need to figure out are: One, how to stop the vehicle without getting caught. Two, how to open the vehicle without it being docked. Three, how to get the boys out without the guards seeing us. Four, what happens when the truck reaches the facility and there are no kids in the back for DNA testing? Okay...," Taylor said with some enthusiasm, "just four things to figure out."

"Four huge things...so far. And that's from what we know. There will be things we don't. We don't know what we don't know until we work it through."

"Yes, but it's the closest thing we have to a plan so far."

"I would call it more of an outline of a plan, really."

Taylor leaned forward in his seat. "Maybe Mike can help with some of the answers. He is a mechanic, after all. He'll know things we don't in that regard."

"That's true."

He leaned forward even more. "So, can I talk to the other parents now?"

Jeremy rolled his eyes and took another look at the wall. He knew this was as close as they could get without some expert help, and time was ticking. He also knew the next step would be to get the agreement—or not—of the other parents. He turned and nodded.

Taylor clapped his hands together. "Right, I'm on it."

"There's one other thing." said Jeremy. "We also need to be able to communicate with the boys in order for them to know what's happening, but I have an idea about that."

Chapter 20

The Porters both worked in education, so Taylor thought it wise not to try and speak with them during working hours. At best, it would be disjointed and rushed. Instead, he waited until the early evening before darkening their doorstep.

It was a modern brick house with decorative flower patches on either side of the front door, but the flowers had seen better days. As he walked up the path, he noticed a few toys scattered around the lawn and assumed they were from the younger daughters he'd read about. When he got close to the door, a security light flicked on, even though it was barely dusk, and made him flinch. They were obviously security conscious. From his research, he knew about the retaliation some of the other kids and families took on them and their house following the incident their son at the school.

When he got to the door, he rang the bell that also doubled as a security camera. From inside, he could hear the usual sounds of a young family—the clatter of dishes, shouting up the stairs. A man came to the door and opened it abruptly.

"Yes, can I help you?"

"Mr. Porter? Mr. Peter Porter?"

"Yes."

"I'm sorry to disturb you. My name is Taylor Price, and I'm a journalist."

At this Peter stiffened, and Taylor had the sense that he was about to slam the door, so he continued quickly.

"I'm not here for a story. I have information about Edward that I thought you'd like to know."

There was a pause in Peter's movement as he stared at Taylor.

"Taylor Price, you say?"

"That's right."

He looked back into the house and weighed up his options against his need to know the information. He turned back around.

"Alright, come in."

Taylor crossed the threshold and was met with a pleasant aroma of cooking, something tomato-based perhaps. He followed

Peter into the kitchen, where Jane was behind a small island, the pans around her steaming away. She looked up in surprise at the visitor. Behind him came the sound of feet clambering down the stairs as the two girls came running into the room.

"Sorry, girls," Peter said. "You'll need to go back to your rooms for a while. We have a visitor we need to talk to for a minute."

The girls each pulled an exasperated face. "First you call us down for dinner, then you tell us to go back up. Make your mind up, will you?" one of them said.

They flounced up the stairs and left the annoying adults to it.

Jane was still staring at Jeremy when Peter began to introduce him. "This is Taylor Price, Jane. He's the journalist."

The journalist. That was a weird way to phrase it, Taylor thought.

Jane turned the dials down on the cooker and moved around to the side of the island. She extended her hand, "Hello, Mr. Price."

"Please, call me Taylor."

"Won't you take a seat?" Peter asked, gesturing.

He sat at the table that was already laid for dinner as the other two sat down across from him.

Peter turned toward Jane. "Mr. Price…Taylor, has some information about Ed."

Jane looked from Peter to Taylor, her eyes widening.

"Is he alright? Has something happened?"

"No, nothing like that. It's about his transfer. As I'm sure you know, Ed is getting to the age where he'll no longer be able to stay in the youth facility he's currently in."

Jane reached out for Peter's hand and found it.

"The date of the transfer is set to be 26th November. Less than three months away."

Jane's hand viably squeezed tighter as Peter put his arm around her. They both sat there in silence, waiting for more.

"You may also be aware of what life is like for kids who transfer into an adult facility," Taylor said. "In fact, I wrote an article about it a little while ago."

"Yes, we read your article," replied Peter.

"Good. That'll save some explaining. Ed is going to be transferred to the California City Automated Correctional Facility B along with four others."

"Your son amongst them, I presume?" asked Peter.

Taylor was taken aback at the question.

"You are not the only one who can do research."

"Yes, well…yes, as a matter of fact, my son will be transferred at the same time."

They both sat still, looking at him. Taylor felt the blood inside him warming to the temperature of the water in the pan, the steam from which did little to help.

"I'm assuming there's more," Peter said, breaking the silence.

"Yes. My husband and I have no intention of letting our son be put through such trauma, especially with the low likelihood of survival, so I'm talking to the other parents about our options."

"When you say options, I take it you don't mean raising a petition or bringing it to the governor?"

"No, what I mean is getting them out."

"You mean breaking them out?"

"Well, yes."

"And you need the support of the other parents to do so?"

"It would be nice to have that, yes."

Peter sat there, thinking for a moment.

"I'm assuming that you intend to break them out in transit rather than from the facility."

Taylor's eyes widened. "Yes, it would make sense to."

"So, how far have you got with the plan and what else needs to be done?"

"Do I take it that you're in support, then?"

"Taylor, don't think that you're the only one who has been thinking about getting their kid out of there before they're subjected to that hell after transfer."

Taylor smiled. He had naturally been inclined to think he was the only one with such thoughts. He was glad to know he was not. He told Peter and Jane about what they had so far and what else was needed, to which Peter just nodded.

"Okay, so what's next?" he asked.

"Well, once I have spoken to the rest of the parents, I guess we'll get together and brainstorm the rest of the answers."

This seemed like an agreeable way ahead, and Peter stood and raised a hand across the table. "Until then."

Taylor followed suit. "Until then."

Jane stood, uncertain, and walked back around the island in silence. She began stirring the contents of the pans to stop them from burning, but really, she was holding on to the side of the cooker for dear life. Peter led Taylor to the door.

"Here's my number and email address in case you need to contact me. Obviously, discretion is needed."

"Obviously," replied Peter, opening the door. "Oh, and Taylor, it might be an idea to call ahead before you descend on someone next time."

Taylor nodded as he walked toward his car.

Chapter 21

Beverley sat at her dressing table, finishing off the last touches to her makeup. She wouldn't normally receive unknown guests at the house, but when the man on the phone explained who he was, her curiosity was piqued. He had been waiting in the drawing room for five minutes now while she got ready, delaying the meeting for a few moments longer. She looked at herself in the mirror, at the lines and aging face, and tried to find some of that courage that had been so readily available when she was younger. She smiled at herself and shook her hair, which gave her enough energy to stand and head down the stairs.

As she entered the drawing room, he stood up, coffee in hand.

"Mrs. Anderson, thank you for agreeing to speak with me."

"Not at all," she replied, gesturing for him to sit again. "I read your article last week and was curious to know why the person who wrote such a thing would be interested in speaking with me."

"Ah, so you read the piece. What did you think?"

"I think it was typical scaremongering from a paper keen on stirring up emotions, especially those of mothers with children."

Taylor blushed and twisted the mug in his hand. "I can assure you that wasn't my intention, but it wouldn't hurt if emotions were raised on the matter."

"So, what was your intention?"

Taylor put his cup down and leaned forward a little. "You see, Mrs. Anderson, I too have a son at the same facility that William is in. He's around the same age and will be facing the same situation in a short time."

It was Beverley's turn to blush slightly now. "I'm sorry, Mr. Price. I had no idea."

"That's okay. It's not something one tends to advertise."

There was an awkward pause before Beverley asked, "So, what is the purpose of your visit today, Mr. Price?"

"I have some information which I thought you and Mr. Anderson would appreciate knowing, sooner rather than later. Is Mr. Anderson at home?"

Beverley looked toward the door. "I'm afraid Mr. Anderson is away on business."

"I see. Is he due back soon?"

"I have no idea. What's this about Mr. Price?"

Taylor shifted in his seat in preparation. "I have the date that William is to be transferred to the adult facility."

Beverley swallowed and tried not to appear shaken.

"It's the 26th of November. At 10am to be exact."

Beverley's eyes dropped. "Less than three months," she whispered.

"Yes. And my son is due to be transferred at the same time."

She sat there, letting this new piece of information merge with the article she had read and re-read, over and over again. "Is that all you wanted to tell me?" she asked, sniffing to hold back a tear.

"No, as a matter of fact, it isn't." In this opulent surrounding, talking to this woman, he suddenly felt a little stupid at what he was about to say. The reality of this world seemed to make his own and that of his idea completely and utterly ridiculous. He contemplated just getting up and leaving, but the thought of Chris and the other parents kept him where he sat.

He looked into the woman's expectant eyes and began.

"Mrs. Anderson, as you know from my article, the survival rate of any transfer from the youth to adult facility is pretty terrible. The exact figure for the facility our children will be going to is 72%."

"A 72% survival rate?"

"No, a 72% suicide rate."

The number hung in the air like a guillotine.

He continued. "If they don't attempt suicide, they are in the minority, but the consequence is pretty much the same anyway. Depression, disillusionment with the world, breakdown, PTSD, amongst other issues."

The sniffing could not hold back the tears that began to seep out of her eyes now. She tossed her head to the side as she wiped away the evidence.

"Yes, Mr. Price. The outlook is not good. I understand that."

"Yes, well, you see, I want to do something about it."

"Do something about the system? Ha! You'd have better luck pissing into the wind!" She surprised herself with her coarse language. "I'm sorry."

Taylor smiled. "If that were the case, you would probably be right. No, I want to do something to help our children, *our* children, now."

"What do you mean?"

"There are five kids being transferred that day: your son William, my son Chris, and three others. I have already spoken to the parents of two of these boys, and they've agreed to help."

"Help with what?"

Taylor coughed. "I intend to break them out."

Beverley sat back and laughed involuntarily, but it was a nervous laugh, a laugh of someone who would either laugh aloud or cry inconsolably. "You want to break them out of a highly guarded, automated prison where no one can even step foot?"

"No, Mrs. Price. We're going to take them while they're in transit."

The clear, calm reply evaporated the laughter from Beverley's mouth. "And how do you propose to do that?"

"The details are being worked out. All I need to know is if you're interested in being a part of it, or at least, not stand in the way."

Beverley's eyes narrowed as she began to examine the man opposite her in much more detail. "Is this some kind of set up? Are you working for my husband?"

She stood up and backed toward the door. Taylor stood but didn't follow.

"I'm serious Mrs. Anderson. This is going to happen. I am not about to let my son be subjected to the inevitable suffering that would follow his transfer. I am guessing this is something you don't want for your son either; I can't speak for Mr. Anderson. You're right in that trying to change the system, even if it could be done, would take far longer than we have. We must be decisive. We have to act now."

Beverley paused. The emotion that flowed over her with those words sparked something inside. She had spent countless nights drinking away the pain and misery, drowning out the thoughts of

William locked up in that place. It had only gotten worse since she had read that article. Was there something she could do about it? More than her useless husband, that was for sure. A light began to pierce through the darkness inside, a light that hadn't been seen since she had been married. It wanted out, to break free from the dizzying concoction of alcohol and drugs that had stupefied it for so long. It wanted out, and it wanted William out too.

She looked at the man, someone who could possibly help. She may have hit the heights of her status, but she'd hit rock bottom with her life. What did she have to lose?

She looked again at him, feeling a surge of energy coming from within. "Alright, Mr. Price. I'm listening."

Chapter 22

The last family on the list needed no research. Taylor had files on Desi Jacobs and Marcus Fuller long before they were involved with his son. The criminal power couple caused almost as many problems for the city before their separation as they did after; instead of the breakup ending their business, it created two where there was once only one.

Although Marcus had custody of Donnie, it was Desi that Taylor would first approach. Appeal to whatever motherly instincts she had.

He sat outside Desi's Hideout Saloon for almost an hour, watching the bikers and scantily clad girls slide off their rides and head in. He was surprised to see other types of customers pull up too, including men in suits, middle-aged women and even some who looked to be mere teenagers. All of them entered and left within five minutes, making Taylor assume they were there to buy product to be consumed elsewhere.

He was thinking about the things this woman had done to his family. Before Donnie's trial, they had suffered with late-night callers, banging and crashing doors, men following Maddie to and from school, intimidation of both Taylor and Jeremy over their phones. It had been a living hell. But these people were good at their jobs. There were no witnesses, no solid descriptions of these people; they were like ghosts that came and disrupted your life only to disappear into the shadows once you were terrified. The harassment had nearly driven their family crazy, broken them down. But they'd held out. They recorded the calls, took photos of anyone they thought was following them, and installed cameras outside the doors of the house. When the trial had ended, they expected a serious retaliation, and for several nights following, a police cruiser kept sweeping past to check on them. When nothing happened, instead of easing the tension, it only seemed to ramp it up more. Like watching a horror movie, waiting for the jump scare, and each time it doesn't come, the anticipation grew.

He took a deep sigh and dug deep to find enough courage to get out of the car, then walked into the establishment. Due to the wide variety of people entering the establishment, his obvious uncomfortable and unfitting presence raised no heads. He walked up to the bar and waited for the bartender to come over.

"The seller's over in the corner," the man said, pointing to the far end.

"I'm not here to buy anything. I'm here to speak to Desi."

The bartender looked Taylor up and down, then went back to wiping down the counter.

"And who might you be?" The Irish accent came through strong.

"My name is Taylor Price, father of Chris Price."

The bartender stopped what he was doing and raised his eyebrows. He looked around before leaning forward.

"Look, man, I'm not sure speaking to Desi is the best thing for you right now. She has a tendency to let her emotions get the better of her, and after these last few weeks, that's likely to mean your head through the window. Why don't I just get you a quick shot of something warm and you be on your way, eh?"

Taylor had to admit it sounded like the best idea he'd heard all day, but he also knew it wasn't something he could do. How would he be able to break his son out of prison if he couldn't even find the courage to speak to this woman?

"No thanks." He swallowed. "I have information about Donnie that she'll want to know."

After a few seconds' pause, the bartender stood up straight again. "Alright fella! It's your funeral!'

He disappeared from the side of the bar and out to the back, Taylor's eyes following him close.

After a quick knock on Desi's door, the bartender opened it up and put his head through the gap.

"What's the fucking point of knocking if you're not going to wait for an answer to come in or to fuck off?"

"Erm, there's somebody here to see you."

"So?"

He walked in a little further, closing the door to the loud music playing beyond.

"He says his name is Taylor Price…the father of *Chris* Price."

Desi looked at him, daggers in her eyes. "What the fuck is that cocksucker doing here?"

"He says he has information about Donnie that you'd want to know."

She thought about this for a few seconds, about what to do, what she'd like to do. She decided to let him in, and if she didn't like what he had to say, she would smash a bottle over his head and hide the body.

"Okay, show him in."

As he left, she leaned down and pulled out a fresh bottle of Jack from a box. She opened it up and poured herself a shot and placed the bottle on her table, within easy reach.

Back in the main bar area, the bartender approached Taylor, who was fully prepared to be punched out and tossed through the door.

"Follow me."

Taylor's chin lifted as he heaved a sigh of relief and followed. The bartender knocked and showed him in, closing the door behind him.

Behind a desk was Desi Jacobs dressed in jeans, boots, and a low-cut, black t-shirt. She was looking at him as if he was a piece of shit rather than the other way around.

"Taylor fucking Price. Nice to finally meet you."

Taylor shuffled his feet a little before replying. "Indeed. I've met several of your people already, of course."

His reply prickled Desi and she stood up, making Taylor take a half step back.

"My people? If you'd met *my* people, then you wouldn't be standing here now."

They stared at each other, the anger rising in both but only one brave enough to show it.

"So, what the fuck do you have to tell me about my son?"

This is a bad idea, he thought. *This isn't going to work, not with someone like her.*

"Well?"

"I have the date of Donnie's transfer to the adult facility."

This gave a pause to Desi's threatening demeanor, for a second at least.

"He wouldn't be in that facility if it wasn't for your rat son."

The blood began to boil in Taylor's veins as this bitch badmouthed his son.

"I think, he wouldn't be in there if his scumbag father hadn't set him up as a drug mule," he rebuked.

Desi couldn't argue with that, but she was not about to let him know that.

"So, what do you want, payment for the information or something?"

"No. He's going to be transferred on the 26th of November to the California City Automated Correctional Facility B."

He could see Desi's eyes turning inward, searching her mind for a memory.

"I know the place," she said. "Is that all, because I would probably have found that out in a few weeks anyway."

If ever there was a place to discuss criminal activity, this was it, and yet it felt completely like the wrong place to say what he had to. He felt like an amateur telling a seasoned athlete that he is going to enter the next race.

He couldn't do anything to relieve that feeling, and he couldn't leave and go home to his husband, who would be waiting on tenterhooks for his return. He couldn't leave his son behind bars, and yet he couldn't form the words that might free him. He took a deep breath, shook his mind clear, and just said it.

"He is being transferred along with four other kids, my son amongst them."

"Ha!"

Taylor ignored the outburst and continued. "I have spoken to the parents of all the others, and we have decided to do something about it."

"What, you and the others going to get a PTA meeting set up and have a fundraiser for the governor?"

Desi started laughing.

"No, we're going to break them out."

At this, she paused, then threw her head back even further and burst out laughing again, uncontrollably. It took minutes for her to regain enough composure to speak, laughter punctuating each breath.

"Wait, you…and the other precious moms and dads… are getting together…to knock over a highly secure automated facility?"

Hearing it out loud again brought more fits, her eyes weeping as the pain from the laughter began to well up in her sides.

Taylor just stood there and took it. Each bout of hysterics cut deep, but he had suffered worse in his time. He waited for calmness to return before continuing.

"We have a plan. Many of the parents are very capable."

Desi tried to suppress the bubble of giggles that were popping inside her stomach.

"I'm sure they are!" She took a breath and suddenly became very serious. "But if you think I'll be part of your special fucking gang to get your kids out, then you've got another fucking thing coming. You understand me? If, *when* I get Donnie out, it'll be done by professionals and not by the bake-a-cake squad."

"Yes, well, I had to try. Thank you for your time."

"Yeah, now get the fuck out of my bar before I have you beaten to a pulp and stuffed in the trash."

Taylor left gladly, moving through the bar and out the door as swiftly as his legs could carry him. He caught sight of the bartender's surprised expression, as if shocked to see Taylor was still alive. He went straight to the car and got in. He took out his keycard to start it, but his hands were shaking so much that he couldn't find the hole. Like a drunk coming home after a night out, he fumbled, slipped, and dropped it in the foot well. He cursed himself as he began hitting the dashboard, anger finally finding its way out.

Back inside, Desi poured herself another shot and was thinking about the exchange. She was impressed they guy had the balls to walk in here and say what he did. Not many people would, but she didn't know if that was bravery or stupidity, and she was not about to let that cloud her judgment. If those fools thought they could get their kids out, then she was damn sure she'd be able to do it too, without them.

***

From across the car park, in an old, beaten pickup that had been confiscated following a variety of traffic infringements and non-payment of fines, Detective Brant looked out at the comings and goings of the bar, taking detailed notes.

Along with the faces and clothing of the strangers, he noted on a separate page the names and badge numbers of almost a dozen cops. They had entered just like everyone else, staying for around five minutes before coming out with much thicker wallets. Brant despised them and the way in which the system kept the wages for officers so low that they almost had no choice but to take kickbacks, just to keep them going. The system presumed that being honest was its own rewards and was enough to keep the lights on and the stomach's full of your family.

He didn't have to worry about that so much. He had no family, no one waiting at home burning fuel and eating through his cupboards. He was alone and knew it all too well.

He paused, his pen hovering above the pad as he saw the journalist, Taylor Price, entering the building…and he didn't write another thing until the man walked out minutes later.

Brant could see him behind the wheel of his car now, trying to compose himself enough to start it and drive away. What the hell was he doing in this place, a place where even if he had a story to chase, his journalistic instincts wouldn't be so dumb as to allow him to enter? Not after what his son had done.

Taylor's car lights flicked on, and the car moved away slowly. Something in the detective also illuminated, an interest, two questions that would need an answer before he could be satisfied. What the hell was Taylor Price doing here, and how the hell had he managed to walk out in one piece?

Chapter 23

Three days later, Taylor and Jeremy were in Mike's garage, waiting for the other parents to arrive. Mike had kindly offered the space for the private meeting and had cleared away the tools and moved out some of the vehicles to make space. He also provided a large old-fashioned chalkboard on wheels that he used to keep track of work; the board had been turned around and copies of the items from Jeremy's wall at home had been affixed to it.

Mary had made tea and a cake served on china plates and cups, all of which looked out of place sitting on the dirty, oil-stained workbench. At 10pm on the dot, Peter and Jane Porter stepped through the door. They looked nervous, she more so, as they introduced themselves to Mike and Mary, then made themselves a cup of tea. They all stood there sipping politely with an awkward silence echoing around the walls. It felt like the first day of school, or an AA meeting perhaps. Each one with a guilty secret, yet in this case, each knowing exactly what that secret was…because theirs was the same.

Jeremy looked at his watch and leaned toward Taylor. "It's quarter past. Maybe she isn't coming."

"She'll be here. You've got to allow time to be fashionably late."

Jeremy smiled and nodded. At twenty-five past, feet were starting to shuffle, and tensions were reaching a point where leaving was a likely option. The fear that someone would walk in and discover what they were doing was palpable, so Taylor felt he had little choice but to begin.

He coughed to get their attention. "Hey, everyone. If you could take a seat, I think we'll get started."

There was a shuffling as people moved to the chairs that had been brought in from the main house.

"Okay, first, let me thank you all for coming. I know this isn't an easy discussion to be having, but it's one that needs to be had."

Jeremy stood, and after referring to his notebook, looked at the map posted on the chalkboard.

"Here is the plan so far… Our kids will be taken from where they are to where they're going at 10am on the 26th of November." He indicated two highlighted routes on the map.

"The journey…"

There was a sudden bang against the door as it swung open behind them. Everyone jumped around and stared, hearts in their mouths.

An expensive pair of high heels stepped over the lip, and a woman entered, trying not to touch the sides of the door frame as she did so. Once inside, Beverley looked up at the wide rabbit eyes of everyone staring at her.

"I'm sorry I'm late. I got lost."

Taylor walked over with a friendly smile. "It's okay. We've only just started."

He led her to a seat next to Mary, then closed the door.

"As I was saying, the journey takes them from Little Rock to just outside California City. It's a fairly straight line, but there are two possible roads that could be taken. The most obvious is the North 14. It's slightly longer, but it keeps the truck on a major road with lots of eyes on it. The other path takes them into the desert and past Edwards Airforce Base. Although this is a protected area, it's also quieter and probably not their preferred route."

Mike put his hand up. "So how will we know which route they'll take?"

Taylor answered, "There is another transfer taking place next week. We'll follow it and see which way it goes. If it stays left, then it's heading toward N14, if it turns right, then it's going into the desert."

Mike nodded and sat back.

Jeremy continued. "In order to pull this off, we've done quite a bit of research, but there are so many things we still don't know. And some of the things we do know are problems that need to be solved. I have put together a pack of information for you to take home with you and read through, including the problems we have so far."

Taylor started handing out the envelopes.

"The problems are basically these. The truck that's being used is an E708 series automated transport vehicle. It has a double locking facility, one manual and one automated. When the truck reverses into the loading port it connects to a frame that acts like a key. The sides guide it into place and then lock to form a coupling that then releases the locking bar. Once that's released, the driver hits a switch that slides the locking bar out of place and the doors open. We need a way of making that coupling and putting it in place to unlock the bar. Then we need the automatic lock to be released or the bar to be cut through, which will then open the doors."

When Jeremy paused, Taylor looked out across the faces, who all shared a common expression of bewilderment at the first problem alone.

"This is even trickier, as there will be two guards in the cabin with video and sound feeds from the back. The truck will most likely be self-driven, which means that any form of collision or diversion will set off the automatic evasion tactics and alert the police, who will be there in no time."

The mouths on the faces now fell open.

Sensing the fear, Taylor decided to step in. "Now, I know this seems all too impossible at the moment. That the answers we have to find are all too daunting, but our kids are counting on us. They need us to step up and come through for them. If we don't, then what we'll have at the end of their sentence would be a shell, a shadow of the child that went in with all their hopes and dreams ripped away from them."

Some of their eyes went down, some heads nodded, but the mood changed enough for Jeremy to continue.

"So, the truck, unlocking and opening the doors, the two guards, the automatic driver, and the likely route are the main things. The next issue is the DNA check. This happens when the boys leave their cells, when they enter the truck, when they leave the truck, and then again back in their new cells. The journey is one hour fifteen. If we manage to get them out around halfway through, that will only give us forty minutes to get away before the van reaches its destination without them and we start being tracked and chased."

The seriousness of the situation and the degree of difficulty of the problems made the air in the room heavy and difficult to take in.

"All of the information is in the packs you have. Take them with you and study them. We need your brains to come up with solutions, even if they seem outlandish. We can meet here in a week's time to see what we've got."

The seats began to creak as everyone shuffled nervously. Mary began to raise a tentative hand.

"Yes, Mary?"

"Shouldn't we let the boys know what we're doing, you know, so they won't be surprised?"

Jeremy smiled at her. "Yes, Mary, we have a plan to tell Chris about it so he'll be able to pass it to the others. It will mean that communication between you and your sons will need to be planned and organized so that the messages they get can be understood, but it's a simple way of avoiding the sensors."

Mary nodded. "Do you mean we need to write in code?"

Jeremy smiled. "Something like that."

Chapter 24

The hard metal toilet seat was cold in the mornings, and Chris had taken to sitting on it in his trousers for a while before allowing his bare skin to touch it. As he sat there, the bottom delivery door opened and in slid a letter and a copy of the newspaper. It took a few seconds to register, as he wasn't expecting anything.

With his curiosity piqued, his bowels took a back seat as he went over and picked them up. He opened the paper and saw an article from his dad about the increasing price of electricity now that some of the government's buy-in tariffs had run out. A frown creased his face. This was not his dad's usual in-depth enquiry or exposé. He shrugged and threw it on the table to read later.

His attention then went to the accompanying letter.

Dear Chris,

We hope you're doing well. Your father and I went to visit your Aunt and Uncle Byron last week ⌐ We had a great time catching up over old memories

Chris stopped and tuned the envelope over again to make sure it was addressed to him. As far as he knew he didn't have an Aunt or Uncle Byron. He continued.

We walked by the sea and 8 a delicious lunch. It was a bargain at less than 5 dollars each.

He stopped again. This was making no sense whatsoever. And why was he writing numbers instead of words? Before he continued, a sudden realization struck him, and he rushed over to the neat line of books on his desk and searched until he found the one he was looking for—*The Silent Killer*. He skimmed through the book until he saw a page of dialogue between Uncle Byron and Detective Wainwright. He flipped to the end of the book where all was revealed…and there it was. A copy of a letter the killer had sent, in which he'd used numbers instead of letters to disguise a hidden code.

Chris's heart skipped a beat as he remembered the countless hours he and his father spent playing these games with clues and codes for his latest book.

He picked up the letter again and sat down, opening his notebook. The first three numbers were, 7, 8 and 5. He wrote out the simple code, A=1, B=2, etc., then wrote down the corresponding letters.

GHE. *What the hell is that supposed to mean?* He looked again at the numbers and realized the 7 was backward. That meant something, he could feel it, but he couldn't remember what.

He picked up the book again and read the whole of the last chapter for the answer. He found it in easily enough. The killer found it hard using the code for letters with double figures because a K with the code of 11 would be thought of as two ones (AA). Instead, he used backward numbers to work from the alphabet backward. So, Z= ſ, Y= ℇ etc.

He put the book down and tried again. This time it spelled, THE. *That's more like it.*

He read through the rest of the letter, jotting down the corresponding codes: THEHIDDENSTEAF.

He broke it down into the words he could see, THE HIDDEN STEAF. The last word was lost on him. The last two numbers 1 and 6 were definitely an A and F. He scratched his head, letting the words flow through his mind. He tried replacing the one that didn't fit with other letters as he went through the alphabet, but there was nothing. He looked again at the numbers and wondered what it would be if it were a 16, the numbers together. That would make it a P. THE HIDDEN STEP.

He knew that name. He searched the book collection again and pulled out the one with the matching title. In here, the killer used another code. Chris flicked through until he came to the ending. The killer was a spy who hid messages in the letters he sent by using the first letter of every new sentence he wrote.

He picked up the letter again and started working his way through, but it made no sense at all. He tried it forward backward, the start of each sentence and paragraph, but it was all gibberish. He felt a sudden wave of annoyance. He was enjoying himself so much, he'd forgotten where he was for a moment, forgotten that he couldn't go running off to his father for help in solving it. He was on his own. He sighed and looked at the mess he had created on his desk. He put the books back in their spaces, refolded the letter, and picked up the pad. Underneath it all lay the newspaper.

That was it! His dad's article. He flipped over to a clean page in his pad and began writing out the letters from each sentence. STAYCALMWEAREGETTINGYOUOUTUSEFOREACHST ORY.

He read it again and again, making sense of what it said and what it meant. *Stay calm* he got, but what did they mean by, *We are getting you out?* Were they planning an escape?

***

The article that followed the next day helped clear up that question somewhat. At least he thought so. The code contained errors he couldn't make sense of. He wrote out the words and tried as before to switch out any letters that didn't seem to fit.

In doing so, he learned they were, indeed, planning an escape for him and three others. At first, his mind raced with excitement at the idea, at the thought of getting out of here, but then it crashed with the realization of what it meant and what it would actually look like. The danger he would be in, that his parents would put themselves and his sister in… He needed to stop them before they found themselves in a similar cell. Yet, when he went to write to them to tell them, he found that he couldn't do it. He wanted out, of course, and the fear of the transfer weighed heavy on his mind. He just had to trust that they knew what they were doing.

The article also told him in which cells the other boys were— at least he hoped it did. He was in cell 113, which meant he was on the first floor, thirteenth room clockwise from the southwest corner. There were ten cells along the width and sixty along the length. That put him three in from the corner. He had to get a message to someone called Miles in 252, Ed in 336, and William in 653, and he no idea how to do it.

He climbed up onto his bed and lay staring up at the ceiling, trying to picture a solution. Cell 252 was on the next floor up, and forty-two cells along. Getting a message to the higher floors was relatively straightforward; he just had to leave the message in the exercise yard and as it lifted to the next level, it would take it with it. What he struggled with was how that message could then be passed along the next. There was a gap of around a foot between one yard and the next, with the squares of the cage wall barely two inches across. Not wide enough to fit a hand, much less an arm, through to reach across.

An idea suddenly popped into his head that made him throw himself off his bed and grab his notepad from his desk. He wrote the message in the center—consisting of just two bullet points—tore out the page, and began rolling it up along the short edge. Once it was rolled, he began pulling the internal tube that suddenly made it stretch to almost double its length again. He unrolled it and rolled it again a few times until he got the tension right to form the longest tube possible. He snapped off a length of tape and wrapped it around the shaft so it kept its shape.

He looked at his work, proud of his solution. He wrote the number 252 along the edge to give it an address. Now he had to hope that other in their cells would pass it along.

Chapter 25

Taylor stormed through the glass-paneled door and into his boss's office. He slammed down a copy of yesterday's paper on the desk.

"What's this?" Taylor asked, pointing to the page now crumpled before him.

His boss leant forward casually, fully aware of the flamboyant tirade writers tended to get into when you messed with their work.

"It looks like an above-average piece on energy prices. Why? Can't read suddenly?"

"I can read my name printed below it. Yet when I read the article, it's not the same one I wrote!"

His boss leaned back in his chair, the old wooden frame creaking beneath him.

"It's called editing, Taylor. Look at my door… Do you see the word 'Editor' printed on it?"

"Why the hell did you edit *my* work. I'm the best reporter you've got in here!"

His boss raised his eyebrows before answering.

"There's no doubt you're a good writer…"

Taylor nodded.

"But if you think I'm gonna just print whatever convoluted piece of crap that comes from your fingers, you've got another thing coming."

"Convoluted!"

"Con…vo…luted."

Taylor had to admit it wasn't one of his best pieces, but he had little time to write it and get the code in, so what was he supposed to do? He couldn't tell him that, though.

"In the future, please don't change my articles without at least allowing me to correct them myself."

"In the future, please hand in articles that don't need editing in the first place."

They stared across the desk at each other before Taylor stormed out, a little less aggressive than he went in.

His boss simply shook his head and continued with his own work before him.

Taylor sat at his desk in a huff. He pulled up the latest article and began to go through it again to make sure it would pass without comment before the inscrutable face of his boss. This was much harder work than he thought it would be. To get a well-researched article written to a very high standard was one thing, but to then add in a code, a restriction on the words you chose to start each sentence…well, it was an almost impossible task. *Almost.*

He took a gulp of the cold coffee from his desk and started editing.

Chapter 26

The days that followed the meeting in the garage felt much longer than usual. Mike spent extended hours at work with the envelope of problems in his hand. He felt overwhelmed by them all and decided to concentrate on just one aspect that he thought he could bring his knowledge to—how to open the truck doors.

He had downloaded the manufacturer's specifications on the E708 series prisoner transport truck, and from what he could surmise, there were two problems with this leg of their jailbreak plan. The first was the manual unlocking mechanism the truck backed into at the loading dock; this acted like a key that clamped around the bottom frame of the truck's rear and physically pushed back the barrier to the bar that locked the doors. This "key" had to be positioned at just the right height and in just the right alignment to fit. There were slanted edges along the key that helped feed it into position, like the old docking system on the Apollo space missions, where the capsule had to turn around and dock with the Lander. The delicate movements of the astronaut at the helm who made minuscule course corrections as they went wouldn't work on a moving truck, though.

The shape of the key was also a problem. Each truck had a slightly different configuration that the loading dock adjusted to upon receiving the truck's signal. They would have to know the shape and size of the clamp at the back of the truck in order for it to be manufactured. He wrote that down to pass along for an answer.

The second part was to unbolt the truck after it had been connected. There was a thick metal bar that slid into place the whole vertical length of the doors. It was activated by the guards in the cockpit once the truck was docked. There was no way of opening up the electronics and searching for the right cable in time while in motion and no way of making the truck stop. The bar was made from some kind of alloy that made it much tougher than steel and impossible to simply cut through. He added this underneath the previous problem.

So far, he had no answers, and if anything, he kept adding more questions. He felt pretty useless. He swiped through the manual again as Mary stepped into the garage carrying a plate covered in tinfoil.

"Thought you might need this," she said as she put it on the work bench.

He looked up; his eyes bloodshot from staring at the pages on his e-reader but remained silent.

"You're going to damage your eyes if you keep this up," she added, his look of deflation not lost on her.

"I just can't seem to find a way to solve these problems," he said. "They're designed so that there isn't a solution."

"I know, honey. Maybe you should give your head a rest for a while and get some clean air."

She smiled at him lovingly, wishing only to help.

He was just about to turn the tablet off when something that Mary had said caught his attention. An image of the air intake manifold floated through his mind, and he flicked to it now. He brought it closer to examine and moved his fingers across the screen to zoom in. He threw the e-reader on the seat and began scribbling away on the notepad to his side. At first drawing a sketch, then adding bullet points along the side. He stared at them for a few seconds, mentally framing each one to see if his idea would fit. Once it did, he ticked them off and moved on to the next. After a minute, all the points had been satisfied.

He threw the pen down and turned to Mary with a grin.

"You're a genius!" he said, pulling her in for a kiss.

Mary smiled back, her eyes moving between the tablet and her husband's face, completely lost as to what exactly it was she had done.

Chapter 27

Miles sat at his desk and closed the course module he had just completed. He leaned back and stretched his arms up to release the tension in his shoulders, grabbing hold of the bed frame above and letting his body hang, elongating his spine. When he dropped back down to his seat, he looked to the package he had received yesterday from his folks. It was unexpected and had thrown him from his weekly routine. They weren't great lovers of literature, so the cheesy-looking whodunit that was included seemed out of place. And the letter that went with it felt weird and unnaturally written. He had kept it on the side of his desk to try and understand it before he put it away. He had tried to read the book a couple of times, but it wasn't his type of thing, and no matter how many times he read the letter, it made no sense at all.

Staring at them now, he decided he was thinking too much about it and reading things into it that weren't there. He found he had a tendency to do that when something seemed out of the ordinary—to his routine, at least.

He picked up the letter and folded it away with the others, then dropped the book in the bin under his desk. He would put it in the trash cage at the end of the day for collection and disposal.

He heard the familiar rumble of the exercise yard being lowered and decided to stay in this time. He hadn't been out that morning, but the day and the package had exhausted his mind. Instead, he climbed up the ladder and crawled onto his bed.

His eyes had just begun to close, his body drifting away into sleep, when an unfamiliar sound crawled into his ears. At first, he didn't recognize it, for it had been so long since he had heard it. It kept crawling deeper inside his awareness until it ran across a memory of something similar. In his partial dream state, he saw himself in the pedal kart he had when he was just three years old. He was riding it around the yard, over the grass and mud, his legs aching from the effort, but he was unwilling to stop the fun. From the back door, his mom called to him to come inside for dinner. The sun had started to sink, and the chilly evening air had started to sweep the leaves around him as he continued to pedal. His vision started to dim until all he could hear was his mother's call, *"Miles…Miles…"*

"Miles!"

He opened his eyes with a start. He lay there in silence to make sure it wasn't a dream.

"Miles!"

There it was again. He threw his legs over the side and dropped down to the floor. He scrambled on his trainers and slapped the green button to his back door. The low sun made him blink as he stepped out into the cold air.

"About time! What were you doing in there?"

"Malik? What are you yelling at me for?"

"Here," he replied, shoving a rolled-up piece of paper through his bars. Miles stepped forward and reached out with his fingers to grab it and pull it through.

"What is it?"

"I don't know," Malik said, looking a little sheepish.

Miles looked at the paper now. It was held together by a piece of tape that had been torn off and resealed so many times it was all but useless. His cell number was written along the edge. He unfurled it and read it several times before he looked up at Malik, who simply shrugged.

"Thanks," Miles said as he turned and headed back inside.

He had passed on several messages during his time here, none of which were for him. Of course, he had taken a look at what they were before passing them on, so wasn't surprised at the state of the thing in his hands. What he was surprised at was the brevity of the words, just two simple bullet points.

- Read the book
- Apply to letter

Chapter 28

Beverley sat in her favorite seat in front of the fire and stared at the flames that licked at the logs. She'd not had a drink for three days, and her body was crying out for one. She wouldn't have said that she was an alcoholic, but the cravings were making her think otherwise. She'd placed the unopened envelope on top of the three folders of company details that were already on the table in front of her. She had wanted a clear head before looking inside to try and understand the problems. She leaned forward now and picked it up, took a deep breath, and opened it.

The front sheet of paper was a list of the problems that needed overcoming. Behind it were maps, diagrams, and the truck's sales manual. She let her eyes skim over the list at the front to find something she might be able to help with. She didn't know anything about mechanics or hijacking, but she did know something about DNA.

She pulled out the vehicle manual and flicked through to the security features to see what DNA machine they were using. It was a DT17V2, an older model but one that was beautifully simplistic and elegant in design. It had two functions. The first was to take a sample from a person who was present. The roller ensured that the DNA couldn't be collected unless it was moved. The second was to match the DNA to its database. The model before this one used to be connected to the cloud, which stored the data and confirmed each sample, but due to the advancement of molecular organic storage systems, this model could hold the entire register within itself, with no need to connect to the cloud. This meant that information currently stored couldn't be overwritten or tampered with.

She put the envelope on her lap and tried to picture the series of events during the transport where the machine would be used. There was a machine in their cell that would be used to register them leaving the room. The one in the back of the truck would register them entering at Point A and exiting the vehicle at Point B. And finally, the DNA machine in their new cells to register that they had arrived.

If the boys were not in the truck when it arrived at the new facility, there would be no way of fooling the system that they were. And even if there was a way of tampering with the machine in the truck, the one in their cells would be impossible to get to. That meant that at best, they had around thirty to forty minutes before being found out and chased. What could you do in that time? Where could you disappear to? It wouldn't even get them back into the city, let alone an airport, before the curtain came down. So even if all the other problems were solved, there was a huge question about what would happen next.

She threw the papers on the table and looked toward the kitchen. There was a chilled bottle of wine in the refrigerator, waiting. The fire crackled and spat, which drew her eyes back to it and then down to the envelope. She felt useless; the spark inside her that had urged her to participate in this plan to free the boys was slowly being extinguished by the hurdles she had no idea how to overcome.

The bottle was calling. It promised to take away the headache that was forming, promised to make the hurdles a blurred and distant memory. She closed her eyes and tried to find that strength again, picturing William in his cell, waiting for his mom to get him out. The memory of his face as he was handcuffed and led away from the house, and another image of the look in his eyes when the verdict had been read in court … These flashes of William went straight through her heart. She held back a sob and leaned forward to pick up the envelope again, this time flicking through the manual without a clear focus, just to get a clearer understanding of the whole vehicle. The automated driving, the guard's security measures in the cabin, the complex locking system of the rear doors.

That's when she read a familiar passage. She read it again before she grabbed one of the folders from the table, searching for one of her companies in particular. When she found it, she quickly flicked through the pages of its product information until she saw the same phrase. *A specialized high-pressure tungsten alloy.*

She read the description that followed:

Today's high-value locations are secured with both physical and electronic locking mechanisms that rely on a variety of conditions to be met before release. The development of this specialized high-pressure tungsten alloy has allowed the physical mechanisms to be as secure as the digital by preventing any traditional methods of cutting, melting or exploding. With this in mind, we have developed an organic amino acid that can dissolve the chemical bonds that hold the metallic alloy together and form end chains that precisely render a break in the material. This has been used by our military to extract high-value persons in several operational theatres such as…

She picked up the vehicle manual and read the details about the locking mechanism again. That would do it.

Chapter 29

William lay in his bed, propped up on his pillow with his head in a book. He was coming to the conclusion of the fiendishly twisty plot where a spy had come to a sleepy New England town to steal secret codes the major kept hidden in his mansion. The townsfolk were great at finding clues after one of the major's maids were murdered and the safe emptied. The local detective was a bit slow, which left the townspeople having to find the killer themselves. The spy was almost caught so many times before slipping through the net. William particularly liked the code the spy used to communicate back to headquarters. Now he had been captured after a thrilling chase through the woods and was tied up in the major's house awaiting the police to arrive, while the people involved in catching him how they'd done it.

When he came to the end, he smiled and closed the book, opening it up to the first page again where his mother had written a message. *My dearest William, I hope you enjoy the book and put it to good use. Love Mom.*

The book had come with a weird letter a few days ago.

He heard the rumble of the exercise yard being lowered and decided he needed some fresh air after his roller-coaster adventure within the pages. He climbed down and slipped on his shoes. He grabbed a sweater and started pulling it on just as the green light came on. He hit the button while his head was still in the confines of the woolen cave and walked out.

As his head popped out of the top, he squinted in the fading daylight. The air was still warm, and the breeze brought with it a faint smell of the ocean, but considering the distance, it was probably his imagination fooling him with glimpses of a past memory. He walked to the small yard at the end of the walkway and lay down. He looked around for the ball to put under his head and found it was wedged in the corner. He couldn't be bothered to get up and retrieve it, so he placed his hands behind his head instead and stared up at the sky, at the wisps of clouds floating so high above. If he focused on them, then the lines of the bars became blurred and almost invisible.

He replayed the book over in his mind again, thinking back on all the clues scattered throughout it. How clever it was, and how clever were the people in the town who'd discovered those clues and found the spy killer. He wished he was that smart, had something that exciting to chase down. Instead, he was in here, the place where the killer would end up. But, really, what had *he* done to deserve it? An image of his father popped into his head. Not so much an image, but more of an emotion attached to a figure. He couldn't see his father's face clearly but was aware of his body, large and commanding, like the major's in the book.

He turned his head and looked back toward his door. Although he was imprisoned here, he somehow felt a little freer than he did at home. Before, he spent the majority of his time in his room, avoiding any drama with his mother's over-friendly and obnoxious friends, the tense atmosphere that swirled around the house when his father was home. He had friends, online, that he spoke to and played games with, and he did miss them. But being here in this place where there was no tension, no drama, made him feel somehow more empowered, even though it was within the confines of a cage.

He wondered if other animals felt something similar if they had been caged at a young age. When the threat of danger had been removed and the constant struggle for survival all but vanished, did they settle back and enjoy their time in captivity? Away from their siblings and the fight for their mother's teat, away from circling predators, away from the pressure of conforming to social expectations.

He lay there a long time until the beeps sounded and he had to make his way back inside. He rolled over to his side and pushed himself up, sitting there a second, allowing the blood to return to his arms. His eyes naturally fell on the ball wedged in the corner and wondered why the people above had done that. As his eyes moved around the globe, he saw something white fluttering from behind it. He stood and walked over, noticing a rolled-up piece of paper stuck between the ball and the cage. He leaned down and grabbed it as he pulled the ball away. Written on the side was his cell number.

He looked around for answers, but it was just him outside now. The beeps sounded a warning that he should be inside. He clutched the paper and ran back to his room, his heart suddenly beating with haste.

He rushed to his desk and peeled back the tape holding it together. He unfurled it like a scroll and read the two lines. Then read them again. He turned the paper over to check the cell number before reading the lines a third time. Did they mean *his* book, *his* letter?

Chapter 30

Jane's hands were warm and wet in the sink, absently swirling a cloth over the dirty plates. Her eyes were focused outside of the window, at the orange glow that spread across the sky like jam. Her mind was deep in thought about her son. She didn't hear Peter's footsteps behind her as he came down from putting the girls to bed, a routine he had taken over since the trial. Perhaps it was a way of making sure the girls were okay, or maybe it was a way for him to hold on to the children he still could. He headed straight for the living room as he had done all week.

She went to pick up the next dish and found there were none left. She dried her hands and reached over to put the kettle on. When two cups of tea were made, she placed them on a tray and took them in.

As she entered, she saw Peter in his chair with the open envelope in his hands, his eyes narrow and focused.

"Do you want me to get your glasses?" she asked.

He looked up with a sigh. "No, not much point. I can't seem to find any way forward with anything in here."

She set the tray on the table and stood behind him, her arms wrapped around his neck. She stayed there while both of their eyes fell on the pages before them. When they started to become a blur, she kissed his cheek and went to sit on the couch.

Peter put the papers back in the envelope and reached for his tea. Jane was unsure how to start a conversation when he was like this. She could feel the weight he had placed on his own shoulders, the blame he had put on himself for Ed and now for his escape.

He looked up at her and tried to smile.

"Sorry, honey," he said, "just can't seem to wrap my head around it."

"That's okay. No one says you have to."

"Well, someone has to, don't they? Someone has to find the answers to make it all work."

"Yes, but there are plenty of us to do that."

"Just makes me feel useless. Like I was with Ed."

Jane leaned forward and took his hand. "You were not useless, you were, *are,* a caring, loving father who tried to do what he could for his son. And now you're putting yourself on the line for him. No one could do more."

He managed a smirk. "I guess I'm not much of a fast and furious kind of person—more calm and steady. Not really the best qualities for a jailbreak."

She smiled back. "Perhaps not, but to me you are perfect."

He looked down, not feeling perfect at all. He put the envelope on the table and stepped over to join her.

"Tell me about your day," he asked.

"Well, it was nice. The kids are getting used to me, and they seem like a good bunch. The school's a lot different than…than the last one, in a nice way. I sat with Stella and Nessie at lunch, and they told all about the staff and parents to watch out for. They're so funny. Stella is having some of her artwork shown in a gallery next month and asked if we'd go to the opening."

"That would be nice. We haven't been out in a while."

"Other than that, it was just a regular day."

He smiled and nodded. She could see his eyes being drawn back to the envelope on the table and tried to hold his focus a little longer before he plunged himself back in.

"So, how was your day?"

"I read Jeremy's mystery book that we sent to Ed. Not quite a classic piece of literature."

"Well, I guess it's not supposed to be."

"I guess, as long as it does the job. It just seemed a little too plot driven, not much work on character development or social conversation, but I guess that's what people enjoy these days."

"Sometimes it's nice to just get lost in a world where none of that matters, where you can just dissolve away into a fantasy and be swept along in the currents without the need to paddle."

"Yeah, you're right. It's nice to switch off sometimes."

His eyes were back to the envelope again, and she knew she wouldn't be able to keep him away from it much longer.

"Well, I'll leave you to it. I have some papers that need grading!"

"Mmmm," he replied, reaching for the envelope.

"Don't stress too much over that. We'll meet back up the day after tomorrow and know more then."

"Okay," he said, not really listening now.

She left the room hoping and pleading that he would find something he could help with. If not for Ed's sake, then for his own.

Chapter 31

Ed hadn't been out of his cell for days. Inside, the air felt as thick as molasses that made his movements slow and full of effort. He had been lying in his bed for the best part of an hour, contemplating getting up and perhaps opening the back door when the yard arrived. There was a voice in his head that urged him to let the fresh air in, to seek out the warmth of the sun on his skin. But there was another voice, one that spoke in a sweet, sickly tone and poured the warmth of the duvet down into his bones.

If he had listened to that voice to begin with, he wouldn't be here. He would have stayed in his bedroom and none of this would ever have happened, so why shouldn't he listen to it now? He had nowhere to be and no reason to remove his body from the warmth of his bed that held him safe.

The other little voice would not stop niggling away at him, poking on the soft parts of his brain with a bony finger, bringing him back into the present and stirring his body into movement. His leg had been tapping away at the metal bed frame for ten minutes or more, and it felt like the theatre for these two voices to finally have it out. One voice moved the leg toward the steps and down; the other pulled it back, and with Ed simply an unconcerned bystander who observed the ravages of this civil war from a distance.

But as with any internal war, there comes a point when the civilian population has had enough and decides to either support the war effort or get the hell out of there, or if nothing else, to pick a side. Ed sighed and made his decision. He swung both legs toward the steps, bringing the conflict to an end. The victorious underdog of his inner voice smiled but knew that although it may have won the battle, the war was far from over.

Ed climbed down heavily and began pulling clothes out to replace his ripe and musty pajamas. Above them lay his soap and towel that would help wash away this feeling of grime, but that was a step too far perhaps. When he had changed, he bundled the sleepwear into a bag to send away to be washed. That was something at least, he told himself.

The rumble of the yard's ascent grew closer, and with a familiar clunk, the green light by the back door illuminated. He took another deep breath and pushed the button. The air around him rushed out, eager to escape the choking confines of the room. He could see the runway and bars glistening in the sunlight; it had obviously rained at some point in the last day or so.

He stepped out and walked toward the yard, his shoes squeaking as he went. When he reached the end, he looked out across at the tops of the thin line of trees that blocked his view of anything beyond. He knew there was a desert out there somewhere, a city and the sea beyond, but he rarely let his mind wander to such places. They were far too distant and felt unreal in his world, in his cage. Instead, he drew his focus closer, to the swaying of the impoverished trees, the sound of their leaves rustling, the tiny specks that flew from their branches.

From behind him he could hear the opening of doors from the other cells, which caused a sudden spurt of anxiety to burst in his stomach. He turned to walk back in, keeping his head down so as not to make eye contact, when he saw something wedged underneath the ball in the corner. He reached down and picked up the damp paper as he passed and continued toward his door. Once inside, he hit the button to close the door and removed his shoes. He sat at his desk with the paper in his hand, curious to know what it was. There was an ink stain on the outside that he couldn't make out. The tape fell away easily as he carefully pulled the edge open. Once unfurled he could see another blotch of ink in the center, the edges smeared all green and purple as the ink spread out into its component parts.

There were definitely words there, but what they may have said had been lost. A thought entered his mind that if he could dry it, the colors would run back together and be whole again, but he knew that some things could not be rewound or repaired. He squinted again, and one word began to appear, "book". He looked up at the mystery book and letter he had received from his parents earlier in the week and wondered if it was talking about that. He turned the paper over again to see the cell number it was addressed to, but it too was lost forever.

A sudden chill caught beneath his muscles that made them shiver. The fresh air had unfortunately awoken them, and now they were starting to complain about it. He shrugged internally and rolled up the paper into a ball and threw it into the bin without a second thought. He stood and climbed back up to the sanctuary and warmth of his bed. He lay there a while, his mind awake and invigorated by the blast of air and sunlight. It began to click and whirr, creating a new conflict to focus on. The word he picked out from the letter had begun a new argument as to whether he should read the damn book he had been sent or not. This battle, however, didn't last for long. His mind was awake enough to request stimulation, so he climbed back down, grabbed the book from his desk, returned to his bed. He had to do something before the drowsiness of sleep found him again, so it may as well be this.

Chapter 32

The house looked tired and weary. It wasn't exactly falling down, but it had seen better days. Its sun-beaten face had begun to peel and its cheeks to sag. As Desi stepped up onto the porch, she could almost feel sorry for it, if it wasn't for the fact that this was the house where her cheating husband had escaped to. She banged on the door.

After a couple of seconds with no movement, she banged again, louder.

"Hold on!" yelled a voice from inside before Marcus shuffled into view and opened the door.

"Late night?" she asked.

"Aren't they all?"

He opened the door and stepped to the side to allow her in. She went only a few steps before she stopped and turned.

"Is the bitch here?"

"We're alone," he replied, rolling his eyes.

This allowed her to continue her way to the kitchen, where she began filling the kettle for a coffee.

Marcus followed and smirked. "Make yourself at home, why don't you?"

Once she had found a clean cup, she turned around.

"So, what have you got?"

"You mean coffee-wise or…"

"Don't be a smartass."

"Okay," he grinned, sitting on a stool at the breakfast bar and lighting up a cigarette. "I've had several guys look into the details and logistics—guys who have experience with similar things—and they all tell me the same thing."

She waited.

"That it can't be done."

"That's bollocks. If a group of nerds can have a plan, then I'm sure as hell a bunch of guys who used to knock off armored cars can have one."

"That's exactly it—they *used* to. Since things have gone automated, there's been a decline in that particular specialty.

116

Money isn't transported anymore, and those precious items that are, are all moved with the latest automated vehicles with security features that make it a nightmare to stop and break into. Now add in the fact that you want to break these kids out without alerting the guards in front or the cops...and that all makes it impossible. The moment you cause the guards to react, the instant you make the vehicle stop en route, all hell breaks loose."

Desi stood there and poured the water, thinking.

"What about Stevie?" she asked.

"He was the first person I asked."

"Nick?"

"He's inside but said the same."

"Old Charlie?"

"Dead."

"For fuck's sake. Can it really be that hard to find some fucker alive who can do it?"

Marcus shrugged. "It's just not a useful skill set anymore, at least not for anyone who knows the details. Look, not only do you have to open the truck, but you have to do it while it's moving. It's the only way. And you have to do so without alerting the guards or making the truck think it's being broken into."

"What about the guards? Can't we get to them?"

He sighed. "Even if we knew who the guards are that will be transporting them, they're nothing more than glorified babysitters with automatic rifles. They don't drive the vehicles; they don't have access to open the doors unless the vehicle is docked; and they sure as shit wouldn't have a job left if they'd lost their cargo along the way."

"Well, there must be a way."

"If these people can figure out a way around all these issues, then I'll be all ears. But I seriously doubt they can."

Desi took a sip of coffee and thought back to her visit from Taylor. The look on his face said something other than failure.

Marcus broke her out of her thoughts. "Maybe we should go along and listen to what they have to say?"

"What? You expect me to suck up to that fucker who snaked on our kid?"

"It might be the only way to get Donnie out."

"This is your fault to begin with!" she shouted.

"Now, there's no use in going over old ground," he said, raising his hands. "We are where we are, and there's no changing that. If we want to move forward and get him out, then we may have little choice but to align ourselves with the other parents. At least to start with. Once we know what they're doing and how they're doing it, there's nothing to stop us from doing it ourselves."

She smiled for the first time since being there. Becoming part of the Brady bunch left her feeling sick to her stomach, but espionage…to infiltrate and steal all the necessary knowledge to do it herself sat much better.

"Okay, I'll do it. But you make sure that we have people who can use the information I get."

"*You* get? I'm coming too. This is my son we're talking about."

Chapter 33

Donnie sat in the doorway to the yard. The morning sun was making its route around the building and had begun to creep its way into the room. As it began to warm him, his mind replayed the letter that was on his desk. He had read it so many times since it had arrived that he almost knew it by heart. Lucy was safe and was looking for a waitressing job. She said she loved him and would wait for him to get out, but he knew it was a long time. She also said she had their money safe, and no one knew anything about it. The letter had contained everything he had wanted it to, and even came with a photo of her, so why was he finding it hard to believe the words? He was raised to be distrustful; it was a part of his survival which meant the chance for any real, meaningful relationship was almost doomed from the start. He didn't want that legacy for himself.

As he sat there now, he tried to feel stronger by having her words close, allowing his natural state of skepticism to be taken over by hope. They would get their dreams, and the extra money that he would demand for getting pinched would be enough to make a start. He had to believe that.

The sound of a basketball being bounced and shot began to find its way onto his consciousness. The guy next to him was out in his yard. He seemed friendly enough and had even tried speaking to him before; not that he had been in the mood to be spoken to back then. He felt different now. The letter and photo had lightened his mind and allowed good thoughts to enter, good enough to even make a friend. After all, he would have to be friendly in the new town he and Lucy would eventually go to.

He stood up, walked along the runway, and stopped as it passed his neighbor's yard.

"Hey," he offered.

The guy with the ball stopped, shocked by the word.

"Hey," he replied, putting the ball under his arm and walking over. "You're Donnie, right?"

"Yeah, how did you know?"

"Word gets around. There's nothing much else to do."

"No, there's not. What's your name?"

"I'm Miles."

Donnie was struggling to think of what else to say. "So, what are you in for?"

Miles sucked through his teeth, "Oh no, we don't ask that question here."

Donnie felt embarrassed at breaking the unknown protocol. "I'm sorry, I…"

Miles burst out laughing "I'm only joking with you."

"Oh." Anger rose, but Donnie gave a crooked smile back.

"I was a runner and got caught after a job. What about you?"

Donnie tried to think of a way of explaining it that didn't make him sound like a loser.

"I got busted smuggling a shitload of drugs over the border."

"Nice, so how long did you get?"

"Five years. What about you?"

"Fifteen!"

"Ouch!"

"Yeah, tell me about it."

Donnie thought about being here for that long and couldn't believe someone who seemed as happy as this guy could have so much time left.

"How do you stay so calm?" he asked.

"Well, I wasn't to begin with, but then you kind of get into a rhythm. It could easily drive you crazy, and it still does at times, but I have a feeling that I'll be alright."

"Be alright? That's a fuckload of years to be stuck in here."

Miles shrugged. "Maybe."

They both stood there, unsure where to go next.

"So, have you tried any of the courses yet?" asked Miles.

"No, not yet. I've looked at them but just don't know where to start."

"I know that feeling! I've almost done them all now. I think they're having to work hard to keep up with me."

"Whoa, how long have you been in here?"

"A little over two years. I don't think they expected anyone to be here that long and to actually do the work." Miles chuckled.

Donnie smiled and nodded.

"If I were you, I'd start with the English and math stuff first," Miles suggested. "Go as basic as you can and build up. There's no rush, right?"

"Right, thanks."

"No problem. It was nice talking to you. Catch you again." With that, Miles bounced the ball and headed back to the net.

Well, that wasn't so bad, Donnie thought. *I could get used to this talking shit!*

Chapter 34

Mike's garage felt a little warmer than it had at the first meeting. Mary was doing a great job at pouring tea or coffee and getting people to relax, as if it were regular PTA session. Each parent had the envelope under their arm like it held a school report with the latest update on their child's progress—and in a way, it did.

"Hi, everyone," Taylor began. "If you could take your seats, we'll get started."

There was the usual shuffling as everyone took the same seats they had sat in before—creatures of habit.

Suddenly, the door banged from behind them. Everyone whipped their heads around with fright at the noise. Taylor and Jeremy felt their temperature rise as Desi and Marcus stepped in, bold and unapologetic.

"Please, take a seat," offered Taylor, gesturing to the empty chairs set out in front.

All eyes were on them as they sat down.

"This is Desi and Marcus, the parents of Donnie, the fifth child being transported."

Some of the faces showed relief, but others remained concerned.

Taylor looked out across the faces, a full house, every boy represented by a set of parents who wanted him out. For the first time that week, he felt optimistic about their chances. He had struggled with any of the solutions to the problems and was relieved when he had the message from Desi that she wanted to join their group. That was before the journalist's skepticism kicked in, firstly on her motivation for joining them, to steal ideas or sabotage maybe, and then to the fact that she, with all her underworld contacts and connections, couldn't find a way of doing it.

"Okay, so we've had some time to look at the hurdles we must overcome for this to work. Anyone want to share what they've come up with?"

The room was quiet except for the creaking of the chairs as people shuffled in their seat, unwilling to answer the teacher's question for fear of looking silly.

"Okay, let's look at one hurdle first. How to open the doors. Now, as we know, this is a two-step system, the manual docking key and then the electrical release of the locking bar."

Everyone's eyes were down on the papers in front of them, all apart from Desi's and Marcus's.

"Mike, what were your thoughts on this?"

Mike looked up, a little flustered at having been called upon.

"Well, the manual docking key is relatively easy to manufacture, if we knew the size and shape of the docking port it fits into. For that, I would need plans or schematics to work from or at least high-resolution images that can be scaled."

"And it doesn't matter that the vehicle is moving for the door to unlock?"

"No, although the pattern looks complicated, the system is pretty simple. It just pushes a lever that will allow the bar to be moved. It would just need to be held steady to keep it attached."

"Okay, that's good. We're unlikely to be able to get the plans, so what about the high-res images?"

Jane put her hand up. "I work in a school, and I'm sure I could borrow one of their cameras from the art department. I think it's pretty good equipment, better than a phone camera."

"That's great. Would they be high enough resolution for what we need?" asked Taylor.

"I don't know for sure," she replied. "I'll find out."

"Perfect. Can you two get together to sort that out?"

The two looked across at each other and nodded.

"Well, that's a good start. There is another transfer happening next week, so we'll need to get ready for that. Perhaps you both could follow the truck and kill two birds with one stone?"

They both frowned.

"You can take the pictures you need and also find out which route the truck takes. The main highway or the desert road."

They nodded again, but the nervousness obvious.

"So, that's step one. What about the locking bar?"

A few seconds passed before Beverley put up her hand.

Taylor gestured for her to speak.

"Well, I've been looking at the composition of the locking bar on the truck. It's a tough tungsten alloy. But I have a company that makes a chemical that should cut through it, and a slight adaptation would also repair it again once it's closed."

Taylor's eyes lit up. "That's amazing! And how does this chemical work? What are the conditions that would make it success or fail?"

"Well, it's a viscous liquid, so there would have to be some kind of spillage containment so that only the affected area is treated. But since its design is formulated to only attack the molecular bonds in just the alloy, it should be safe to use anywhere."

"Okay. Could you look into this further and come up with the best way to get it done?"

She nodded, looking pleased.

"So, we may have a way of opening the truck. That's great news. Next is the guard issue. Now, we don't know who they are, so we just have to assume they'll respond as instructed, which means activating the automatic response and call for back up with their guns aimed at us."

Mike volunteered his answer this time.

"I've had a thought about this. The truck is on autopilot, right? Which means the guards are only there if things go wrong, not to actually operate the vehicle. So, why don't we just knock them out?"

There was a collective chuckle around the garage. Even Marcus laughed until Desi shot him a look.

"How do you think that can be done?" asked Jeremy.

"Well, according to the truck's specs, the air intake system is classed as a secondary function, so it's not tied into the higher-level security system. We could pierce the intake hose for the cabin and fill it with a knockout drug."

The chuckling stopped as minds began racing.

"How do we get the drug into the hose?" asked Peter.

Mike walked over to the shelves on the back wall. He reached inside a plastic crate and pulled out a small, electric, remote-controlled car.

"From the looks of the engine, this thing could be driven underneath with an attachment that pierces the hose and delivers the drug."

"What sort of attachment?" asked Beverley.

"Something like an industrial syringe. The hose only takes air, so it isn't made of thick rubber, just wired plastic."

"And what drugs would you use?" asked Marcus.

Everyone stared at him. Even Desi looked up in surprise.

"Well, I don't know," Mike said. "What would you suggest?"

Marcus thought for a second. "What about some Mexican valium?"

Eyes of confusion looked back at him.

"Rohypnol!"

"Isn't that a liquid, though?" asked Jeremy.

Mike shrugged. "Yeah, but there must be a way of changing that."

"You could vaporize it," said Beverley.

"Would that be hard?"

"Not at all. It's the same process that's used in vapes and e-cigarettes. You would have to experiment to get the temperature right, though."

"Great! Marcus, would you be able to get some of this drug for Beverley to test?"

He shuffled in his seat, the eyes of Desi burning into the side of his head.

"Yeah, sure."

Beverley looked just as nervous about the idea as he did.

"Okay, you two can liaise about that. Next is the fact that we have to do all of this in transit. We can't stop or even bump the truck too hard as it will trip the automatic defense system."

Eyes were down in thought until Mike spoke again, more thinking out loud than offering an answer.

"What you need is another vehicle to come up behind it to attach," he said, then looked up, a little embarrassed that the words had come out.

He continued nonetheless. "I guess I could retrofit a vehicle with the docking key, but with the emergency response, it would need to be driven calm and steady and connected gently no matter what."

"Well, that's something that can be done," Taylor said.

"What about witnesses? Surely there'll be cars passing by that would cause a problem" Peter said.

Minds began to whirr again.

Jeremy spoke next. "What about making this vehicle look like it's part of the truck?"

Everyone frowned.

"I used something similar, but the other way around in my book, *The Long Road*, where a vehicle looked like it was just a single piece, but in fact, it was two separate vehicles that could be detached. Maybe we could make it so the vehicle we use looks just like an extension of the truck itself?"

"If we turn the vehicle around," Mike said, "so that the cab's at the rear, then we would have an area in the front for people to work and the boys to get into. Kind of like a truck in reverse, you would have a concealed area that's attached to the truck. A safe place to do all that's needed."

"That's an awesome idea!" said Taylor, a broad smile across his face. "Is that something that can be done?"

"Well, I have an old van frame that might work...maybe use some parts I have lying around, but most of it I would have to buy."

"Okay, do it," Jeremy said. "Let us know what the costs are, and we can help divide that out."

Mike nodded.

"Thanks, Mike. It looks like there's a lot of this falling your way."

He just shrugged a reply.

"Okay, finally, we have the DNA machine. We don't have access to the ones in the cells, but what about the one in the truck? If it gets to its destination and opens up without it being swiped, then it would give us thirty to forty minutes tops to get out of there. If we can trick it somehow, that may give us an extra five minutes."

"And then what?" asked Peter.

"What do you mean?"

"Well, say that we pull off all these crazy things, then what? We'd have forty minutes to do what, go where before they come looking and arrest us all?"

There was a murmur of agreement spreading as the thought sunk in.

"Well, I can't speak for anyone else, but Jeremy and I are going to move away. He has family in Canada where we can stay before figuring out where we go next."

"But I have two young daughters. I can't just pack up and disappear."

Frustrated words echoed off the walls and grew louder as each voice strained to be heard, worries and fears began to explode.

"What the fuck's the matter with you all?" shouted Desi, standing up.

The room fell silent.

"You've got your precious lives, in your precious homes with your bullshit jobs, and you're putting that above your sons?"

They all stared at her now.

"Fuck it all!" Desi continued. "You have the balls to pull off a job like this but then shy away from the consequences that might come afterwards. You don't deserve to get your kids out, if that's the case."

Mary stood up in the back.

"Well, most of us have lived our lives within the bounds of the law, and whatever change that's coming as a result of what we're doing, should naturally be of concern. We do have houses and other family to consider that shouldn't be discarded without a second thought. That doesn't mean we aren't committed to our sons—if we weren't, then we wouldn't even be here—but this is a huge personal hurdle that cannot be overlooked."

Everyone was staring at Mary now.

Desi sat down, angry inside but also knowing that she didn't really have a plan for afterward either.

Mary continued. "We all have our own circumstances to deal with and what that might look like, but these gentlemen did not offer to fix that for us. They offered to help save our children, and I for one am thankful of that. What we do after needs to be a personal choice."

"Thank you, Mary. It's a concern that we all need to sort out for ourselves, and the longer we have after we get them out, the better," Jeremy said, waiting a beat before continuing. "So, what are people's thoughts on the DNA machine?"

Beverley's eyes fell to the floor before she spoke. "It can't be altered."

"Are you sure?"

"Yes, the model is self-standing with no memory override or adaptation. New information can be added from central, but none can be altered or removed."

"Couldn't we build something that mimics the movement with their DNA on it?"

"The DNA that's present on the finger is contained within a variety of substrates like sweat, skin molecules and proteins. What parts and to what degree the machine analyzes these is a trade secret. It won't sequence the whole strand, but enough to know it's got a match. Not to mention the method of extraction is unknown. It could be phenol/chloroform, magnetic beads, ballistic motion, or some new DNA extraction technique kept under wraps. Whatever it is, it needs a live sample to be sure to work."

The disappointment from these words was felt around the room and almost removed all the positive steps forward they had made. Jeremy felt the room shift and stepped in.

"Thank you, Beverley. That's really useful to know."

She smiled, not feeling very useful at all now.

Jeremy said, "So, we have ways of overcoming the vast majority of these hurdles, and we all have things we need to get moving on. Can I suggest that you exchange information if you have to get together after this and we'll meet again in a couple of weeks to see where we are with everything. But remember, discretion is of the utmost importance."

When everyone started gathering their things to leave, Taylor placed his hand on his husband's shoulder as a thank-you for stepping in. He wasn't sure which he preferred: the unknown answers to the problems or the weight of the answers they did know that now required action.

The parents began to file out, each pair having quiet conversations on these very things.

***

From down the street and in a much nicer car, Detective Brant had been watching the garage. The meeting had apparently adjourned, and it looked like the end of a church service as the people exited, their mood somber. He didn't recognize some of the faces, and some he had a vague recollection of, but the others he knew without doubt. It was these faces that made him gasp. What the hell was going on here? The two simple questions that had formed a week ago and had urged him to tail Mr. Price when he had the chance suddenly exploded to an overwhelming number as these people dispersed from the scene. He couldn't understand it or make sense of this congregation, but he was sure as hell going to find out.

Chapter 35

Detective Brant woke with a start. The sheets around him were scattered to the edges of the bed and beyond. Memories of his fitful dream floated around the edges of his mind, vignetting his thoughts that now, with his eyes opened, began receding into the darkness, but some of the faces remained.

He got up and tried to shake off the emotions that kept drawing him in, to keep pulling apart the details of the nightmare, as he went about his morning routine.

When he was dressed, he sat on the single kitchen stool with his morning coffee and tried to pull a distant memory from the past into the present, but it kept swirling around with the ghosts from his sleep until he couldn't tell which was which.

Absentmindedly, he took a sip and placed the mug down on the counter a little harder than expected. The clang reverberated around the sparse room. The echo wasn't lost on Brant as he looked around, noticing the single mug, the set of four plates on the side and knowing that only the top one had ever been used. The room was small and functional and missed all the homely comforts a woman or a family would bring.

In his tired state, he allowed his mind to wander, wondering what it would be like to have pictures on the wall, drawings on the refrigerator, noise of laughter floating in the air. He had prioritized his career over his personal life, a cost taken willingly. But recently, he thought that price may have been too much.

He recalled the officers that he had seen the other night picking up their bribes from Desi's, the look of distrust he received at the station from guys who knew he wasn't on the take. The fact that he wasn't made him a liability, someone not to be trusted, which he thought was ironic. When was it a bad thing to stay true to your principles and uphold the law? As a police officer, it was surely part of the job. But that part was being controlled by corrupt politicians and government officials who had their own interests in mind. It was becoming clearer to him that he was not a man on the street making a difference, but a pawn in a game played by wealthy and influential criminals. Maybe it had always been that way, and it had taken time for the rose-tinted glasses to slip. Either way, he was getting sick of it.

He drained the last of the coffee, washed his mug, and placed it on the side. He grabbed his jacket and, with a last look at his empty life, left for work.

It wasn't until he arrived at the station and closed the door to his office that he let the memories of the night before replace those of his dreams. He called up the computer system to start a new search and typed in the first name, *Taylor Price*. Up came his details, addresses and contacts, known associates and any past dealings with the police. Brant hit the button for links and typed in another name, *Desi Jacobs*. A much denser file filled up the right-hand side of the screen, pushing Taylor's measly details to the left. Across the top, over the full width of the screen was a section that housed several notes pertinent to both. The first ones concerned the trial, the information from Chris regarding Donnie, and the sentences. As he scrolled down, this took up most of the window. It wasn't until he got to the last two points that he stopped. Both children were being detained in the California Automated Juvenile Detention Center, and both were due to be transferred on November 26th.

On this last note there was a hyperlink tab. He pressed it and up came the details of the transfer, including the other youth being moved. As he clicked on each name and their details emerged, the parents' images and information appeared, and each time a familiar face stared back at him.

He sat back in his chair and let out a long, slow breath.

Chapter 36

They sat across from each other with the remnants of large glasses of wine in their hands. Jeremy swirled the deep-red liquid around the bottom of the glass, creating spider legs that ran back down to join the rest before being thrown back up again by the turbulent wave. Taylor picked up his glass and downed what was left. The silence between them was a mixture of anticipation and dread as if the atmosphere were both as thick and heavy as a coal mine yet as devoid of air as a mountaintop—both making it difficult to breathe.

A noise from above brought them out of their thoughts and when footsteps skipped down the stairs, that was a signal for Jeremy to swallow his wine and prepare himself.

Maddie came swinging around the bottom of the stairs and into the room.

"Hey," she said as she went about looking for food to devour before heading out.

"Hey, honey, can you sit down a moment? We want to talk to you," Taylor said.

"Can't it wait? I said I'd meet Beth at her house and then we're going to see a movie."

Jeremy shook his head somberly. "No, we need to have a chat now, really."

She looked over at them for the first time and saw how they were sitting, huddled over empty wineglasses on the table.

"What's up?"

"Come and sit down, honey," Jeremy said as he pulled out a chair next to him.

"Okay, you guys are scaring me now. Has something happened to Chris?"

As she sat down, they all looked at each other for a moment.

"No, honey, nothing's happened to him…yet," began Taylor.

"Yet? What's that supposed to mean?"

"It means that he's due to be transferred to the adult facility in two months, and once there, who knows what will become of him."

Maddie looked down. Although she was Chris's twin, she had been trying to dismiss the dark feelings she had about him being in prison. When he first went in, she thought that the strange twin feelings that happened between them sometimes would mean his feeling of depression and being trapped would transmit itself over to her. But, to her relief and guilt, it hadn't.

"I know," she said finally.

Taylor and Jeremy looked at each other again, stealing themselves for what came next.

"We have a plan to help him," said Jeremy.

It took a second before a small crease formed on the smooth skin of her forehead. "What do you mean?"

There was a pause, neither man wanting to be the one to say it. Taylor took a deep breath and spoke.

"We're going to break him out of prison."

Maddie's eyes widened. Her face drained of color.

"What?"

"We can't sit by and watch him be destroyed by a system where he'll be left to rot or worse."

"So, you're going to break him out? You two?"

"Not just us," took up Jeremy. "There are four other children being transferred at the same time, and all of those parents are involved as well."

Maddie's eyes began darting around the table as if chasing the elusive answer to an unknown question.

"How…when…" she began.

"The details don't matter. What does matter is what happens afterward. Once we do this, they will be looking for him and us, which means that we have to leave."

"Leave? You mean, like, *move?*" her voice was beginning to rise.

"Leave the country. We're thinking of heading to stay with Grandpa Belanger for a while."

Her mind took in the words, then handed back the implications of such an action.

"You want to break Chris out of prison, cross the border to Canada, and somehow hide out at Grandpa's? That's the first place they'll look. And how do you expect to cross into Canada if our names are on a watch list? Do you know what you're doing? How is this going to affect me and my life?"

"We know it will be a big shift in—"

"A big shift? You're basically making us fugitives for the rest of our lives!"

"But if we don't, then the consequences to Chris will be catastrophic."

"Chris made his own choice and has to live with the consequences. You can't expect all of us to do the same. I did nothing wrong; neither did you! Why should we have to pay for his stupidity?"

She stood, the chair scraping behind her. "No, I won't do it. I won't go anywhere. Just leave me out of your plans. I'll go and live somewhere else and deny all knowledge."

She turned and walked out, heading for the front door. Taylor stood to follow, but before he caught up, Jeremy grabbed his arm.

"What are you doing? We can't let her leave with that information, as upset as she is," said Taylor.

"She's not stupid," Jeremy replied. "It was bound to cause a reaction, and we have to just give her a bit of time to process it. If we chase her, she'll just continue to run."

Taylor knew he was right, but that didn't stop his blood running cold as the front door slammed behind her.

Chapter 37

"Okay, Mrs. Anderson. We'll have the equipment and a private lab space available for you tomorrow. Is there anything you'll need?"

"Umm, yes. Will Rosie Woods be in the building tomorrow?"

There was a brief pause on the line.

"I would think so. Miss Woods is always in. She's the one who will have to sign off on your request."

Beverley's stomach heaved. She did not want to bump into her old colleague under the best of circumstances, let alone when she was up to no good.

"Yes, of course. Thank you."

"Okay then, we'll see you tomorrow."

We'll see you tomorrow. Great.

Beverley hung up the phone as several messages came through, inviting her to a brunch and a dinner party. She clicked on them and declined the invitations with a pitiful excuse of a cold. She tossed the phone on the table and sat back into the sofa. She had barely taken a breath before the front door opened. Only one other person had keys and would come in through that entrance. She checked her watch and was surprised to see the time that had passed. As she looked up at the door, in strode her husband. He looked at her for a moment before putting his briefcase down and heading toward the bar to pour himself a bourbon.

"Thanks for coming over," she said.

"I was surprised to get your message," he said, dropping a large ball of ice into his glass. "From the tone of your voice, it sounded like I'm going to need this."

She couldn't deny that. She had been dry for weeks now, but she suddenly felt the need for something strong. David crossed the room and sat on the couch opposite her, taking a good sip.

"So, what's all this about?" he asked.

Beverley leaned forward. She had been preparing for this conversation and had a checklist of steps to take.

"First, I want you to read this," she said, handing over Taylor's article.

It took him a minute to skim through before throwing it on the table. "Alright, so this is about Will?"

"Yes."

He sat back, looking a little relieved.

"Okay, so what do you want to do about it? You know I've spoken to the Governor and several people in the justice system, and there's nothing that can be done."

"There is something that can be done, and I'm doing it."

A look of incredulity swept across his face. "What can *you* do about it?"

"I…we are breaking him out."

David paused for a second before he threw his head back and laughed. Beverley felt her cheeks flush as she remembered reacting the same way when Taylor had made the suggestion to her, right in this very room.

After a few seconds, he managed to calm himself enough to continue. "What on Earth do you mean, you're going to break him out?"

"Me and the parents of the other kids being transferred have a plan to get them out."

He looked at her closer this time and took another sip of his drink. "You're serious?"

"Yes."

David's demeanor suddenly switched from mocking to anger. "What the fuck have you done? You can't get yourself or me mixed up in anything criminal. What the hell are you thinking?"

Beverley's stomach tightened, "I'm thinking that I'm not going to let our son perish in a prison that you should be in instead of him."

"Pfff."

"I'm thinking that as a parent, I need to do everything I can to ensure the safety and future of my son."

"And you don't think I want that too?"

"I don't think you think about it at all. You're too busy with your other babies."

"Don't be ridiculous. I think about him all the time, but there's nothing that can be done, and to go on a foolhardy path that will only get you locked up in the same place is absurd."

"As absurd as putting your fifteen-year-old son's name on a company that you knew was being bled dry?"

"I didn't know what was happening until it was too late."

"But you did put his name on it. Who does that?"

"Look, there's only so much apologizing I can do for that."

"Words are meaningless, David. Actions are what matters now."

"Actions! Are you insane? You'd risk everything for this ridiculous idea? No, I won't allow it. You need to stop now and distance yourself from these other crazies as much as possible."

The internal battle that had been raging ever since he'd stepped in the room suddenly stopped, as if all the combatants ceased fighting and looked up at her to see how she'd react.

She lifted her chin, resolute, and spoke softly. "This is going to happen, so you need to get ready for it and do whatever you need to, as do I."

David slammed his glass on the table, spilling its contents, and stood up, towering over her. "Do whatever I need to? You expect me to be able to convince the police that I had nothing to do with it? To sort out twenty companies, houses, bank accounts, assets that will all be frozen the minute you break him out…in how long?"

"Two months."

"In two months! To live the rest of my life as a suspected fugitive. You may as well lock me up right now!"

A thought flashed across Beverley's mind.

"Nope, I won't allow it," he continued. "And if you think I'm just going to stand by and let you ruin us, you've got another thing coming."

She looked up at him, feeling stronger than she'd felt in a long time. "As I said, you need to do whatever you need to do. But don't think for a minute that I won't have a backup plan if anything happens to me. I have enough shit on you to make sure you spend the rest of your life behind bars."

"Pfff, you have nothing on me."

"No? What about Texas?"

"What about Texas?"

"About the land you bribed your way into when you forced a lease to expire early. I have the documents."

"How the fuck did you get the…"

"And New York. The illegal company asset strip. Chicago, the illegal price fixing. New Orleans, the property…"

"Okay, Okay. You've made your point. I can't believe you'd ruin us over this…this…"

"Ridiculous idea?"

He stared at her as he slumped back down on the couch. He took up what was left of his drink and drained it dry. His mind was whirring away as he stood to pour himself another. Beverley waited.

With drink in hand, he walked over to the window and looked out. This was not the way he imagined it to end. All the work he'd done to build a business and amass a fortune all undone by one mistake and one woman. But perhaps it wasn't the end. If he could put enough cash away to get through whatever investigation might happen, he'd be okay while she alone took the fall.

He returned and sat down. "Okay, I may be able to liquidize some of our assets and put them into the offshore accounts to get me by, but you do know that you'll be hunted for the rest of your lives, don't you?"

Beverley nodded.

"I want a letter from you absolving me of any knowledge and responsibility of this. I want you to make it clear that I had nothing to do with it. God knows they're going to lock everything I have away for years until they're satisfied, or you're both caught. So…this is it, then. If you do this, I don't want anything else to do with you. I'll give you some money to disappear, and you give me all the evidence you have."

"That can be arranged."

David slumped back, deflated, defeated, now needing to prepare to weather the storm that was to be brought to his doorstep.

Beverley stood. "I'll keep you updated," she said as she left the room, placing her shaking hands in her pockets so he couldn't see them but with a smile on her face.

Chapter 38

Mary stepped through the garage door carrying a tray with a pot of coffee and cake. The garage had been temporarily closed so Mike could focus solely on refurbishing the vehicle needed for the breakout. She placed the tray on a bench and walked over to where his legs were poking out from underneath the chassis.

She touched his leg to let him know she was there, but the unexpected sensation made him jolt.

"Ow!" came the groan from the floor.

"Sorry, love. Just wanted to let you know I'm here with refreshments."

Mike slid out from underneath, one hand rubbing his forehead. "Thanks, honey."

"It's coming along."

He looked back and nodded. "It's getting there."

They headed over to the bench and took up their cups.

"Will it be ready in time?"

"It has to be!"

Mary simply nodded with a faraway look, as if another question was floating around inside, trying to find its way out.

Just as Mike bit down on a slice of cake, her query found an exit. "So, what happens to us after we break them out?"

Mike stopped chewing for a second and stared at her. He resumed mastication as quickly as possible in order to not let the question hang in the air for too long in case it found its way out of the confines of the garage.

He swallowed hard. "I'm not entirely sure," he relented.

Mary nodded again.

"Is there a way we could run?" she asked.

"We could give it a go. Move inland, somewhere small. I could pick up work in another garage."

"Would we have to sell everything here?"

"I'm not sure we'll have time. Besides, it might be good to rent the house and lease the garage for extra income."

"But wouldn't they trace that to us?"

"Perhaps. That's your specialty, honey."

Mary looked down to access memories and information stored within. After a few seconds she shook her head. "I'll have to think about that one."

Mike smiled and leaned forward to kiss her cheek. "It'll be okay."

She half smiled back at him. The life they had created and worked for was about to be blown to smithereens, and the law that they had always stayed on the right side of would soon disappear into the far distance behind them. But what else could they do?

Mike drained his coffee. "I'd better get back to it."

Mary watched him slide back under the vehicle. She stood there for a while, looking at the man she had always loved all of her life and wondered what their life would soon become.

Mike felt her gaze from where he lay, staring up at the undercarriage, looking over to where his wife's feet pointed toward him, and thinking about what the hell he could do to protect her and his son.

They remained there for a second or two until a loud bang sounded, the entrance door closing, causing the rolling doors to shudder. Mike slid back out in time to see one of his mechanics stepping farther into the space.

He rushed to his feet, giving Mary a start as he bounded over.

"Hey, Mike," Josh began.

Mike extended his arm around his shoulders, turning him back toward the door.

"Hey, Josh, now's not a good time."

Josh tried to look back across his shoulder at the unusual van Mike had just come out from under, but the pace at which he was being led back through the door gave him little chance. Before he knew it, he was back on the sidewalk.

"I'm sorry, Josh," Mike said to his bewildered colleague. "I'm just in the middle of something that needs my focus."

"But what could need your focus so much that you close the garage?"

That's a good question, thought Mike. "Listen, Josh, I'll be in touch soon about coming back. You're still getting your salary, right?"

"Yeah, it's not that…"

"Okay, then. Sorry to rush off, but I've got to get back to it. We'll speak soon."

"But me and the boys want to…"

And with that, Mike closed the door.

Josh stood there a moment, scratching his head at a loss for words and actions until, eventually, he shrugged, kicked a stone that lay by his foot, and walked off.

With the door still open just a crack, Mike watched him leave, then he closed the door completely, leaning against it to catch his breath.

Mar walked over. "I'm sorry. I should have closed the door behind me."

Mike placed a hand on her shoulder and gave her a lopsided grin. "Might be good for next time," he said.

Chapter 39

When Peter arrived home late, Jane was clearing up the food from dinner. She had saved him a dish that was in the oven drying out under tinfoil. She looked up as he entered the kitchen and slung his bag on the floor.

"It's done," he said.

She walked over to him and held him tight. She could feel that the energy had been drained from him and squeezed tighter to keep him upright. He sighed a deep mournful sigh, somewhere between defeat and comfort.

"What did they say?" Jane finally asked.

He stepped back, pulling away from her grip and sat down. The weight of the words just too much.

"I handed my resignation into the head of department who wouldn't accept it. He took it to the Dean, who called me into his office after lectures. He couldn't understand why I was leaving and didn't believe the half-assed reason I gave." Another sigh. "He finally took it but said he would keep it open, just in case I came to my senses."

Jane pulled his head into her chest and began stroking his hair. The job had been everything to him, his dream position in his dream university. Now he was giving it up to go on the run. It just didn't seem real, like some dream that had somehow morphed into a nightmare.

After a minute he forced a smile. "It'll be worth it though, right?" he asked.

All she could do was smile and nod. She had been planning how to tell the girls about their new life, how to tell their family that they were going to disappear and leave everything behind. She was going to tell him about the realtor who came today to view the house for a quick sale, that she had said that there have been a few properties coming onto the market at a low price recently. She wondered if these were the others preparing to disappear as well. But she said nothing. She just kept stroking his hair and holding him close.

Chapter 40

The phone rang just once before it was answered.

"Hey, Desi."

"Hey, Ozzy, what have you got?"

"I've got his new passport and social security sorted out, and the apartment is clean and ready. Bobby has agreed to take him there and get him settled in after the, uh, event."

"Who did you go to for the documents? Not Grayson, tell me not Grayson."

"No, not for this. I went to Lukas. More expensive, but you get what you pay for."

"Good. Is the apartment stocked?"

"Yep. They've got enough food and drinks for three months of lying low. We've even got his games console set up! He'll be fine there, and Deacon will get him in the shop to make ends meet when the heat has died down."

"And is Bobby gonna stay with him for the whole three months?"

"Yep, everything's sorted, Desi. Don't worry."

"It's my job to worry."

"Okay. Now, about paying for this…"

Desi pulled her chin back and narrowed her eyes. "What? You worried I'm not good for it?"

"No, no. I just mean this is already costing me a small fortune, so any upfront help you can give would be appreciated."

"What number are you thinking?"

"Twenty."

"I'll send it over via the usual means."

"Great, that's great. You know I'm not making any money on this. This is done at cost, just for you."

"If I thought you were making money on this, Oz, then I'd be more than a little upset. And you don't want me upset with you."

"I know. I'm just saying, that's all."

"Is there anything else?"

"Umm, nothing that can't wait."

"Spit it out."

"Well, are you sure about doing this? You know it's gonna bring a lot of heat onto all of us."

"Are you saying I should let Donnie rot in there, or end up dead?"

"No, no, I'm not saying…"

"You know what it's like in there now; there's no way to keep people safe anymore. No way to make sure he's looked after."

"I know. I'm not saying he's not worth it. All I'm saying is the heat that'll come from it will be more than some people can cope with."

"Who? What people?"

"Desi…"

"No, Ozzy, tell me who the fuck you think will buckle, and I'll make sure they won't get the chance."

"No one, Desi. No one will buckle. I'm just talking out loud."

"Well, talk in definites, not some *maybe* bullshit."

"Okay. Sorry, Desi. I didn't mean anything."

"Hmmm."

Ozzy put the phone down and breathed a sigh of relief. Desi was an unpredictable character at the best of times, and he was glad to finish their conversation. He couldn't talk to her about the chatter that was circulating on the streets. This was going to have a more far-reaching impact than she realized, and he had no idea how to smooth any of it.

Chapter 41

Jane stood on the corner clutching the camera she had borrowed from school. She'd told her colleague that she wanted to take some nice shots of the girls, and they didn't question the overkill of the camera she'd asked for. With 150 megapixels and all the built-in functions you could ask for, it should get the high-rez shots they needed, but it was the range guide that would really help to get the dimensions accurate.

As her mind began to wander back to her husband and the desolate look on his face, a car pulled up. She dipped her head to check, then got in.

"Hi, Mike," she said as he pulled away.

"Hey, Jane. How're you doing?"

"Honestly? Pretty shitty."

Mike looked across at her. "Yeah, I know that feeling."

They drove for a while in silence, until the noise became unbearable.

"I mean," she continued. "It's just so massive, isn't it? So huge, thisthing we're doing, that it doesn't seem real until you actually start putting the plan in action, doing the things you need to do. Then suddenly, you find yourself in the middle of something you had no idea would change everything."

"Yeah."

"Pete's handed in his notice, as have I, but we haven't even told the girls yet. We don't know where we'll end up, and that's the most frightening part of all." She paused then glanced at Mike. "What are your plans for after?"

He sighed. "Well, I guess we're in a similar situation. There's not much time to sell everything, so Mary's trying to figure out how we get by with what we have. I know Miles is our son, and we'd do anything for him, but..."

"It feels too much?"

Another sigh. "Yeah. Is that bad of me?"

"No, I think we're all feeling something similar."

"I mean, when is it too much? Where is too far to go for your kids? Me, personally, I'd do anything for my son, but the effect it will have on Mary, and even Miles when he's out, feels overwhelming."

He glanced across at Jane who was silent.

"I'm sorry. I shouldn't be saying things like that."

"No, no. I was thinking about the impact it's going to have on the girls. It's already a strain for Pete. I'm not sure there's an easy answer for that, Mike."

He just nodded, and the car fell silent again.

Before long, they pulled up at a McDonald's on the 318 and parked close to the exit. The truck would pass here before either continued on the same path or turning onto the desert road past the Air Force base. They were a little early, and the breakfast crowd was still in full force. They looked at these large individuals entering and leaving, not quite understanding why they ate there; yet, at the same time, the smell of the food being pumped out made their mouths water.

"So, how is your son doing?" Jane asked finally.

"Oh, he's doing okay. It was tough at first, but he's seemed to have got into a rhythm."

"How long's he been in there?"

"Over two years now."

Jane nodded. "And if you don't mind me asking, what is he in for?"

Mike shuffled in his seat. "Umm, well, he got mixed up with the wrong people and, well, became a runner. You know, the getaway driver. It was a bank robbery."

It was clear that the words coming out of his mouth were causing him pain, so she proceeded carefully.

"That must have been terrible for you and Mary."

"It was unbelievable, really. He was just getting started on a great career as a driver. He had it all at his feet, and then he threw it away."

Jane paused a moment before asking/ "Was anyone hurt when he was caught?"

At this, Mike drew in a sharp intake of breath through his teeth and gripped the steering wheel tighter.

"He actually saved a life, *lives*, during the escape. That's what got him caught, but it also reduced his sentence somewhat." He didn't want to elaborate further. "What about yours?" he said, hoping to change the subject.

It was Jane's turn to feel uncomfortable now.

"Ed was being bullied badly at school. We didn't know at the time, but it was pretty extreme. Then one day, he just snapped and hit one of them. The kid fell awkwardly and broke his neck."

"I'm sorry."

"It's okay. I should have known. I taught at the school, so I should have been aware of what was going on. It's my fault."

Mike turned in his seat and stared at her. "None of this is your fault. None of it. We can never know what someone else is going through if they don't talk to us, and when something like this happens, it feels out of the blue, even though it may have been building for a while."

He paused a moment before continuing.

"When I spoke to Miles about why he did it, the answer he gave didn't make much sense for a while. He said that he felt invincible. That nothing could touch him. He said when he was behind the wheel racing, controlling the uncontrollable, the world flying by in a flash, he was unstoppable. And when he got out, that feeling went away. When the season was over, he looked for ways of getting that feeling back again and being a runner seemed like the only way. It's like he was addicted to the speed, to the thrill of the chase, to the adrenaline, so you can imagine what it's like for him in the tiny cell. It took many, many months for his body to change and his addiction to reduce. But it will always be there, in some form. The memory of that emotion and the need for that thrill will always be there, and that's what frightens me the most. What he may return to once he's out." He half smiled. "But maybe that's just my issue."

Jane reached over and placed her hand on top of his.

Just then, Mike's alarm on his watch sounded.

They both withdrew their hands and took in a deep breath. Mike started the engine and waited for the truck to pass.

After a short moment, the vehicle drove by. Its serious white armor charging down the street like an albino rhinoceros.

Mike pulled out and started following. Even though they were a few cars back, their hearts were racing, the adrenaline pumping.

A car in front pulled away, and they moved closer. Jane felt the weight of the camera in her damp palms growing heavier.

The truck drove straight past the 82nd Street turnoff and continued along Pearlblossom Highway, which meant it was not going through the desert. The cars in front began to overtake the truck, so there was now no obstruction between them and it. Jane checked around her before lifting the camera to her eye. She checked the settings, then pressed the button. The shutter rapidly fired three rounds. She looked down at the image displayed on the back of the camera and couldn't understand why she saw the windshield of the car and not the truck beyond.

She began pressing buttons furiously, trying to figure out the problem.

"Everything okay?" Mike asked.

"No, it's not working."

She raised the camera again and took another burst. When she looked down again, she saw the same image as before.

"What is it?"

"I'm just getting pictures of the windshield."

"Maybe it's picking up on the dirty glass?" Mike suggested. He pulled a lever and water began to coat the dusty glass as the wipers began to sway. "There. Now try again."

Jane focused and shot.

"Shit, it's still not working. I think the range finder is picking up the glass."

"We can't stay behind the truck for much longer before looking suspicious."

"I don't know what to do."

Mike thought for a moment.

"You're gonna have to lean out of the window."

Jane stared at him. "There's no way I'm doing that. They'll see me."

Mike thought some more.

"There's a turn coming up for the N14. When the truck takes it, we'll keep going straight and you can take the pictures as we pass."

"That'll only give us one chance."

Mike glanced over, his eyebrows raised, but said nothing.

"Okay," she relented.

He pulled a little closer as the turn came up, and Jane made sure that everything on the camera was ready. The truck indicated the upcoming turn and began moving to the far side of the road. Mike slowed down to match its speed. The camera was up to Jane's eye as she tracked it across the windshield, past the small side panel and as soon as it reached her open window, her finger pressed down. A long, continuous flutter sounded as the truck turned away and Mike kept going straight ahead. As her finger released, they both allowed themselves a breath.

She looked down at the camera and flipped through the images.

"Well?"

"I think we got it."

Chapter 42

The floor stuck to the underside of her red-soled shoes as she walked across to the far side of the bar. Neither one of them had wanted to meet in the other's neighborhood for fear of sticking out, so somewhere in between had been chosen. Although, looking around now, Beverley thought it was a little lower than halfway, but she took a seat in a side booth anyway.

She studied the clientele, the mid-morning drunks and jobless with nowhere else to go. Her eyes landed on the bar next, the couple of bottles lined up at the back, and her throat suddenly felt dry. She presumed they didn't do table service here, and there was no way she was going to stand at the bar and order a wine. Who knew where the grapes were from!

She checked her purse, more for something to do than to look for anything. As the minutes passed, her eyes kept returning to the meager selection of drinks on the shelf. She was just about to say *fuck it* and get one when the door opened, and a silhouetted figure came strolling over.

Marcus sat down opposite her, a smile wide across his face.

"Hi," he said.

"Hello."

"Fancy a drink?"

"Can we just get this over with?"

"Wouldn't it look strange? Coming into a bar for sixty seconds and then heading out again? May cause some suspicions."

Beverley looked around at who might be watching.

"And besides, one drink won't do any harm."

Her eyes returned to the bar before meeting his gaze.

"Okay, I'll have a white wine spritzer please."

Marcus started laughing. "I'm not sure they know what that is here, but I'll ask."

Her cheeks flushed as he slid out and went up to the bar. Her eyes followed him. He was a rogue, no doubt, but he was kinda good looking, and he kept himself in shape. As her eyes wandered down his body and back up, she caught him staring at her in the mirror, catching her checking him out. Her blush deepened as she reached to fumble with her purse once more.

As he came back with the drinks, he asked, "Like what you see?"

"What?"

"The drinks. They don't have a wide selection, so I wondered if there was anything else you liked the look of?"

"No," she said, picking up her glass. "Thank you."

"No problem."

They both took a sip in silence.

"So, what is it you do, Beverley?"

"Well...I was a chemical engineer."

"Wow! That must pay well."

"It can."

"It must. That dress isn't cheap!"

She looked away, trying to derail the train of conversation before it went any further.

"So, what is it *you* do?" she asked.

"Ah, well, I'm in the entertainment industry."

"You mean movies and TV?"

"Let's say, more the personal, adult kind."

"Oh, I see."

"Now don't get me wrong, I'm not a bad guy. Just trying to make it through."

"I'm sure."

The air suddenly became a little frosty as they took another sip. There was something whirring away in Beverley's mind, working itself into a frenzy, trying to find a way out.

"So, when you say *personal, adult* entertainment, you mean prostitution, right?"

Marcus's eyes widened at the outright question. "I provide opportunities for people to come together. What happens after that is their business."

"And are those opportunities at a specific location or more street based?"

Marcus squirmed in his seat a little. "What is it you want to know, Beverley?"

"I'm trying to understand the person opposite me who's part of this incredibly stupid thing I'm doing, and if they can be trusted."

"Trust is an interesting concept. For this, you have no concerns. I want my boy out just as much as you want yours."

"I have no doubt, but what I'm trying to assess is if you'll screw us over in the process."

He leaned forward and placed his elbows on the table. "You don't have to worry about me princess. I've actually come to like the group and think it will do what needs to be done. And if there's any screwing, you'd know about it."

His stare turned cold, but a twinkle remained in the corner. She tried to hold his gaze for as long as she could but had to turn away, taking a gulp of her drink.

He reached inside his pocket and produced a glass vial of colorless liquid and slid it over. Beverley snatched it out of his hand, her eyes darting around, and placed it in her handbag.

"Are you insane?"

"I have my moments."

She pushed what was left of her drink away from her.

"Thank you for the drink."

"Anytime."

The warm glow of the alcohol began to spread through her body as she stood and strode toward the door. She could feel his eyes on her, which didn't help. She pushed open the door and exited without giving him the satisfaction of looking back.

***

When she reached the lab, her temperature had returned to normal just in time to rise again. As she approached the wide glass doors, she could see Rosie inside waiting by the reception desk.

"Fuck," she whispered to herself and wished she'd had more of that disgusting wine.

Stepping inside, she steeled her nerves and walked over to her.

Rosie's face was stern, as if it had been chiseled out of granite, and stared at her across the desk.

"Hello, Rosie," Beverley said in a voice as calm as possible.

"Hello, Mrs. Anderson," she replied.

The silence between them started to make the receptionist squirm in her seat.

Beverley looked around. "It's a lovely building you've got here, and some interesting work you've got going on."

"Not the most interesting work I've done, and certainly not life-saving."

Beverley looked down at the keyboard, the receptionist's fingers paused above them.

"Well, I'm sure it has its purposes," she smiled, looking up again. "If you'll excuse me, I'll head in."

She turned to go when suddenly the receptionist came to life.

"Umm, who are you? I need to sign you in."

From beside her, Rosie cackled. "Why, this is *the* Mrs. Anderson. The new owner of this whole company and payer of your wages, so I'd let her in if I were you."

Both Beverley and the receptionist blushed.

"Is there anything you need me to sign?" Beverley asked, returning to the desk.

"Oh no, don't worry," the receptionist replied, her hands waving.

Beverley looked up at Rosie, who was smiling at the scene, and turned on her heel. She headed for the space that had been set aside for her and tried to ignore the stares of the employees as she walked through the building. She knew Rosie had every right to be angry at her, that she had sold her out along with the company they had worked on together. And here Rosie was, working once again for the woman who had betrayed her.

Once inside, she locked the door, hung up her handbag, and donned her lab coat, glasses, and gloves. Putting on the garments helped her slip into a professional frame of mind.

She moved to the gas chamber that had been set up and placed the glass vial on the counter. It contained around 30ml of liquid, enough to put down an elephant, if an elephant frequented the local nightclub and had their drinks spiked, that is. In a gaseous form, however, it might be a different story. She had to work out the exact pressure and temperature needed to vaporize the liquid and then see if that gas would have the desired effect in the volume of space in the cab.

She syringed out a sample and placed it in a machine to the side. She hit the button and waited for the results. After a few minutes, a printout of its characteristics would be produced that would show the details she needed to see.

While she waited, she recalled the lecture notes she had written so many years ago about the structure of compounds and properties of vaporization. She knew that at any point on the characteristic curve of a compound, the pressure and temperature allowed only one phase to exist at a time, either a liquid or a gas. At only one point on the curve will the temperature and pressure be just right to allow both phases to exist in equilibrium—this was the boundary between liquid and vapour. Only liquid can exist on the high-pressure, low-temperature side of the line, while the substance must be liquid on the low-pressure, high-temperature side. The place where this line vanishes, the critical point, is where the liquid and its vapor become indistinguishable. That was the line she had to find.

If the temperature was too high for the pressure, then the molecules of the structure would break down, and although a gas would be released, it would not be in its original form or have the desired effect.

The almost silent noise of the machine changed from a buzz to a purr as a thin, white sheet began to be fed out. Once it had stopped, she tore it off, looked at the results, and smiled. *Piece of cake*, she thought.

She went back to the table and made some notes on the graph that had been produced and thought for a moment. She went over to a tote bag that was in the corner and pulled out the selection of vapes she had bought earlier. She had read their operating structures and temperatures to make sure she had a good range to choose from.

Finding the one she wanted, she pulled it out of its packaging and took it to the gas chamber. She unscrewed the lid and poured a sample into the housing. She flipped the switch on the side of the chamber, which started the fan unit, and then hit the vape button. An invisible cloud emanated from the mouthpiece, and the red light for the fan illuminated. A foreign substance was detected. She checked the panel on the side and saw the intact molecular structure identified. *Excellent.*

Now all she had to do was to calculate the amount required to take out two averaged-sized men in an enclosed compartment. She looked toward the corner of the lab, at the rat that was staring at her from inside its cage.

"It's okay, buddy. You may wake up with a hangover, but I'm not going to fuck you!"

Chapter 43

The evening air had a bitter sting to it, despite the heaters that were dotted around this half of the garage. Everyone had assembled as before, but the mood was quiet, tense. The outcome of their efforts was becoming a painful reality and the aftermath to follow all too real. Jeremy stood at the front with his clipboard.

"Hey, everyone, thanks for coming along again. We have a bit to get through, so I thought we'd start with an update. Mike, the vehicle looks incredible. Can you talk us through it?"

Mike stood up and walked over to the other side of the garage that was blocked by shelves and tarpaulin to the weird-looking vehicle he had been building. Everyone stood up and followed, the scraping of chairs echoing off the grease-stained walls.

"This was a Ford E-Transit in its former life, but I've turned the cabin around so that it essentially runs backward. I've built a frame around the sides that should line up with the transport truck and appear simply like an extension to anyone looking. The flatbed inside will give you plenty of room to work and get the boys out. I've added lights and holders for tools and stuff."

Everyone began to move around the vehicle.

"This is incredible, Mike; it looks just like a normal van," Jane said. "You can't even see that the driver sits at the back."

"Really great work. I love the fake windows at the front. It looks so real," Taylor agreed, running his hand along the side. "What about the front?"

Mike moved around and pulled down a heavy sheet that covered the front hole. "I've made it look like the front of the driver's cab as best I could. It's not perfect, but as long as you don't inspect it in detail it should be fine."

As Mike raised the cover again, Beverley and Peter stepped up into the back.

"When the two vehicles are connected, the doors should come in to about here," said Mike, pointing to a line of black tape on the floor. "I've put a couple of boxes there to hold anything you might need to cut through the bar."

Beverley nodded.

"And how are you supposed to drive the thing while you're sitting at the back?" asked Marcus.

"There are cameras all around to show you what's ahead, to the sides and behind. It may be a little strange at first, but if you imagine it like driving a simulator, it'll be fine."

Desi started to examine the solid metal key welded underneath, which was to secure to the back of the truck and free the first lock.

"Is this thing really gonna fit?" she asked.

Mike and Jane glanced at each other. "From the pictures we got and information we pulled from them on its dimensions, it should, yes."

"Should? We need a fuck ton better than should!"

Mike was about to answer until Taylor stepped in.

"Is there a problem?"

"Yeah, there's a fucking problem. So far, I'm only hearing shoulds, dos, and maybes. There's a hell of a lot riding on possibilities."

"And what would you suggest? Do you have any better ideas you're not sharing?"

Desi stood there, holding back the burning desire to break his nose.

"Then I suggest you stop with the negativity and contribute." He turned to Mike and put his hand on his shoulder. "You've done a great job, Mike."

Mike smiled with a blush, knowing she might have a point.

"What's this hatch here?" asked Peter from inside the van. He was crouched by a trap door, lifting it up to see the ground beneath.

"Ah, that's for the radio-controlled car to drive out." He walked over to the far table and picked up the toy car. "I've put an arm on the back that should...that *will* reach the intake pipe underneath the truck. I don't know what will go on the arm just yet."

Everyone looked at Beverley.

She walked over to her handbag and pulled out a strange-looking syringe and handed it to Mike.

"I've modified the vape stick to be forced through the syringe head. It's an industrial needle, so it will puncture most things."

Mike examined the device.

"It's activated by remote," she added, handing that over as well. "But we need another 40mls of product to be sure the guards are unconscious for the length of time we need."

Marcus gave a whistle. "Do you know how much that stuff costs?"

"I'm sure we can cover whatever costs there are," replied Taylor.

"Okay," he answered, hands up.

"Thank you, Beverley. That's great work. And what about the locking bar?"

"That's coming along. The compound will do the job; it's just a case of getting it deep into the cut once we start. It would be easier if it were lying flat."

"I'm sure you'll work it out."

She nodded.

"Shall we return back to our seats?" said Jeremy, gesturing the way.

When they had all sat down, he continued.

"So, we have a vehicle; a way to render the guards unconscious; a way to open the doors. That's pretty impressive stuff. We'll drive to the rear of the truck, deploy the RC car and its syringe to knock out the guards, latch onto the back carefully to unlock the doors, cut through the bar, and release our boys."

Apart from the creaking seats, there was silence.

Jeremy continued. "All we have to do now is assign who will be doing what."

Everyone's eyes fell everywhere but on Jeremy's.

He coughed. "We need a driver for the van, another for the radio-controlled car, and someone to cut the bar."

He looked at Beverley, who was intently focused on the clasp of her handbag.

"Beverley, I guess you would be the obvious choice for cutting the bar, with your expertise."

"Really, there's no expertise needed. I'll make it simple for anyone to use."

Jeremey shuffled his feet. "We also need someone with steady hands to drive the van."

They continued to look away.

"I can drive the car," said Mike. "I'm used to the thing."

"Okay, great. I guess I could do the bar if needed," added Jeremy.

"If we're to keep pace with the truck and have the maximum amount of control, we need as few people in the front as possible," Mike added.

There was a relaxing of shoulders in the room. Then a hand was raised.

"Yes, Mary?"

"I'm not sure about everyone else, and I know it was mentioned at the last meeting, but…well, there are a couple of things that are on my mind."

"Go on."

"First of all, and I'm not being negative, but what if we fail to get them out?"

"We're doing everything we can to ensure that doesn't happen."

"I know, but what if it does?"

"Then we're fucked," offered Desi.

Taylor frowned. "If there's an issue while we're in the middle of it and we can't pull it off, then we get out of there knowing that we tried our best. I know stopping is not going to help our boys, but that's why we're planning this, to make sure we cover everything that may happen."

Mary looked down and nodded. "And the other thing is about what happens afterward."

There was a collective sigh.

"To be honest, Mary, I don't have an answer. We're struggling to find a solution to that problem ourselves."

There were nods.

Peter said, "The window of time for getting them out is such a short one that if we go over, we'll have no time to actually escape before the truck arrives at the prison and all hell breaks loose."

A mumbling began to spread.

"And then what? We would have done all this for nothing!"

The noise continued with no answer forthcoming. The realization of the question of "what will happen next" punctured through the bubble of contented ignorance and washed over everyone, drenching them all in fear.

Beverley gripped her handbag tighter. She'd been thinking of a solution to this problem but was afraid of sharing it for what it would mean. The noise began to grow into a chatter of discontent. She knew she had to say something.

She began to stand, the weight of her intended words making it difficult to get to her feet.

"Beverley?"

The noise settled down.

"I have a solution to this," she said, "but you're not going to like it."

The noise started again with anxious words. Taylor raised his hand to signal for silence. "Go on."

"Well, the DNA machine is pretty foolproof, as in we can't tamper with or change the code that it's looking for…but it's not laboratory standard, meaning it will only look for specific markers and not run the whole sequence."

"So?" asked Desi.

"So, it can be fooled with a DNA sequence that's close enough to have those markers."

"What the hell does that mean?" Desi replied.

Beverley shuffled on the spot, knowing that once what she was going to say came out, there was no taking it back. "What that means is it's looking for confirmation of a male person who is close in that bloodline." She was hoping they would understand without having to say the rest out loud. The blank faces staring at her told her she was not going to be that lucky.

She finished with, "In other words, their DNA can be replaced with their father's DNA."

Everyone looked down, processing what she'd just shared, what it actually meant. Jeremy got there first.

"You mean the fathers could replace the children?" he said.

There was an audible gasp as everyone else caught up.

"That's ridiculous," said Marcus.

161

"Is it?" replied Peter, looking down thoughtfully. "If we replaced our sons, then they would be free, and we'd be in a much better position to survive what happens in there."

"But they'd know it wasn't a bunch of teenage boys who'd arrived!"

"How?" asked Beverley. "They process the DNA for confirmation and would only check the camera footage of the transfer if there was a problem en route."

Marcus struggled to find a comeback.

Jane's hand could feel Peter's body rocking as if it were getting ready for action. It increased until he suddenly stood. "I'm willing to do that, for my son," he said, his voice trembling but sure.

Jane held his hand, tears flowing down her cheek, fear erupting in her stomach.

"Me too," said Mike standing now to join him.

Jeremy and Taylor looked at each other. A silent communication flowed between them, then a nod of agreement.

"We'd do that as well," Taylor said.

Beverley was the only one without a male present, and she knew it would be a near impossible to convince David to do something like that.

"Well, fuck that," shouted Marcus. "You're all fucking crazy if you think I'm going behind bars."

He headed for the door. Desi hastily stood and followed.

Chapter 44

The door burst open, and Marcus strode out, closely followed by Desi.

From where Detective Brant sat in his vehicle, he could see the argument between these two starting to unfold. Their gestures and shouting were all a mime show but with obvious connotations. He had been following the group for a while and had some interesting, if contentious, ideas as to what they were doing. He wasn't surprised at all at the fireworks show that was going off. In fact, he was surprised it had taken this long for there to be an issue with these two and the odd mix of others.

As Desi and Marcus walked away from each other, still shouting, the doorway remained unoccupied and partway open.

It was a bit of a risk, but one worth the chance.

He waited until they two had driven away before he got out of his car and skipped across the street toward the garage. As he drew nearer, he could hear the muffled voice of a man and a woman in discussion—loud enough for everyone on the inside to hear but just quiet enough for the edges to be indistinct to him. He looked around for passersby before walking up the driveway toward the light that was streaming out. He pressed his ear close to the gap in the door and listened.

"So, it's agreed, then. Beverley, let us know that it's been confirmed your end, and I'll talk with Desi and Marcus."

With that, the chairs scrapped back as the people stood.

Shit, though Brant, his heart in his mouth. He turned and ran for the corner of the garage. His old knee injury stung with the unexpected spurt of pace, and he only just managed to disappear around the corner before the door was pushed all the way open.

He edged back deeper into the darkness as some of them began passing by, too lost in thought or conversation to notice him in the shadows. He looked toward the back of the garage, the dark, overgrown brambles that led to the rear, and began to edge toward it. He turned to face the garage wall, palms flat on the bricks as the thorns began to get closer, the prickles scraping across the backs of his legs as he pushed through to the end.

Here, he had some space and noticed an old fire-exit door that looked like it hadn't been opened in decades, but from which came a few piercing shards of light from the cracked and splintered wood.

He went to peer through the cracks, and the light was so bright, it caused him to wince and step back. Then he tried again, more cautiously.

A smell of rotten wood and grease filled his nostrils as his eye scanned through the pinhole camera, trying to make sense of what he saw. There were chairs laid out in front of a board like he remembered from Sunday school. He moved across at the workbenches that were lined down the middle. Farther still, he saw the white side of a vehicle until, just like that, darkness swallowed everything. His eye opened wider, enough to see the silhouette of two people walking out of the door at the front and then closing it behind them.

He removed his face from the hole and leant back against the door. He replayed the images as his mind tried to make sense of what he had seen. Something didn't feel quite right, maybe not the seats or the worktops... Perhaps it was the vehicle. What was it that had been so odd about it?

Chapter 45

Miles's eyes were already open when the double beeps sounded. His sleep had not been great since he had decoded the letter. His dreams had become a mixture of thrilling excitement and fearful dread. The old sensation of speed had resurfaced, not as strong as before, but it was there. His recurring dream of racing around the track had some additions to it. Now as he went around, his father would open the exit gates on each lap, but whenever he drove through, he would always end up crashing into the traffic on the other side.

As the lights came on, he sat up and shuffled to the ladder. The nervous energy that had been growing in his stomach was tingling, hoping for some activity, the memory and thrill of speed just under the surface. The adrenaline that accompanied it meant the minutes and hours that followed took forever to pass. His mind elsewhere, he jumped down to the floor, his ankle twisting beneath him as he landed, forcing the entire weight of his body through the unnatural curve in his bones. An explosion of pain erupted through his foot and traveled at the speed of light up his leg and into the rest of his body that instinctively collapsed under the sensation.

He began yelling and cursing, rocking back and forth on the floor, wanting to grab hold of his ankle but not daring to. Instantly, his computer screen flashed on, and a face and voice emerged.

"Miles, are you okay? What's happened?"

"What's it fucking look like?"

The face frowned, wanting to admonish the language but, knowing that it would probably result in more, instead spoke calmly.

"It looks like you might have sprained your ankle. See if you can carefully stand up and show me."

Miles looked at the screen, his eyes boring into the pixels that made up the image. With an intake of breath, he slowly raised his body to a sitting position. A throbbing sensation began to take over his thoughts, images of his skin being torn open, like the

Incredible Hulk's shirt, by the swelling of his ankle. He shuffled to the desk and pulling himself up onto his good foot. He managed to stand with only minor groans of agony.

"Show me."

"Alright, hold on!"

He shuffled to the side and pulled his bad leg up by the cuff of his pajamas and carefully placed it on the desk. Pain shot through his leg, as if he'd placed it in a raging fire.

The face stared hard at the ankle with a look of concern.

"Yes, looks like a sprain, a bad one."

The face looked away for a moment and seemed to be tapping away at a keyboard. The next second, the delivery slot opened, and in came a tray carrying three boxes.

"Okay, here we go. I want you to get the tray and bring it to the table."

"And how do you expect me to do that?"

"Carefully," the face smirked as it watched Miles lower himself to the floor and slide on his bum to grab the tray. He shuffled back and raised it above his head to put on the desk before pulling himself back up.

"Great. Now, in the biggest box is a portable x-ray camera. Take it out, turn it on, and I'll tell you how to work it."

Miles opened the box and removed the rectangular item.

"Okay, the power button is on the top there, see?"

Miles pushed the button, and a deep sound began to whine from inside. "Is this safe?"

"Perfectly. See the green button on the side? Press that while slowly moving the open end over your ankle."

He did as he was told, only once catching it on his skin with a wince.

"Slower…"

His movements slowed as his patience wore thin.

"Okay, great. You can stop now." The face was looking at a screen to their side. "Mm-hmm. Yes, no breaks luckily."

"Yeah, real lucky."

"Now, in the other two boxes are bandages and a cold compress. Put the compress on your ankle and wrap the bandage around it firm. Change it every couple of hours with the spares in the box and rest with your leg up in the air. I'll send more compresses in the morning."

"And painkillers?"

"Hmmm," he said again, tapping again while reading. "When you send the camera back, I'll send you some aspirin to take the edge off."

"Thanks," replied Miles, some calmness beginning to settle.

"I'll inform your parents of the accident, so they know the prison service was not at fault."

"Great," he replied as the screen went blank. *Yeah, real great*, he thought. With the escape only days away, his mind raced with fear. *What the hell am I going to do if I've just fucked up the whole plan?*

Chapter 46

The battle inside Ed had steadily grown to a world at war. There were no bystanders and no part of him that wasn't affected. He paced the floor, back and forth for hours, his feet unable to remain still, his stomach caught between the elation of being free from this place and the fear of what that would mean. His fingers twitched to his mouth to nibble away what skin remained around his decimated nails. He had not spoken to his counselor in days for fear of saying something incriminating, so his mind was left to wander through the battleground of his head alone.

Questions formed on repeat, with no one to answer them. So, he answered them himself, and kept answering them with all the possible solutions he could find. The reasonable, the outlandish, and the downright insane whirred around and detonated in every corner.

He had finished the book, twice, and had unfortunately been curious enough to use the code to decipher the newspaper article that had been circled in the paper he was sent. He wished to God that he hadn't. The words he began to spell were exciting to start with. He couldn't believe he was decoding an actual message. Then comprehension took over as he read it again and again. Surely it couldn't mean what he thought it meant. That would be insane.

If he was broken out, then where would they run and live? What would happen with his sisters? Would their lives be ruined all because of him? What would become of his parents?

His dreams had become filled with nightmares. In them, he found himself wandering back along the corridors of his old school. It was fine at the start, until everyone stopped and stared at him as he passed, and the sudden realization of what he had done flooded back, making him want to run away from their gaze. But no matter how fast he started, his legs became slow and tired, as if wading through treacle. There were children and adults staring and pointing along every wall, the corridors extended to infinity, the exit doors nowhere to be found. And then it came into view, the way out. He pushed forward toward it, but as he got closer, he would see Hunter standing before the door, his neck twisted and deformed, his face bloody. Suddenly, the floor that had been so difficult to make ground over became a conveyor belt, dragging him toward the grotesque figure that grew larger and larger the closer he got. He was unable to move or turn away as Hunter reached for him, and he woke with a start, his lungs gasping for air, his hands raised to protect his head.

The insomnia allowed the incessant internal chatter to begin; it drilled into the folds and recesses of his brain so much so that the rumble and clunk of the yard coming up outside barely registered. It was only the green light that drew his attention. He had to get out, had to escape the confines of this room. He rushed toward the door, hitting the button and running outside. He stumbled along the walkway to the far end of the cage, his fingers hooked through the squared gaps of the cage to hold himself up. He leaned back, sucking in as much air as he could, then exploded forward, his head toward the sky with an almighty "Fuuuuuuuuuuuuccckkk!"

It continued until his lungs began to collapse, all the air being forced out in one bellow. The word was being carried on the wind across the barren landscape of the desert beyond, birds suddenly taking flight at the cry. When all remnants of gas had been expelled, he slumped to the ground as if all the bones had suddenly vanished within him. His body struggled to take in the next life-giving breath that simply would not follow. His chest felt as if it had imploded, and he just didn't have the energy needed to expand it again. Time had stopped. The line between life and death came ever closer until he was standing with his toes right on its edge, kicking in his body's automatic response, forcing his muscles to spasm and draw in the air it needed to keep from crossing over where there was no coming back. His heart hammered at the bars of his chest to wake up whoever was in charge and kickstart his mind into action.

It took several minutes for the fog of asphyxiation to lift, and when it had, he unexpectedly felt some kind of peace. All of the unknowns inside had been expelled beyond the bars, beyond the trees, and for a moment, he had space to think.

He was not a bystander; he did have a choice—and when the time came, he would choose to stay in his room. He didn't have to take part in any of it. He could stay in his room, in his bed, and ignore all attempts at getting him out. He could let the world pass by without his input. That was it. When the time came, he simply would not go.

Chapter 47

William's fingers were happily typing away as he came to the end of his essay. He scrolled through it, squinting at the screen, and when he was happy, he hit the *save and send* button. He rolled his chair back from the desk, stood up and stretched away the aches from the unforgiving chair. As he pushed it back under his desk, he looked at the picturesque town printed on the back of the spines of all the books that now spread across the back. He grabbed the next book in the series and headed up to his bed. He had enjoyed the first one so much that he asked his mom for more. She'd sent him the whole collection.

As he got to the foot of the ladder, he turned to his clothes behind him. They were all neat and tidy, but one set stood out. One set of clothes he had folded and kept slightly separate from the others. To the untrained eye, it wouldn't look unusual, but to Will, they stood out like a beacon. On the bottom were his favorite pair of jeans, then a new undershirt and shirt, and perched on top like a cherry was a fresh, unused pair of socks. As soon as he had realized he wasn't going to be in here for much longer, the first thing he did was to prepare his clothes. These were the ones in which he wanted to celebrate that wonderful upcoming day.

He found himself staring at them sometimes. Just catching glimpses from the corner of his eye, and every time, a thrilling rush of adrenaline shot through his veins. They had taken on a whole new persona; they now represented the day he would be free from this place, free to live his life again. They caught his attention now as he paused before the ladder. He turned toward them and straightened the socks that had turned slightly from their position. Smiling, he climbed up the steps and almost leaped onto the bed.

He propped his pillow up on the back and got comfortable before opening the first pages. *The Red Star* was the fifth book of the series and one where the blurb promised a communist infiltrator was amongst the villagers—quiet for years, they had now been activated to steal secrets from the local military base.

It began with the mailman going about his business on a regular morning in the village, but William didn't make it past the third line before looking over at his clothes again. He smiled and returned to the pages as a special letter was being delivered to one of the residents, a letter upon which was a foreign stamp with a red star.

He looked over again; the clothes hadn't moved.

He gave a cough and shuffled his body deeper into the pillow and tried again, but as he did so, the corner of his eye began to draw his attention away again. He wrestled for a few lines more until he gave up, closing the book with a slap. He lay it on his chest and stared at the socks, a resigned sigh floating from his lips as he freed his imagination to play out the adventure of his escape to come.

He saw himself putting the clothes on in the morning of that day, looking smart and ready. The walk down to the truck. The actual escape became a mixture of movies and TV shows he'd seen. Sometimes it would involve shooting the tires out and blowing off the doors; others would cut through the side of the truck and have them jump across to a flatbed truck driving beside them. The one he went to now was where a helicopter flew in above the truck, picked it up, and disappeared into the sunset.

He played each scene back and forth several times before moving on to the next, enjoying the thrill of each part, especially the sensation that came from being lifted into the air. What came next was also a smorgasbord of delights. The helicopter would drop him off at a runway, where a private plane waited to whisk him away to safety. To a secret island perhaps, where he could live out his days in the sun, drinking cocktails, surrounded by scantily clad girls. He stayed on this scene for a while, savoring the sights, letting the thrill of white-bikinied females linger.

When he came back to the room again, the buzz of adrenaline came with him. He shuffled to the end of the bed, climbed down, and grabbed the remnants of the chocolate bar from his desk. It had been decimated over the last few days. The two months' worth had now been recalculated to two weeks, which meant he could practically gorge himself daily. He was pleased about that...but a little sad too. The preciousness of each piece had lost its thrill somewhat. He no longer craved the thing that he would soon have in abundance as much as when it had been a rarity. But he had the clothes now, and what they represented provided more than enough gratification. The adventure to follow gave him a wealth of material with which to fill his mind.

He put a handful of chocolate in his mouth as he looked back toward the socks and turned them again, his brown, sugar-filled mouth opening into a wide smile.

Chapter 48

Chris had just finished his breakfast when the delivery door opened, and a small package was shoved inside. He had gotten used to the regular delivery of his father's articles and had become very proficient at decoding their messages now. He reached down and snatched it up as he picked out remnants of breakfast from his teeth with his finger. He tossed it on his desk and began loading his tray to be sent back.

Once it had gone, he sat at his desk and opened it up. There was nothing much of interest on the front cover, but he still opened the pages with care, knowing that when he got bored, he would eventually end up reading the whole thing. He found his father's article, picked up his notepad and pen, and nonchalantly started to write out the letters. After the first two words were spelled out, he stopped and checked the article again. *That can't be right!* He continued writing, each letter that followed filling him with a greater sense of dread than the one before. Once complete, he sat back and read it again and again.

Donnie Fuller will be taken too. Send him message. 251.

That couldn't be *the* Donnie Fuller, surely. Not the Donnie Fuller he ratted out to get a lighter sentence. The same one who had vowed to kill him and his family for causing him to be put in prison? But how many Donnie Fullers could there be in juvenile prison in California?

Chris's heart rate rocketed as he remembered the nights of fear that were his life after the trial, after he had spoken of the things he was told never to utter. The nightmares that haunted him about what would happen to his fathers and his sister as a result filled his nights with torment and his days with anxious ignorance of their well-being. He knew a little of the intimidation they had faced, the people following them, waiting outside of the house, the psychological torment, but nothing to their bodies thankfully—not that he knew of, anyway. It had taken a long time for those feelings to settle, but now they threatened to return with a vengeance. He sat there, mouth dry, hands flat on the desk as if to steady himself.

He had been imagining the breakout often, and his worry had always been about his parents getting caught or something going wrong in some way. Now they took on a whole new dimension. His nemesis, his reason for being here who was safely stowed away, would now be his accomplice. What the fuck were his parents thinking to include him in the plan? Perhaps they had no choice. He wondered if Donnie would know he would be there on that day or if it would be as surprising to him as it was now for Chris. How would he react? Scenarios began to play themselves out in his mind. The look of shock, the change to anger, the beating that might follow. The collapse of the plan as guards were called to break them up. Those and a hundred other images streamed dizzyingly around his mind.

Their motion started to make him feel nauseous, the room began to spin along with them. He staggered back off his chair and lurched toward the toilet. The fresh bread and eggs that he had just enjoyed made their return with full force, splattering the sides of the bowl as his mouth only just managed to find the target.

He breathed in a mixture of breakfast and bile as his stomach lurched again, emptying out its contents completely. As he lay there, slumped to the side, the room began to slow somewhat; the sensation of the world in turmoil began to decrease. He opened his eyes, which helped stabilize the disparity between his mind and his inner ears. His drunken sea legs began to find land.

He slowed his breathing and allowed his mind to return from the edge of panic enough to be able to look at the problem. Of course, Donnie's reaction would be one of anger, being face-to-face with the rat that had snitched on him. So, Donnie had to be told about it beforehand so it wouldn't be a shock and he could control his reaction, at least until they were free. And then what? The moment they were out, would he then receive the street punishment for his crimes against the code? Maybe. Maybe the fact that it was his parents who'd come up with the plan to break them out may compensate somewhat. Either way, all that was beyond his control.

He stood up carefully and returned to his desk. He picked up his pad and pen and began writing the note.

Chapter 49

Donnie had been getting used to going out to the yard each morning. The ease with which he could speak with Miles was refreshing. There was no need to put up a front, no need to be coercive or threatening. No expectation that followed his name. They had begun sharing things about themselves that Donnie had never spoken about before, and a realization found its way to them both at just how much they had missed out on in life.

Miles told him about his driving career and the races he'd won. His parents and how they were just regular people, slightly older than most. It made Donnie feel like a freak with his background and parents. The drugs, the crime that was his normal everyday life. He had not had the opportunity to change what he had become, and when he finally realized he could make a different choice, he was put in here. He talked about Lucy and their plan of getting out and away from everything. He was surprised when Miles admitted to never having a girlfriend, never even kissing a girl, in fact, and for the first time, Donnie understood just how long Miles had been in here and what had been taken away from him. Away from them both.

As he stepped outside this morning, Miles was already waiting for him at the end. Donnie could sense a feeling of excitement from his movements, hopping from foot to foot. When he got close enough, he could see a beaming smile on his face, as if he had just been handed the keys to the door.

"Hey, Miles, what's up?"

"Okay, so before I give you this, I have to tell you something."

"Okay," Donnie replied, noticing the tube of paper in his hands.

"I had one of these weeks ago but couldn't say anything about it for obvious reasons. So don't be mad at me for keeping it from you."

"Keeping what from me?"

Miles threaded the note through to Donnie, who immediately stepped forward to grab hold of it.

He peeled away the loose tape and read. He looked up at Miles's face that was still beaming and read it again.

"Is this for real?"

"Yeah. My folks are involved in it, as well as yours now, I guess."

"Your plain old boring as shit folks are involved in..."

"Shhh!" Miles rushed forward to the fence. "Don't say it."

Donnie looked around for anyone who could be listening.

"Yes," continued Miles. "They may be boring, but they know their stuff. But my note didn't have the extra details as your does. I don't know who Chris is."

Donnie's lip began to curl. "I do. He's the bastard who put me in here."

"Oh."

"And I promised him that I was gonna rip his fucking head off the next time I saw him."

Miles looked away from the scowl on Donnie's face.

"Listen. I don't want to speak out of turn, but this is an opportunity for all of us, me included. Please don't fuck it up."

Donnie's hand began to screw the paper into a ball, his anger rising as the red mist began to descend. Miles could see it, and the feeling of excitement he'd felt slowly began to turn to dread.

"Lucy," Miles blurted out.

Donnie's eyes focused a little at the name.

"Think of Lucy. This will get you to her in a matter of weeks, not years. How would that feel?"

Donnie pictured Lucy and the dream they shared. But the doubts he had begun to have about how she really felt about him didn't help keep the image strong, and before it became solid, it was snatched away by the rage. The anger exploded in his stomach as his mind instead presented the memory of Chris at the trial. He tried to hold onto her image with everything he had and the trust that she would be there for him when he got out, but it was almost impossible to keep between his fingers, like grasping water.

He tried to control his breathing, closing his eyes to make the picture of her stand out more, to increase its power.

Miles could see his color start to return from lava to tanned, and when his eyes opened again, they were mostly clear.

"Alright," Donnie said. "I get it. I won't kick the crap out of him until after we're out."

Miles smiled, a little relieved, but Donnie's eyes began to glaze over as he returned to his internal thoughts once more.

Chapter 50

The station was busy, but Brant was in his own bubble, oblivious with his office door closed. In here, he didn't have to deal with any of the bullshit. He leaned forward to rub his knee. It hadn't quite recovered from his exertions of the other night.

His fingers had been playing with the corners of a manilla folder that had been sitting on his desk for a while. The size of it had grown over the last few days as more and more information had been gathered. In his mind, there was only one possible deduction to be made from it all, so why was he hesitating to take it to his captain? There was something holding him back, a memory perhaps.

He opened the folder and flicked through the information inside. Each family's details were paperclipped together, with scraps of paper and handwritten notes added along the way. Absently, he began to turn the pages of each, his eyes not really settling on anything in particular. He had read the contents several times so wasn't looking to read them again. He just wanted the overview, the feeling of them all together. Perhaps he was looking for the thing that would make his suspicions wrong. The thing that would collapse the house of cards he had built that was becoming more solid with each new piece.

He stopped at one of the families. His eyes flowed over the words but lingered on the images. Was he trying to see something that wasn't there?

He stuffed the papers back inside and, with a sigh, slid the folder inside the top drawer of his desk. He would ponder on it a while to figure out what the problem was. There was time enough to act if he was right, and he was sure he was right.

Chapter 51

The sky outside was blanketed in gray that threw a consistent gloomy light through the window, diffused further as it scattered between the fibers of the curtains and into the bedroom beyond. Taylor had been awake for a while, watching the day increase in brightness if not in contrast. He looked across at Jeremy with envy as his shoulders slowly rose and fell on the gentle swell of his breath.

He had been playing out different scenarios in his head in which either he or Jeremy would take the place of their son. He calculated different factors including, money, jobs, family, and friends, but no matter which way he turned the dials, the answer always came out the same.

Jeremy began to stir, feeling the weight of his stare no doubt, and turned over. His blurry eyes blinked open and caught sight of his husband staring back.

"You been awake long?"

"Yeah, a while."

He shuffled to sit up.

"Something on your mind?"

Taylor just looked at him with a frown.

"Sorry, stupid question."

"It's okay."

"Want to talk about it?"

"I don't want to, but I think we have to."

Jeremy nodded, wiping away the crust from the corner of his eye to appear more awake.

"I've been thinking about who will go in place of Chris."

"And?"

"Well, I've broken it down into four categories. The first one is job. Who would still be able to work inside and who wouldn't? That's also linked to money, who would still be able to earn a wage from behind bars."

Jeremy just nodded and listened.

"The second is appearance. Who would be missed by friends and family. Not missed as in they don't matter! Missed as in it

180

wouldn't cause as much of a stir if they were suddenly not around."

Jeremy remained still.

"And then there's still the matter of dealing with life when he's out and what that looks like. I...I've thought about all of it and..."

Jeremy placed his hand on Taylor's and smiled.

"It's okay. I know it's me."

"I'm sorry. I just can't come up with a sensible way in which it's me."

A look of pain shot across Taylor's face at the words coming from his mouth and the shared realization of what it meant. Jeremy turned and stroked the side of his husband's face, pulling it up toward his own.

"It's alright. I know if it could be any other way you would do the same."

A tear broke free and started to trace a path down Taylor's cheek.

"I bet you're wishing we didn't have the stem cell treatment so he had both our genes now!" Jeremy said, trying to lighten the mood.

Taylor just looked at him, unable to answer or smile along.

His husband saw the pain and tried to ease it as best he could. "It won't be for long. And besides, think of all the peace and quiet I'd get to write!"

They leaned forward and held each other tight, neither one wanting to let the other go.

"I love you."

"I love you."

Jeremy said, "We have to tell Maddie."

They pulled away slightly, looking at each other.

"Well, that's something I can do at least," Taylor said, hoping her reaction would be less violent than the last time. She hadn't spoken to them since and had avoided them very successfully. Now she was in for another shock.

Chapter 52

"Hey, Josh, thanks for coming over."

"No problem, Mike. Is everything okay? The garage's been closed for weeks now. Don't get me wrong—I don't mind staying at home and being paid for it, but my fingers are itching to pick up a wrench, you know."

"I know. I'm sorry. And I'm sorry also for the way I spoke to you when you came over the other day. It was a surprise to see you."

They both sat there for a second, neither one good at expressing their thoughts to the other. Mike finally coughed and began.

"Listen, I'm going away for a while, and I need someone to look after the garage while I'm gone."

Josh's eyebrows raised high. "Where are you going? Are you and Mary okay?"

"Yes, we're fine. There's some family issue in Australia that I have to go and sort out. I might be some time."

"Australia? I didn't know you had family out there. That's a hell of a way to go to sort out some family strife!"

"Yeah, tell me about it. Anyway, in the meantime, I need this place to keep running and naturally thought you'd be interested. You'd get paid a manager's wage, of course, and be able to hire your replacement."

"Jeez, I've never really thought about running a place. I kinda just like showing up and getting my hands dirty."

"I know, but you'd be doing me a massive favor. And Mary will still be here to take care of the paperwork side of things, so it'll only really be scheduling and ordering parts that will need your extra attention."

Josh looked down at the floor, uncertainty on his face.

"And I'm only in another country, it's not like I'll be dead! So, I'll still be able to keep my hand in and be there if you need anything. I'll just be a message away!"

Josh still wasn't looking up.

Mike searched for some other button to press, another point of leverage he could pull.

"Of course, you'd need to look after Korinna for me as well."

At this, Josh looked up.

"Are you serious?"

"Absolutely. I won't be able to drive her from across the ocean, will I?"

"But she's your baby!"

"She is. That's why I know she'll be in safe hands with you."

Josh had suddenly found something to be excited about. He had wanted to drive Korinna for as long as he'd been working at the garage. She was Mike's 1955 Ford Mustang GT500 that he'd practically rebuilt from scratch, and the thought of being behind the wheel of her began to make his mouth water.

"Well, if you're sure. I'd be happy to look after her."

"Great," said Mike, trying not to let the fear for his car show on his face. "I'll have her ready for you next week when you pick up the keys to the place."

Mike reached out a hand that was met enthusiastically by Josh's. He tried to ignore the damp palm and the thought of them on the wheel, tearing around the neighborhood in his Korinna.

Chapter 53

"This can't be good," said David as Beverley strode past his glass paneled office and straight into the conference room of DMA Investments.

He sighed from behind his desk and walked out, following her in.

When he pushed open the heavy door, she was already at the window, looking out at the Los Angeles skyline beyond.

"What's going on, Bev? If it's nothing important, I have a load of work to do to be ready in time for your stunt."

She turned to him, looking unfamiliar, as if he was staring back at her twenty years in the past.

"That's what I wanted to talk to you about. Would you be interested if I'd found a way to get William out without it being discovered, where you didn't have to sell anything and everything else wasn't frozen?"

David made sure the door was closed and sat down in one of the junior chairs, midway along the table. It felt unusual, but he let the feeling pass.

"I might be. It depends on what else it would cost me."

"Nothing much. You can keep all your businesses, all your money, all your investments. I'd just need some of your time."

"How much time?"

"Just under four years."

"Beverley..."

She raised a hand to quiet him before he started.

"There's a problem, which may turn out to be some kind of solution for you."

"Okay, I'm listening."

She moved to the end of the table, sat at the head, in his chair, and stared across at him.

"After our conversation, I realized the expectation I put on you to get ready for the scrutiny and danger from the police was slightly unfair and possibly unrealistic."

"Slightly?"

"There's an alternative which would allow you to keep everything you have with no disruption or loss."

David leaned forward, eager to hear more. He'd been having nightmares trying to liquidize his portfolio without it looking suspicious. He wasn't about to admit it, but an alternative sounded good about now. He kept silent and waited for the offer.

"Everything is set to go. All the details have been worked out, and next week, William will be free."

He brought the tips of his fingers together in a pensive movement but continued to hold his silence.

Beverley looked down at the impossibly shiny surface of the table for a second before returning her gaze to him.

"In order for you to keep everything you have…you'll need to swap places with William. You'll need to serve the remainder of his sentence in his stead."

David tried not to react but couldn't help but let the corner of his eyebrow raise slightly. They sat in silence for a good minute.

Finally, he plopped back in his seat, the shift in power having skimmed across the table from her seat to his.

"I see. And what makes you think I'd let myself be locked up for four years?"

"What makes me think that?" Her temper started to catch around the edges. "Well, for one thing, it's your fucking fault he's in there to begin with!"

He simply waved her words away with a flick of his wrist.

Her temperature continued to rise at his impassivity.

"Secondly, I still have all the information on you, which would probably see you behind bars anyway."

He smiled, "It may, but it will also mean William stays there as well, and possibly you too for not sharing it with the authorities sooner. We could be a nice happy family behind bars, together at last."

The fucking bastard, she thought. She knew what he wanted and had nothing left but to give it to him.

"Okay. And you can have everything else. I will sign over everything to you."

He leaned forward, suddenly interested.

"The businesses?"

"Yes."

"The savings fund?"

"Yes."

"The house?"

She paused. Where would she go with William if she didn't have a home anymore? She looked across at him. He had all the power now, and he knew it. But she had to have something.

"Yes…on the proviso that I get the beach house. We'll need somewhere to live."

He thought about it, making her sweat. He could run things remotely without too much of an issue, and he could prepare for being a remote CEO much easier than having all his assets frozen for God knows how long. He would need to set it up with Frank, but if he got everything from her for the inconvenience, it might just be worth it. His mind tried to show him the negative side of the deal, the white room, the feeling of incarceration, but his greed swatted them like flies and fed him the taste of victory.

"I guess that's something I could do. It would need a hell of a lot of preparation to be able to run the business from inside, but it's not impossible. Give me the details."

She looked across at him, perhaps seeing him for the first time—his sleaziness masked behind a thin veneer of charm. *That's fine*, she thought. *You can take it all. At least I'll have my son and my life back.*

Chapter 54

"Open the fucking door. I know you're in there!"

Reluctantly, Marcus's silhouette appeared from a doorway inside. He shuffled forward.

"What do you want?"

"Open the fucking door. I'm not talking through the wood."

He sighed and opened up. Desi barged through, slamming it behind her.

"What was that about? You didn't think I'd come here to find you?"

"No, I knew. I was just hoping it was after I had slept."

"You're staying up all night with your bitches doesn't concern me. Our son is what concerns me and what you're going to do to help him!"

Marcus walked toward the kitchen, picking up a crumpled pack of cigarettes from the counter as he went.

"Coffee?" he asked as he lit up.

Now she was inside, her anger started to abate, but only slightly.

"Sure."

He filled the kettle and began getting the cups ready when Desi's patience had used up its short lifespan.

"Well? Are you going to willing take his place, or am I going to have to force you?"

He turned and looked at her.

"Look, we were only going to be a part of this group until we had a plan of our own. One that doesn't involve me going to jail preferably."

"Well, if you hadn't noticed, we've got shit-all of a plan, and definitely nothing better than they have. Would you have known or cared about the DNA machine? Or been able to cut through the bar?"

He smiled at her. "Sounds like you're getting to like them!"

She stiffened her back in response. "I don't fucking like them, but they serve a purpose, a purpose that you suddenly don't seem bothered with."

"It's not that I'm not bothered. But I didn't sign up to be banged away."

"Maybe you should have thought of that before sending your child across the border to pick up drugs!"

"He knew what he was doing."

"He's seventeen years old! And, for some godforsaken reason, looks up to his father."

Marcus winced as he turned to finish off the coffee.

"I can't do it. It's not just me! The business would collapse if I wasn't there to keep it straight."

"There are ways around that. Someone could take over while you're away. Hell, I'd even run it if it came to it."

"You'd look after my whores?" He laughed.

"If it meant you standing up to be a father to your son, I would."

"And how long before you ran it into the ground or pissed everyone off enough to leave?"

"A lot longer than you'd survive if you didn't."

A look of anger flashed across his face. She needed a different tactic.

"Look, Marcus, I know we've had our issues, and…well, things aren't great between us at the moment." She moved closer. "But this is our son, our boy, and no matter how big he thinks he is, he's still just a child. He's not like we were at that age. Remember?"

Marcus smiled as he remembered. They were younger than that when they'd met. Two runaways who survived by knocking off gas stations and convenience stores. They needed each other back then. Maybe it was love, maybe it was something else, but they had always been there for each other, and despite his affair, he knew she'd have his back if it came to it.

"There's no getting away from it, is there?" he said.

"No, but maybe we should be seeing this as an opportunity rather than a problem."

"An opportunity?"

"Sure, I mean, we have the chance to get good a quantity of product into the system. Imagine…you could be loaded up with it at the switch and sell it inside for whatever you asked for. You'd be their only source, so you could set the prices sky high.

He thought about it for a moment. "What happens when I run out?"

"You'd need to pace yourself. Sell slowly, keep the demand up and the prices high. If you're smart, it'll take all that time to get rid of it. Then you'd not only leave a hero, having saved your son, but with a healthy profit to boot."

His mind played with this thought as an unconscious smile began to form.

Desi smiled too. *I've got you.*

Chapter 55

The girls were asleep when Jane came down into the living room. Peter was on the sofa with a pile of papers he was going through to mark. He looked up with a smile as she entered.

"Well, one thing's for sure," he said. "I won't miss marking incompetent undergrads!"

She tried to smile back, but there was a weight upon her that made it difficult for the edges of her mouth to turn up. Peter noticed it.

"What's up?" he asked, moving the papers so she could sit next to him.

"I've got to tell you something, something that's not going to be nice."

He sat there, his mind suddenly panicking, trying to second guess what she might say.

He held her hand. "What is it?"

His hand felt warm on hers, comforting, secure, all the things that she loved him for. She wondered if it would feel like that in a minute or two. She cleared her throat of the lock and chain that had been tied around it for so long.

"Peter," she began. "You know I love you right?"

"Of course, honey." He squeezed her hand firmer.

"And we have a pretty good family here."

His eyes looked up at the stairs, to the girls fast asleep, and nodded.

"What I have to tell you is in no way a reflection of my love for you or the life we've built up over the years. This is something I thought I wouldn't ever have to tell you or ever say out loud."

Peter's mind was gripped with fear, blank and empty, waiting to be filled with the horror of what she might say.

"Before we met, I had been single for a time. I'd broken up from my boyfriend a year before, and to celebrate, my girlfriends took me out for a drink before the start of the academic year."

"Okay."

"Well, we'd all had too much, and before you knew it, we were at a honky-tonk, taking shots and dancing with the cowboys."

"Uh-huh."

"And, well, this guy had just left the Army and was out celebrating with his buddies too, and…well, one thing led to another. You get the idea."

"As disturbing as that image is, I'm not sure what that's got to do with us now?"

Jane looked down at their hands, still clasped.

"It was just that once, and I never saw him again. A week later, you and I met at college, and I fell in love."

"I remember that very well. You were the brightest thing in my lecture hall. I was nervous in my first year and couldn't believe my eyes when you walked in."

She blushed at the memory. The flirting with each other while he tried to give lectures, the private tutoring and help with assignments that actually led to less work being done. Those were happy, frivolous times. Different than now.

"I became pregnant with Ed very quickly, didn't I?"

Peter's eyes glassed over as he looked back. A realization beginning to dawn.

She pressed onward. "And Ed was born a little early, wasn't he, but a good size?"

She hoped all the clues would help him understand before she had to say it outright.

He looked back at her now, puzzlement and pain in his face.

"You mean…Ed…isn't mine?"

Hearing those words in the air was too much. She began to cry.

Peter sat back and pulled his hands away onto his lap.

"I'm so sorry," she said, struggling to speak.

"Are you sure? How do you know?"

She sniffed back the tears to answer. "Because it just makes sense. The timing of the pregnancy and birth, the fact that he looks just like him now. I've wanted to tell you of course, but it didn't seem to matter. We were all happy together."

"But we were living a lie."

"It wasn't a lie. We were a happy family."

He paused a moment, thinking. "Would you have told me if my DNA wasn't required to get him out?"

She knew the right answer, and she knew the truth, both of which refused to come out.

"I see. And what about the father? Have you spoken to him and told him?"

"No, I've only just managed to track down his number."

"And how's that going to go? *'Oh hello, yes I know we haven't spoken in a long time, and you probably don't remember me, but I'm that girl you shagged in the car park that night and…well, I became pregnant with your son, and now I need to break him out of prison and for you to take his place.'*"

Those words bounced off the walls and kept going around and around. Peter hated them and hated that they had come from him. He stood up.

"I'm going out."

"Please don't. Let's just talk about it. We can sort it out."

He walked toward the door and pulled on his jacket.

"I need some air." He looked back at her in a way that broke her heart. He opened the door and was gone.

Jane sat there for a while, the tears flowing easily. She tried to keep from making a noise as best she could, not wanting the girls to wake and find out who was making it and why. She had just destroyed her marriage and broken the heart of the one man she loved more than anything. But what choice did she have? It was going to come out sooner or later on this path they had taken.

Eventually, her eyes began to dry as the stock of tears ran out and reality came back into view. She had tracked down this man over the past week, calling his old unit to trace where he lived with no joy, scrolling for hours through the search results on his name. Finally, by narrowing the search to likely career paths chosen by ex-military, she managed to find him. It was an image she saw that stirred a vague recollection, a memory of a much younger face. From there it was easy.

She dried her face and blew her nose before picking up her phone. She dialed the number and waited.

"Hello."

"Hello, Jack? This is Jane Porter, I mean, I was Jane Simmonds when we met. It's been a long time I know."

There was a pause on the line. "What can I do for you, Jane?"

"I was wondering if we could meet. There's something important I have to tell you."

Chapter 56

Beverley sat in her chair by the fire, stirring the chai latte on her lap and staring at the golden tongues of the flames licking around the logs. She looked around at the shadows dancing across the walls and windows of the room that suddenly felt so empty, as if all the furniture and fixtures had been removed to leave nothing but the bare shell behind. She had spent the day packing her bags with the essentials and had loaded William's too, to take to the beach house. She had filled and refilled them several times. Not out of errors particularly; more from a need to keep occupied and focused on something other than the following day.

She looked across at them, now piled up and waiting to be put into the car. She still couldn't quite come to terms with the changes that were about to happen. She was on the precipice of becoming an accomplice to a jailbreak; she was leaving behind her home, her friends, and everything she had sacrificed her life for to save her son. But was it anything she had wanted anyway? The money and security had been nice and needed at one point, but as she sat there now, tallying up the costs, she realized she had paid too high a price for these things that once seemed so important.

The years that had been lost in either a stupor or through willful ignorance of the world outside had amounted to half a life lost, the potential she had once had, diminished—but she was not dead yet. She had made a choice and was about to begin a new chapter in her life, a chapter that was as frightening as anything she had endured before. She was to be alone without the support and finances she was used to, to disappear from the world. She would have to rejoin it at some point, she knew, and be a part of life again. The responsibility for the income and level of living that would follow was daunting. But this thought, instead of one of just fear, made her feel alive again, as if her heart had been between beats for the years since her marriage and was on the verge of pulsing once again.

She had no idea what life would be like after tomorrow, but the fact that it would be in her hands made it okay somehow. That the challenges and struggles to come were hers to face and overcome, that the purpose of her life was once again open for discussion, the direction of which was led by her and her alone.

She took a sip of tea and allowed its sweet warmth to drain through her body. She looked at the mug now, her mind imagining the day to come, and ran through a checklist in her head. She had ensured the compounds were ready to go and that they would do what was needed to the bar. She listed anything that would be a problem and checked it off with a solution. She thought about the syringe attached to the radio-controlled car and the status of the battery of the vape that she would double check at the garage in the morning. Then she thought about her husband. Would he actually turn up and go through with it? Was this part of a game he was playing, which would mean the failure of everything to everyone would be her fault? She had no control over that. She had done everything she could. She had signed documents relinquishing herself as owner of the businesses, signed over the house to him, and filled out the forms to remove herself from the bank accounts. This and the electronic evidence she had against him was all together in a thick envelope that sat on top of her bags now. Everything that gave her power and leverage over him was placed neatly together there, convenient for anyone to just pick up and walk away with.

She felt vulnerable now, suddenly aware that she wouldn't be able to stop someone from breaking in and taking it if they wanted. The thought sent a chill through her and erased the warmth from her tea instantly. She placed the mug down, went over to her bags, and picked up the envelope. It felt heavy in her hands, as if the whole world had been stuffed inside.

She turned and headed for the kitchen counter to peel off a large carving knife from the metallic strip on the wall. Well, if they were coming, they wouldn't get it without a fight.

Chapter 57

Mike had been sitting in the deep stitched leather seat of Korinna for a while before Mary found him. She opened the passenger door and sat in elegantly, bottom first with legs and knees twisting in together like Jackie Onassis. He looked at her as she closed the car door and made herself comfortable.

They both sat there then in silence, just sharing the space for a while before the air was broken.

She looked across at him. "We going somewhere?" she asked.

Mike smiled. "Anywhere you want, Mary Lou."

"Anywhere with you," she replied almost automatically, until the realization occurred to them both that in the place he was going tomorrow, she would not be able to follow.

The weight of the air around them changed. Mike felt it, so he reached out his hand and turned the key. The engine roared into life with deep vibrations that pulsed through their cores.

"Oh, so we really are going somewhere," Mary said.

Mike grinned, shifted into drive, and edged out toward the road. "Just a little spin," he replied.

Although it was still early evening, the sun was already setting below the horizon, painting dramatic firelight on the undersides of the clouds that seemed frozen in place. The soft golden glow reflected off the buildings as if they were gilded, made up for a special parade that only Mike and Mary were a part of. No spectators, no waving or cheering, just a motorcade of one following the well-known streets of their home.

All of a sudden, Mary leaned forward and pointed across the dash to a park they were passing.

"Remember when we used to take Miles to that park when he was young?"

"I used to chase him around that climbing frame until he was dizzy."

Mary's hand touched Mike's arm with a gentle squeeze.

"There's the launderette I used when our washing machine broke down, remember?" she said. "We switched to using cloth diapers to be environmentally friendly at the same time Miles was having a diarrhea episode as if he was possessed!"

They both started laughing at the memory, the smell returning as if still caught in their noses.

"Those were some toxic explosions, luminous yellow and green!"

"I was so embarrassed. Everyone just stared at me with this disgusted look on their faces whenever I went in there. It was like there was a huge cloud of it following me!"

Their laughter continued as they passed the rank of stores and turned down another street. It took another ten minutes before Mary realized where they were heading next. She turned to him and saw him smiling out of the corner of his mouth.

She swiveled back in her seat and stared through the screen, "We really are having a tour, aren't we?"

A little while later, they were pulling up outside a dilapidated house surrounded by similar structures, all of which were on their last legs. The paint had been sun-peeled from its surface, and the windows were shattered, a fun game for the local kids no doubt.

They both stared at it with different eyes, eyes that saw past its faded façade back to a time when it was loved and cared for, when it had been a home.

"I can't believe you used to climb up that trellis to my window, you old romantic you," said Mary.

"I don't think it would take the weight these days!"

"I remember so clearly kissing under that porch. My mother switching off and on the light above our heads as if she worked in a disco."

"That didn't stop us."

"Nothing could stop us." She smiled at him. "Not even my father." Her mind drifted to the man she had all but erased from her memory.

"It feels so long ago and yet only yesterday."

"It was. Time has a way of doing that."

"Do you want to get out and have a look?" he asked, reaching for the handle.

"No," she replied, grasping his arm. "I'd just like to sit here for a while."

197

He removed his hand from the door and placed it on hers. They both sat there as if looking at an old movie at a drive-in. The actions and sounds happening only in their minds. When enough time had passed for them to reach the present, they both sighed in unison and looked into the others' eyes.

"It's gonna be okay," he tried to reassure her.

She looked down, unwilling for him to see her lie. "I know."

"Are you sure you're gonna be okay at your sister's?" Mike asked.

"Yes, it's about time she had more company than the spinster life she's been leading."

Mike looked over at the rundown shell. "That house really took it out of the both of you."

Mary just continued to stare.

Mike turned the key once more and broke the spell of the moment. "I'm sorry. I shouldn't have brought you back here."

"There are good memories here too. The ones with you. Those are what I can see now."

They drove off without another word, back to their own home for possibly the last time together.

Chapter 58

Jane closed the book and looked at the two faces staring up at her. They were unusually quiet during the reading as they had been for the last few days. She stood and put the book back on the shelf to join its many companions as the girls snuggled down in their beds. When she turned to see them, she had to catch herself from not bursting into tears at their little faces, eyes wide, anxious and expectant, poking from the tops of the duvet. She held it back and walked over between their beds.

"Mummy, when's daddy coming home?"

The question that had been on the tips of their tongues all night. The question that she dreaded the most. Her tears began to well again as she tried to formulate an answer.

"Soon, honey, he'll be back soon."

"But why has he been away so long?" the other one added.

"I told you, Daddy had to go away with work for a while, but he'll be back real soon."

There were more question lurking beneath, more things they didn't understand that they so desperately wanted to. But they kept it to themselves for now. For that she was grateful. She didn't know how many more lies and half-truths she could tell them.

She tucked them in tighter and kissed them on the head, avoiding their wide, pleading eyes.

"Goodnight, my beautiful girls," she said as she opened to the door to leave.

"Goodnight, Mummy," they said in unison.

As the door closed behind her, she leant back on it, relieved at making it out before the floodgates opened. They were cracking now as she walked down into an empty, lonely space; a space where her husband should be sitting, working, waiting for her to come down the stairs. Instead, there was the memory of the last time he was there, the time when she'd broken his heart. The devastated look on his face flashed before her eyes at the thought of what she had done to him. A sob burst out and with fear she looked up toward the girls and covered her mouth with her hands.

She walked out to the kitchen, still holding any noise in place, only freeing her lips long enough to pass wine between them, to appease them with a task of drinking instead of creating sound.

She stood behind the island, looked out across the kitchen, and remembered the day when Taylor had come in with Peter. How he'd explained his plans to free his son, plans that ultimately would change the rest of their lives. The fear she'd felt that evening as he explained it, as Peter listened, having already spoken about the need to do something, his feeling of guilt at not being able to stop what had happened. All the while without knowing that he wasn't even Ed's father.

But wasn't he? He had been there through pregnancy, been there at his birth. Loved him, cared for him, raised him. Wasn't that what made a father? Not the single piece of genetic material used in his creation.

Could Ed feel that in some way? Could he feel that the bond wasn't there at the molecular level? Did he have an innate sense that they shared no blood?

There was a sudden noise at the door as Jane's wet and red eyes looked up. A familiar jangle of keys filtered through the air, and the pressure in the room dropped when the door opened.

Jane's heart and lungs had paused in anticipation of who it was and exploded as Peter walked in the room. He looked across at her, and she at him. Her body was caught between fear and love. She tried to predict which one it should be based on the look in his eyes. He stood there, and she could see he was unsure of what to say or where to start. She reached behind her and grabbed another glass from the side and poured some wine in it, sliding it forward for him to take. He smiled and stepped forward, lifting it up for several gulps, his eyes focused on the bottom of the glass.

As he lowered it and caught his breath, he looked up at her and spoke.

"I'm sorry."

"*I'm* sorry," Jane burst out as the tears fell, and she rushed to hold him. He swept her up, and they held each other tight, their bodies shaking with adrenaline and relief.

"I'm so sorry," she continued, her voice quivering. "I should have told you. I should have…"

"No, I'm sorry. I shouldn't have reacted that way. I know you wouldn't have done anything out of malice. I just didn't know what to do."

"I didn't know what to do either."

They were both crying now, the noise traveling up the stairs and into the little ears of two girls who couldn't help the excitement of hearing their father's voice. They clambered from their beds, leapt down the stairs, and practically bowled him over.

"Daddy, Daddy, you're home!"

"Hey, girls," he said, stroking their hair as they held on tight. After a minute, when their arms were getting tired, he knelt down to them. "I'm sorry I was away for a while. But I won't ever be away again."

They flung their arms around his neck and kissed his cheeks, wet with tears of love.

"Right, why don't you both get back up to bed, and I'll come up and read you another story before sleep?"

They both smiled wide and nodded before racing up the stairs again.

Peter stood and turned to Jane. "I guess I won't have to go away now, will I?"

"No," she replied.

"Have you spoken to him?"

"Yes, a few times now."

"And has he agreed?"

"Yes, I'm pretty sure he has. He seemed genuine and wanted to know about Ed. I just hope he doesn't change his mind or rat us out."

Peter nodded. "I guess we'll find out tomorrow, won't we?

"You're still coming?"

"Of course! Somebody has to keep things calm and steady."

Chapter 59

Desi sat there tired and worn out and looked down at the pile on the floor. It had taken a while to get together all the drug-mule paraphernalia...the body packs, the secret containers that fit around the legs and torso to transport all manner of powders and pills across borders. Each had been filled with a select range of products for Marcus to take with him. She had also prepared the invoice to cover the cost of them but removed—very graciously, she thought—the usual markup.

She had closed up the bar a little earlier tonight in order to have some privacy. The place was eerily quiet as she waited. She picked up the glass of Jack and brought it to her lips, and the image of her father floated into her mind like an unwelcome specter. She wondered what he would be thinking now. Would he be looking down at her and laughing, would he be angry at what she was doing, or would he be as concerned as she was now, anxious to find out which way it all went?

There was a knock on her door as it opened and Marcus stepped in.

"It's quiet," he said as he closed the door behind him.

"Yeah," she replied.

He looked down at the heap on the floor. "Jesus! You expect me to be able to carry all that on me?"

"What's the matter? Don't think you're strong enough?"

He stepped over and picked up a pack, weighing it in his hands. "It's not that I'm not strong enough, but more like it won't actually fit around me and still leave space to move...or to breathe, for that matter."

"So, what's your point?"

He looked at her as a smirk began to show in the corner of her mouth. "Where did you find all these bags?"

"I had to go hunting!"

"Jesus, I think I recognize this one," he said, picking up a battered waist band. "Isn't this the one we used on the streets the first time?"

"It sure is."

"Wow! I didn't know it was so sentimental that you kept it."

She snatched it from him and tossed it back on the pile. "It's a useful piece, that's all."

"Alright, I was only kidding. Jeez, you need to lighten up."

"Don't tell me to lighten up, not tonight of all nights."

He looked down, feeling the weight of the night as heavy as the bags before him.

"I'm sorry. I know I can be a bit of a dick sometimes."

"A bit?"

He picked up another bag, one that went around the thigh, and began fiddling with the strap. "I'm sorry for a lot of things, Desi."

There was a moment's pause, a brief ceasefire.

She grabbed the bag from him. "You think you can remember how to wear all these?"

"It's been a while. I'm not sure I ever wore them all!"

"This one is great, especially if you've got skinny legs like you do." She knelt down and began placing it on his thigh.

"I don't have skinny legs!"

"Uh-huh!"

She fed the strap around the top part of his leg, brushing his groin as she went. She could feel a reaction as she clipped it into place and stood, allowing her fingertips to slide upward as she went. They stood there as the electricity of anticipation and the adrenaline of the day to come swirled around them. He could feel her touch on his leg and the thrill that shot through him. She always had a way of stripping down his defenses. Her head was close enough to feel her warm, sweet breath on his tongue. It created a tingle that went directly to his penis. He couldn't take any more and grabbed her, kissing her hard.

The intensity grew as their lips became reacquainted, finding old familiar angles and tastes until suddenly it stopped. Pain soared through him as he opened his eyes to see Desi looking up at him, her teeth clamped tight to his bottom lips. She bit harder and then pulled away.

"Fucking hell, Desi!" he yelled as he felt his lip with his fingers and saw the blood, felt the swelling start.

"Don't think for one second I'll let you back in my bed after what you did." She backed away from him and pointed to the bags on the floor. "Get this shit out of here."

He stepped forward and began picking them up, his eyes hurt and angry, watching her as an animal would a predator who was close by.

"And don't even think about not showing up tomorrow."

She turned, poured herself another glass of bourbon, and picked up the invoice from the table.

He had managed to pick up all the bags by the time she walked back to him. He stepped back, aware of the vulnerable position he was in.

"Look, Desi…"

"Shhh," she said, placing the paper in his mouth, the blood staining the edge. "I'll need that taken care of before you disappear tomorrow."

He tried to reply, but the mumbles fell on deaf ears. She returned to her chair and busied herself with papers on her desk. He stood there a second before turning to leave, fumbling for the door handle with no look or help from her.

She could hear him leave through the outside door a moment later; she stopped pretending to work. She picked up her glass again and drained the rest with a look of pain that spread over her face. Her plan was in place, she had no choice but to go through with it now.

Chapter 60

John Williams played through the speakers as the credits rolled, the three of them sitting there, Maddie in the middle, sandwiched between her fathers. A rose between two thorns she'd like to say. Although the movie was her choice, she picked one they would all enjoy, and even though it was made way before she was born, *Raiders of the Lost Ark* still held some kind of magic for her. Maybe it was the class of Indie, or maybe it was the dramatic landscape and story. Whatever it was, as soon as she heard that music, her heart raced in search of an adventure.

It was an adventure that she seemed to be on now, not knowing exactly what was going to happen with the huge thing her fathers were planning to do. They were characters in their own movie that featured her, and although they all should be the stars of the show, she felt more like a side character.

"That was amazing. Great choice, Mads," said Jeremy.

"Yep, top choice."

"Why, thank you!" she replied, smiling.

"Of course," continued Taylor, "it all boils down to the amazing filmic education we've given you growing up."

She turned with her eyebrows raised. "Really? What about that one where this guy's locked in a room for fifteen years only to be released and cut his own tongue out."

"Well, there's more to it than that! It's a classic. The best of the Vengeance Trilogy."

Jeremy nodded in agreement.

"It was disgusting. And in Korean!" he said.

"Just because it wasn't American, doesn't mean it's not good!" Taylor countered.

"I know, but I mean, I was only ten when you showed it to me."

"Really?" said Jeremy. "You seemed older somehow. Chris loved it!"

"Yeah, he would!"

There was a brief pause as they remembered where Chris was at this very moment. But not wanting a depressing feeling to overcome their night, Jeremy continued.

"So, what would you say was your favorite movie?"

"Oh my god. You can't ask me that!"

"Why not?"

"Because it's like asking what favorite molecule of air you like to breathe," she said. "If you narrowed it down to genre, director, style, I might be able to answer!"

"Well, that sounds like hard work."

"Yes, it should be. It's like if I asked you what's your favorite book you've written, or what is your favorite article. It can't be narrowed down like that."

The two men sat there and thought for a second before answering simultaneously:

"*Midnight is a Place.*"

"The corruption of the prison system."

They all looked at each other and laughed. The mirth of the evening was a much-needed remedy, tonight of all nights. As the noise quietened once more, it lingered, casting a shadow over their faces.

Maddie looked to Jeremy. "I can't believe you're going to prison tomorrow."

He giggled. "Well, technically yes, but hopefully I'll be out in no time."

She looked down. "In years maybe."

He stroked her hair and drew her closer, kissing the top of her head. "It will fly by, and I'll only be a letter away."

"Won't I be able to do video chats?"

Her fathers looked at each other before Jeremy answered. "It's probably safer not to show my face on video, just in case it's monitored."

At this she looked devastated and worried. "But don't they have cameras in the cells?"

"Yes and no," Taylor chimed in. "The cameras are monitored by an AI unit that watches for dangerous or suicidal behavior. As long as he behaves himself, he'll be fine."

Jeremy tried to show a brief smile that all would be okay.

"And I'll have my writing to keep me busy," he said. "You'll be able to send me all my stuff once I'm in."

Maddie began to think about that, about life without him there. "But what about my graduation? My prom? You'll miss it all!"

"Then we'll have to have another one when I'm out, so you get two!"

"It won't be the same."

"No, honey, it won't be the same," replied Taylor, shuffling in closer. "But your brother will be here and able to enjoy it with you to a degree, and that's more important."

She nodded, although not whole-heartedly.

"And besides, you'll have me!" Taylor joked as he tickled her sides.

She laughed, and Jeremy joined in, bringing some kind of happiness to the end of the night.

"Well, I'd better be heading to bed," Maddie said as she stood. "Thanks for a great evening."

"Thank you for picking a great film!"

She walked a step before looking back. The banks suddenly burst, and she ran into Jeremy's arms, crying uncontrollably. He wrapped her up as she shook beneath him.

"Shhh, it's okay, honey. I know it's tough, but we're tougher, right?"

She nodded as she pulled her head away. It was all he could do to not join her in the mire of his own tears, but he couldn't allow her to see that.

Her grip was still tight as he asked her, "You wanna sleep in with us tonight?"

She nodded feverishly with a half-smile.

"Okay."

They switched the TV off and headed upstairs, trying to squeeze out as many minutes as they could together before the morning.

Chapter 61

Brant now knew it all. He knew the times, the location, and all the people involved. The final pieces had been gifted to him, and now he had a decision to make. Should he hand it all to his superiors so that action could be taken, or should he allow it to take place? It was a bold plan, and one that came with so many risks for them all. How they had worked together to get this far he would never know. It was almost too beautiful to ruin.

After all the children he had put behind bars, here were parents who actually gave a damn enough to put their own lives on the line. What would a good parent do for their kids? The thought encircled his mind as he got up and went to the freezer, dropping a few ice cubes in the bottom of his dry glass. Then he filled it up with what bourbon was left from a bottle on the counter.

He looked around his empty apartment. There were no photographs of a special woman, no images of children growing that he could use as a source of knowledge or understanding. He was alone and had been alone for a very long time. He'd thought he liked it that way. It kept him safe and focused on his career, on doing his job, but as he looked around now, he knew it hadn't been worth the price he'd paid.

He sat back on the sofa and looked across at the laptop before him. On the screen was an email he had drafted to his chief. He read it again now, knowing what it would mean if he were to send it.

He looked around the room again before returning his gaze to the screen. He reached forward and hit the send button, and with a *whoosh*, it was gone.

He closed it up, removing the glaring light from the room, and took another sip. He had to do what he had to do.

Chapter 62

Chris's eyes were already open and staring at the ceiling when the morning alarm sounded. His heart rate hadn't dropped below a hundred as his mind raced through the day that was to come, not least of which facing his enemy. All night, his mind kept showing him the dangers of all that could go wrong as it scrambled for solutions and ways to prevent them, but every time, he came up short. Even the things that could presumably be prepared for, like Donnie attacking him...he had no influence over. He couldn't preempt a strike, as it would cause a commotion and bring the whole thing to a very messy end. If he reacted to being hit and a fight ensued, then it would end in the same way. He had to walk willingly into the lion's den, fully aware of all the dangers, with nothing but the shirt on his back. No wonder his mind was unable to find the off switch.

He also tried to figure out what exactly was going to happen that day. Details had been minimal for obvious reasons, but he would still have liked to know how it was going to be done. Were they going to blow up the truck or kill the drivers? How were they going to solve the fact that they wouldn't be arriving at the new prison? The swirling of questions and possible answers did little to settle his nerves from the other thoughts.

And as if to add insult to injury, he thought about what his life would be like out there. He'd only been confined for a few months but already he had a nervousness about being free. Perhaps it wasn't just about being free. There were feelings of guilt and a desire possibly to be punished. He had made mistakes, and he should have to answer for them. He tried to push the feeling aside, to convince himself that he should feel glad about getting away with it, but it wouldn't quite go away. His life outside would also be one of hiding and solitude for who knows how long. He had no idea where he was going or what he was going to be able to do once out, and the idea that he would be just as much a prisoner outside as he was inside couldn't escape his mind. Sure, he'd have a lot more room to walk around, but the limits would be the same, if not more painful, with real life and people living their lives freely around him. At least here he didn't have to see that. He could live in blissful ignorance of the world outside and what might or might not be going on. He was on pause in here, safe in a kind of stasis where one day he could wake up and walk outside again once his journey had ended. Now he was heading out into the void of a space without knowing what to expect.

The thickness of all those thoughts made his head heavy, and yet, with a heavy sigh, he lifted his chin and began the day.

Chapter 63

Miles's eyes opened seconds before the morning alarm sounded. He lay there for a while and wondered if he would always wake up at this time in the future, if his body clock had now been programmed with an unmovable switch.

He sat up sharply with instant regret as pain swelled up within his ankle. He would often wake having forgotten the sprain, but that memory was never lost for long. He shuffled up slowly with some effort and looked down at his room. His contents had already been packed up and transported away, using the boxes and QR code stickers that were provided. All that was left was a change of clothes and a small brown paper bag for his nightclothes and toiletries. The bareness of the room surprised him. It was amazing how somewhere as foreboding as this could feel like home. The slow integration of your own possessions, pictures, clothes, books, can take over a place, and it's only when those things are removed that you can see just what it had become.

He often tried to recall his own bedroom at home, to remember the posters on the walls, the furniture and things that were around it. He still had the image, although he was sure that it had changed somewhat over the years as he filled the gaps in his memory with best guesses.

He pulled away the duvet and looked down at his bandaged ankle. The days since his accident had gone by very slowly and had almost driven him insane. With his movements limited, he was only able to open the back door and poke his head out, talking with Malik and sometimes with Donnie when Malik wasn't in earshot. The initial anger that Donnie had toward Chris had mostly abated with just flashes of it now and again. At those times, Miles asked him about Lucy and the things they would be doing once they were out. That seemed to work.

He shuffled down his bed toward the steps, sliding his ankle over the edge with care. He turned over onto his stomach and groped for the ladder with his good foot, hopping down the rungs until he was on the floor. He gingerly placed his foot down to take some of his weight. It hurt, but it wasn't as bad as it had been. The pain had been easing each day, and he was able to place a good deal of his weight on it now, although it had to be done with care.

He hobbled over to the toilet and slumped down on the seat, squirming to pull his trousers down. As he relieved himself and stared across at his solitary pile of clothes waiting for him, a cold shiver ran through his body. At first, he thought it was just the temperature drop from the warm liquid running out of his body, but then the shiver was accompanied by an increase in heart rate and breathing. His eyes fell to the floor as he tried to understand the emotion. Was it nervousness and anxiety of the day to come? That would be understandable. Or was it the excitement and thrill of what was waiting to happen, the chase, the speed?

The sensations from these two opposite emotions were so similar that it was often difficult to tell them apart, with one easily mistaken for the other.

As he sat there, the slight difference began to make itself known. The chemicals coursing through his veins made his fingers twitch and focus shorter until the pulsing growth of excitement was undeniable.

He tried to shut it down, to stop it before it took hold, but he was fighting a losing battle. After all this time inside, caged, it wanted out—and what was a more thrilling way to let it out than to escape?

He pictured his mom and dad, the look of devastation on their faces at the trial, but that was a distant memory that held no sway over him now. He gripped onto the seat beneath him and began willing his heart to slow, his breathing to change. He knew only too well the damage that came from allowing that addiction out, and as he sat there, he couldn't believe his mind had ultimately learned nothing, that the punishment of solitude in this room for those years had done little to remove these feelings.

His mind tried to find an answer, a way forward where it couldn't hurt any more people. The idea of staying in his room, or even staying in the truck to his new destination, occurred to him but was simply pushed away. He was in trouble, and there was nothing he could do to stop it.

Chapter 64

William sat on his bed, unable to move. The day had finally arrived, and he was now stuck between the anticipation of it and the excitement of it beginning. He wanted to give the anticipation a few more minutes of play before he allowed the day to take place. After all, it would only happen once.

His clothes were the only things that remained in his room, which left nowhere else for his eyes and mind to go. They stood out like a beacon, dulling everything else around them into insignificance.

After he had allowed the sensations to grow and swirl around him for a while, he made a move toward his ladder. Once down he stripped off his pajama shorts and t-shirt and stood there naked. He reached out his hand toward the pile of clothes, and an odd sensation of arousal tingled in his groin. It lowered as he moved his hand away and increased as he moved it forward. He played with the feeling for a few seconds before finally picking up his socks and underwear and slipping them on. Next, he slid into his shirt before finally stepping into his jeans and shoes. Once complete, the day had officially started.

In his eagerness to begin, he had forgotten to use the toilet and became a little annoyed with himself as he had to undo his jeans again and pull them down with his underwear to sit on the seat. In all the excitement of the adventure, he had overlooked the normal, mundane aspects such as the toilet, deodorant, combing his hair.

That's okay, he thought to himself. *It all adds to the flavor of the day.*

Once he'd finished, he stood and turned to use the sink and his toiletries next to it. All done, he placed them inside the brown paper bag by the door and folded inside his sleepwear.

A few seconds passed before he ducked under the bed to his desk and awoke the computer. When he stared at the screen it read 8:37am.

He slumped on his chair and looked at the time again. Another thing he hadn't accounted for was the wait. His feet began tapping the floor like the wings of a hummingbird until the muscles in his legs began to ache and cramp, which made him stop.

He sighed and walked to the back door. He slid aside the cover to the small spy window to reveal a day that had already begun and was in full swing, yet here he was having to wait.

He returned to the computer that now read a whole minute later than the last time. He slapped the *off* key and stomped back toward his ladder. He banged up the steps as he climbed and slumped onto his mattress, his arms folded across his chest as he forced himself to lie there and wait.

Chapter 65

The stark room reflected the bright white light from the ceiling with almost no interference. Ed sat there in his empty room staring at his clothes. He had reluctantly packed and sent his belongings off after several prompts by the computer, and now they were all that was left. He looked up at the blank room that had somehow become blanker and actually liked it better. It felt like he was inside of a white void, a shell of nothingness. All apart from his clothes. They now stood out as a foreign object rather than personal belongings. They represented a choice.

When the packing bags arrived several days ago, he had the choice to pack them or not. He chose to, albeit reluctantly. He made a choice to take one step closer to leaving. Then came the information and forms he had to read and sign through his computer. He could have ignored them and refused to sign, but he didn't. And now the clothes were his penultimate decision. If he put them on, he was just one step away from choosing to walk out that door.

As the two options battled it out, he began rocking his body back and forth. He felt the war in several parts of his body now, his stomach leaning him forward to stand, his back pulling him away. His hands clasped to the seat with his palms lifting him forward, his fingers pulling him back down. His heels raising to take his weight, his toes forcing him to stay. He was in turmoil.

He could feel the decision he had made slipping away from him, as if he were on a conveyor belt trying to run back but being taken forward anyway; his pace slowing the speed of travel but not enough to stop it. And now he was getting tired. Fatigue had begun to set in, and his body was beginning to fail as his energy drained.

What would it be like to rest, he wondered. To just stop running against the flow and simply allow the conveyor to take him where it will. Would that give him peace or would it be handing over the final piece of himself to fate? He felt like he had been fighting against the tide all his life. That living had become a battle of wills. Now perhaps, he should just let it go. Concede defeat and surrender to whatever life had in store for him next without trying to resist.

At this thought, a sudden wave of relief washed through him. The battle stopped, and his mind was clear. He had stopped struggling, raised his hands above his head, and allowed his body to float freely with the tide.

He walked over to his clothes and began dressing as if it were a normal day back at home. His movements were smooth and his mind empty as he went through an almost forgotten familiar routine.

Once dressed, he packed his final belongings in the paper bag and sat facing the door. His blank expression now matched the room completely. He had let go of the controls and was in the hands of everyone else now.

Chapter 66

Donnie was up, dressed, and ready to go at first light. He had been counting down the hours as they passed by like years. He was stood facing the door, bouncing from one foot to the other like a boxer in the ring, waiting for the bell. His mind was blank, allowing his stomach to continue to do all the thinking. It wavered between the anger he felt toward Chris and the relief he'd feel at being free. From the hatred he had built up toward his parents to the love he felt for his Lucy. All of this switched around with every bounce of his foot.

For the first time in his life, he felt able to make decisions for himself. The veil of his childhood had been lifted to see the puppet strings he had been tied to that led back to the fingers of his parents. He could see the coercive nature of their love, the anger and control they had over him that had now been broken. He was a free man in mind and about to be in body, and the anticipation with what he was going to do with it was intoxicating.

He took a deep breath and bobbed his neck from side to side, loosening some of the tension that was forming. He had to stay loose and calm. His mind showed him the photograph of Lucy that she had sent that was now the only image he could recall of her. She had no idea he would soon be there with her again. He could imagine the look of shock on her face, the overwhelming happiness as she ran forward and grabbed him, as he held her close enough to smell. He pushed away those nagging doubts that she had run away with the money—as best he could, at least.

But then he switched foot, and the image of Chris was there, somehow sharper and clearer than Lucy. The exact details of her face he had forgotten, which made him angry. Why did the good memories evaporate away to leave the negative ones clear as day?

He breathed out in several short bursts to dispel the anger that formed. *Got to keep loose and calm*, he said to himself as above him sounded two soft beeps, the bell for round one sounded.

He stepped forward and rolled his finger over the DNA machine, and a second later, the front door clunked. He opened it and stepped forward. *Here we go.*

Part 3

Chapter 67

The early morning dew had begun to give way to the sun as a low-level mist floated above the stems of the glistening grass outside the garage. Although the day had begun several hours before, there hung around it an air of anticipation, a quietness that was as fragile as a glass balloon. It would take very little for it to shatter and the day's events to start—just a word or a presence would be enough.

Mike sat there in the garage, motionless, sensing the delicate nature of the moment, not wanting to be the cause of its collapse. He was thinking about the fragile nature of life, of the moments we so often miss and the things that can affect them. That, in this moment, everything was still, waiting, the outcome of the day yet to be decided. He wondered if the results were already calculated and the consequences simply waiting for them to play out their parts or if there were some tiny actions that would make all the difference.

A shadow passed in front of the door as Mary stepped inside, and the moment was gone.

She looked across at him and felt as if she had disturbed something.

"Are you okay honey?" she asked.

"Yeah, just getting ready."

He stood and began taking the van and the radio-controlled car off charge, both batteries showing green across the board.

She came over to him as he checked the readings and held him from behind. He stopped and took the embrace, their bodies naturally swaying in unison.

"Hello there," came a voice from the door, and another moment was lost.

They separated. "Hi, Taylor, Jeremy."

The two men walked toward them.

"Everything ready to go?" asked Taylor.

"Yeah, just double checking the battery levels, but it's all good."

"Great."

The four of them just stood there as a pensive silence fell.

Taylor hated the silence so burst it quickly.

"So, we're all set and ready to go," he said, just for something to say.

Mike nodded and continued with his checks.

Jeremy turned to face Taylor and straightened out his shirt. "You nervous, babe?" Jeremy asked.

"Me? No…well, maybe a little."

"Anyone would think that it was you switching places!"

He tried to smile. "No, it's just that this is all my idea. I'm the one who started this, and now the fate of all these people's lives are in the balance."

Jeremy raised his hand to Taylor's cheek to stroke it.

"You've done what you needed to save our son. And you have given these people hope that they can do the same for theirs. That is an amazing thing, and don't ever forget it. No matter what the outcome."

Those last few words stuck in deep as he tried to take the reassurance it was meant to offer.

"Hi, Beverley," said Mike from behind them.

They looked across as she silently came in. They instinctively looked down at where her heels would normally have been clicking to see a pair of flat sneakers below jeans and a loose shirt. Her hair was tied back in a high ponytail that took at least ten years off her. She looked like a completely different woman.

She held in both hands a heavy bag. Taylor and Jeremy approached her.

"Here," she said handing the bag to Taylor. "In here are the chemicals that will take care of the bar. Come over here, and I'll show you how it works."

As they moved to the side another pair entered the garage.

"Are we ready to get this thing done or what?" said Marcus, rather over-excitedly clapping his hands. He looked like he had gained fifty pounds in his sweatpants, t-shirt, and loose shirt over the top.

Everyone just looked at him, including Desi at his side.

"What?" he said looking at her.

She just shook her head.

"So, who are we waiting for?" Desi asked no one in particular.

Taylor left Jeremy with Beverley and looked around.

"We're still waiting for Jane and Peter, as well as Beverley's husband."

Beverley's eyes turned to the side, hearing her name. A blush and wash of anxiety rising in her, hoping that David would be there.

Desi nodded and checked her watch.

"Well, I don't know about you lot, but I can't wait to get going and get my boy out, and I bet he can't wait either!"

Mike came over to join them.

"Well, I know Miles will be itching to get out. He damaged his ankle a few days ago, and he's been in a great deal of pain.

Beverley's ears pricked up again. She turned her body to face them.

"Damaged how?" she asked.

"Oh, nothing serious," he replied. "Just a sprain."

Her eyes fell to the floor as the gears in her head began turning. Taylor could see a look of worry on her face.

"What is it?" he asked.

"Remember I said that the DNA machine could use one of a number of techniques to sequence the information? Well, some of the methods include taking the white blood cell count as a marker."

They all looked at her blankly.

"Sooo…"

"So, it means that the machine on the truck could have the latest updated sample with the raised white blood cell count because of the damage to the ankle."

"You mean it might not register a match with Mike?"

"Exactly."

"Whoa, wait a minute," said Desi. "How can we know if it does or even if it measures the white blood cell count?"

"We can't," Beverley answered.

"Fuck!" Desi yelled, and it echoed around the walls.

"So, we can't get Miles out?" asked Mary.

All eyes were on Beverley now, her face red.

"Not unless we duplicate the raised white blood cell count."

"How do we do that?" asked Mike.

Beverley coughed. "The best way would be to duplicate the injury."

"You mean I would have to sprain my own ankle?"

"I'm sorry, Mike."

The attention fell on Mike now as he thought about this new detail.

"Hey, everyone," called out Jane from the doorway as she walked in. The tense look from everyone told her there was an issue. She squeezed Peter's hand as she asked, "What's wrong?"

Beverley said, "Miles has been injured, which may have affected his DNA result on the scanner."

"Oh shit," she replied.

"Oh shit indeed!" agreed Desi.

"Okay, I guess I'll have to do it," said Mike. He looked down at his ankle. "Although…I'm not quite sure how."

Taylor looked around the room. "Come over here, Mike," he said, gesturing to a chair in the corner.

They all walked over as if they were in a playground, going over to watch a fight.

"Sit there and put your leg up on that block of wood, and we can hit the ankle for you."

Mike's heart started to race at the thought of the deliberate act of violence and pain he was going to allow. He nodded and sat in the chair. Mary came over behind him and bent forward, wrapping her arms around his neck.

He raised his leg onto the block of wood. "Okay, do it," he said, holding Mary tight.

Taylor looked around. As it was his idea, he guessed it fell to him to do it, to give that ankle a hefty kick. He took a deep breath and leaned back, but no matter how he tried, his foot wouldn't leave the floor. He stood up and took a few more breaths.

"Okay, I've got this," he said, leaning back again, but his body wouldn't do what his mind was telling it to. Mike peeked out from Mary's arm to see what the holdup was.

"Oh, for fuck's sake," said Desi as she stepped forward, pushed Taylor aside, and kicked Mike's ankle hard.

"Ahhhhh!" His shout was quickly muffled in the folds of Mary's arms. She let out a yelp of pain herself, and tears began streaming down her cheeks.

All eyes turned to Desi.

"What?" she said. "It had to be done."

Beverley walked to the wall to retrieve the first aid kit. She brought it over to Mike, whose eyes were as wet as Mary's. He began removing his boots to wrap his ankle for support.

As the room grew quieter, Jane began to shuffle her feet anxiously. "There's another problem," she said.

They all looked at her now, Mike hoping it wasn't something that would make this pain worthless.

Jane shuffled again until she was calmed by Peter's arm reaching around and drawing her close to him. His comfort gave her the strength to speak.

"Well, Peter is not actually Ed's biological father."

An audible gasp slipped out as the realization of what that meant occurred to them all.

"Well, fuck! I'm sorry, honey, but in case you didn't know, we kinda need the real guy who knocked you up for this one," said Desi.

Jane blushed. "I know. I've spoken to him and explained the situation. He said he would do it."

"Jane, you told someone else about this without consulting with us first?" asked Taylor.

"Well, I didn't have much of a choice, did I?" she answered.

A low mumbling began as the displeased crowd let loose their thoughts.

"What if he goes to the cops?"

"What if he doesn't show up?"

"We could all be in danger now!"

As the anger began to circle around her, a man's voice spoke from behind them.

"Hello?"

They all spun around, hearts in mouths.

"David," Beverley said as she rushed forward.

"Fucking hell," said Marcus, echoing everyone's thoughts precisely.

Beverley brought David over. "Everyone, this is David, William's father."

They all nodded at him with relief.

"So," David began, "what's the plan?"

Chapter 68

The mist that had been hovering around the grass was now completely evaporated, leaving the dry stalks to shimmy in the breeze. From across the street and down the road, Detective Brant counted the last person into the garage. He had been leaning back, out of sight, as they arrived, and now they were all present. He closed his eyes for a moment. His mind piecing together the events that had led him here and to the moments that would come. He felt his nerves begin to shudder somewhat like a mini earthquake, a foreshock that sent vibrations to every corner of his body. So, without thinking any more, he sat up straight, got out of the car, and locked it up.

He crossed over and slowly began to make his way toward the entrance. When he reached the corner of the garage, he looked down at where he had hidden the last time and thought of the fire exit door at the back that he knew would be jammed. He continued moving toward the open door, his feet curling beneath him to make no noise as they rolled over the surface. He paused at the entrance and strained his ears inside. He could hear voices—talking, explaining, questioning—and the shuffling of feet. It felt like they were all together at the far end of the garage.

Okay, he thought. *This is it.*

In he stepped, his movements naturally stealthy as he approached them. They were all huddled in a loose circle, all eyes on the speaker until a pair looked up and over the shoulders of the person in front of them, straight at him.

"Fuck!" yelled the voice that accompanied those eyes.

They all spun, recognition on many of their faces. Marcus instinctively reached behind his back and barely managed to remove his pistol from the bulk that was strapped to him and the tight pull of the stretched elastic of his waistband.

"What the fuck is he doing here?" he yelled.

"That's the detective who arrested William," gasped Beverley.

Jeremy and Taylor grabbed each other as they remembered the face from Chris's arrest.

Fear spread like wildfire around the room and took hold easily from the fuel of panic being given off from everyone. Everyone except Jane.

"Jack," she said, stepping forward.

Everyone stared at her in disbelief.

"You know this cop?" asked Marcus.

"Yes. Everyone, this is Jack, Ed's biological father."

Jaws collectively hit the floor as Marcus lowered his weapon until a sudden thought forced it to be raised again.

"So what? Is he here as his father or as a cop?"

Jack Brant stepped forward. "I'm here as a parent of a child, just like you," he said, his hands raised slightly.

"How can we be sure?" asked Desi.

Brant lifted his shirt slowly and turned around to reveal no weapon and no badge.

She scoffed. "Whatever... You could be the infiltrator, giving your buddies the intel to arrest us in the act."

"I can assure you, that's not my intention. And if I were here as a cop, I wouldn't be foolish enough to put myself in this situation in the first place. I'd simply wait for you all to make your move, arrest those who remained here, and let my colleagues take the rest out during the event. Anyway, I don't even think I'm a cop anymore. I sent in my resignation last night."

Marcus looked across at Desi, who was frowning heavily as he lowered the gun.

"Okay," he said. "But if anything happens or you act in a way that's suspicious, then I'm gonna end you."

Brant simply nodded and lowered his hands.

"Thank you for coming," said Jane, stepping forward again.

"Well..." He paused, not quite knowing what to say or how to explain his decision. "That's okay."

Peter came up and stood beside Jane, his protective arm around her once more.

"So, I guess we're all here," said Taylor. "We'd better get started."

Chapter 69

Peter slowly edged the unusual van around toward the exit of the garage. While the others were getting the equipment ready, Mike ran through the controls with him. It was all standard, apart from the cab's position at the back, which would take a little getting used to. "The main thing is," said Mike, "to get used to the accelerator so that you can ease up and connect to the truck as softly as possible." He slowed now and stopped several feet short of the doors to allow room for people to climb in without being seen from outside.

Taylor pulled Jeremy close and held him tight.

"It's okay," reassured Jeremy. "Everything will be alright."

Taylor pulled away and looked at him, nodding as tears filled his eyes. Jeremy stared up at the van. "Right, well, here we go!"

He stepped into the opening and walked to the rear.

Jane opened the cabin of the van and stepped up to the driver.

"Thank you for doing this," she said.

"How could I not? He's my son after all."

Those words broke her heart with love. She kissed him, her lips shaking through the tears.

"Come back to me safe," she whispered.

"I will," he promised.

Mike's arm was wrapped around Mary's shoulder as he limped across the floor to the van's opening. He sat heavily on the lip and winced.

"Oh, Mike," she said.

He just smiled up at her, his eyes full of the love that had never diminished over the years.

"It's okay, honey. Just make sure you give our son the biggest hug from me and tell him I'll be seeing him soon."

"Of course," she replied and leaned in for one last hug and kiss.

"Make sure Josh takes care of Korinna, won't you?"

She nodded in response as he shuffled to the back of the van.

"Right," said Marcus. "I'd better get our son out!"

Desi nodded at him, not quite knowing the right words to say.

As he began to step up onto the van, she grabbed his shirt and pulled him back down. She stared at him. All of their history, all of the emotion and memories swirled around her mind and generated a new sensation that she didn't know quite what to do with. She wanted to punch him and to hold him, to swear at him and to tell him what she had done. But none of these were able to come out. Finally, she looked down at the bulk of his shirt, "Don't forget to spread out the distribution of that stuff. Don't want the price to drop."

He smiled and patted the bags strapped around his stomach. "You got it."

He turned and struggled to haul himself up.

"And don't forget to leave that fucking gun in the van. You don't want to set off any alarms on the way in!"

He smiled and winked at her as he disappeared into the back.

David walked over to Beverley and gave her the once-over. "You look different," he said.

"Good different or bad different?" she replied.

"Good, very good."

She smiled and looked down. "I have all the documents signed and ready," she said.

"That's fine. Take them over to Ted at the office. He's expecting them."

She nodded. "I'm sorry I put you in this position," she said.

He laughed. "You did what you needed to for our son. I shouldn't have underestimated you for so long."

She nodded again.

"Will I see you when I get out?" he asked.

She thought about it for a second. "That depends on you. You know where we'll be."

He nodded and took a deep breath. "Right, well, wish me luck!"

"Good luck," she whispered as he climbed aboard.

Jane now stepped toward Brant who had been standing to the side, watching everyone.

As she approached, he said, "You don't have to keep thanking me, Jane."

She smiled and nodded. "Perhaps, one day, we could talk about it?"

"Sure," he replied. "Just do me a favor, will you? Tell our son about me before I get out. It would be good to be able to see him and build a relationship."

She nodded. "I'm sorry I hadn't done that already."

"You did what you thought was best. Who could have anticipated this situation would ever arise?"

They smiled. Brant made his way over to the van and climbed up.

Peter turned on the van as Marcus stepped to the edge and lowered the sheet that covered the front and kept them hidden inside.

Mary, Beverley, Desi, Jane, and Taylor stepped back and watched it roll out the garage doors, then turn into the street and drive away. They shared a collective moment of anxiety, a pause, none of them wanting to believe their partners were on their way and there was nothing more any of them could do.

Mary said, "Tea anyone?"

Chapter 70

The drive was a little shaky to start. Although the van steered like any other vehicle, the fact that Peter sat at the rear took a while for his senses to become accustomed to. Visibility through the cameras wasn't the best, and it was hard to rely solely on the screens that Mike had put in the cabin, and the covered windows made him claustrophobic.

He needn't have worried though—to the outside world, it looked like a regular van traveling along. Mike had added parts to the frame that made it look as normal as possible. If you really stared you could tell, but it would fool most passing glances.

Inside the front area, the occupants were being bumped and shoved around. They either sat or knelt down, but their lower center of gravity did little to steady them. As Peter turned a sharp corner a little too fast, Jeremy fell into Marcus, who then tumbled into Brant.

"Fucking hell!" Marcus said as he tried to right himself.

Brant, pushing himself up, couldn't help but feel the packages covering Marcus's body.

"What you got in there?" he asked.

Marcus looked up at him. "Never you mind, pig," he replied.

Brant's nature couldn't let it go so easily.

"You're heading to break your son out of prison and you're taking a ton of drugs with you? You're thinking of making money on this?"

Everyone else looked at Marcus now, seeing the bulk around him for the first time.

"Jesus, Marcus!" said Jeremy.

"What? I'm not going to waste my time in there with nothing to show for it."

"Isn't getting your son out enough for you?"

He blushed in the semi-darkness.

Mike was silent, trying to control the pain.

David looked across at Marcus and nodded with a grin, *You have to make money somehow*, he thought.

Brant just shook his head. He knew the life and crimes of Marcus well, but even he wouldn't have guessed the guy would stoop this low.

Marcus felt the look.

"Don't you fucking judge me, you piece of shit. You're in here breaking the law just as I am, so you can cut the righteous crap."

Brant couldn't deny it. In a way, he thought perhaps he was worse. At least Marcus had declared very early what side of the law he was on. Brant had also, but now he was crossing over, so he was really the traitor to his own moral code.

The van slowed to a stop as they heard Peter say, "We're at the place. We've got a few minutes before it's due to leave."

They all reshuffled into position. The air in the enclosed space began to get warm as the sounds of cars passed by outside. The noise was mostly lost on them, however, as the thumping of their hearts bounced around the hollow shell.

Chapter 71

As Miles hobbled down the tunnel toward the truck's opening; the pain in his ankle eased somewhat with the motion. As he got close, he saw another person in there already. He was looking up expectantly, his leg jittering on the floor. Miles bent his head as he stepped in and sat down.

"Hey," he said.

"Hey," replied the boy.

"I'm Miles."

"I'm Will."

As they smiled at each other for a second, another pair of footsteps could be heard. They looked up.

"Donnie!" yelled Miles.

"Hey, buddy. Who's this?"

"Donnie, I'd like you to meet Will."

Donnie nodded in his direction. William smiled back nervously.

Donnie sat and stared up through the tunnel. Miles could see his face flush a little.

"Donnie..." he said.

Donnie turned to him. Miles gave him a look. Donnie rolled his eyes and turned his head to look over at Will and asked, "So, what are you in for?"

Will looked at him, his eyes bulging. "Umm, uh..."

"You can't go asking questions like that," cut in Miles.

"What?" replied Donnie, shrugging.

Another look from Miles.

A small bang rang from outside as a door closed, and another person could be seen. They all looked. He was walking slowly toward them. Miles looked over at Donnie and noticed his chest starting to rise and fall that much quicker.

"Donnie...Donnie."

Donnie snapped around to him.

"Not now."

William sat there, his anxiety rising even more as the tension mounted.

Chris walked closer, his eyes rising occasionally to meet Donnie's. The fire in them obvious. He came in and sat down on the opposite side of the van.

"Hey there, rat," hissed Donnie.

Chris looked away as Miles spoke.

"Donnie, for fuck's sake," said Miles.

"What's going on?" asked William.

"This little rat," replied Donnie, "snaked me out and got me thrown in here."

All eyes were on Chris now as he tried to ignore the comments.

Miles tried to get Donnie's attention but was failing. He shuffled around closer to Chris so that he was in Donnie's line of sight. Chris jumped at the feeling of someone moving closer.

"So, Chris," Miles began, "it was your dad who came up with this plan?"

He nodded in response.

"Cool."

"Let's hope he doesn't fuck it up," added Donnie.

Miles stared back at him.

After a minute, Donnie spoke again.

"Where the fuck is the last guy? Who is it we're waiting for?"

Miles shrugged as they continued to look back across the empty tunnel.

Another minute passed before the far door opened and a figure shuffled through. He moved forward in smooth, robot-like steps.

"Come on!" Donnie shouted.

Ed stopped for a second, wavering on his decision. He looked behind him, but the gate was already closed and locked. He looked forward at the enclosed truck and the people waiting, his heart crashing against his chest. He looked away from the one who had yelled at the other three, whose eyes were much kinder. His body began moving forward again as he released the brakes, the automatic feeling taking over again. He looked down at the floor and felt dizzy, as if he were sat in the cockpit of his head, looking out through the windows of his eyes at the huge distance to the floor.

Once at the truck, he bent inside and sat down at the back next to William.

"About time," said Donnie as the automatic doors began to close. There was a clunk as the secure bar slid into place and a bump as the truck moved forward and disconnected from the key. They were on their way.

Chapter 72

Jeremy looked down at his watch. "They're late."

They all instinctively checked their own watches.

"They were a minute or two later when Jane and I followed them," said Mike as he looked down at the hands on his wrist that pointed to five past.

"Is there any chance they could have gone another way?" asked Marcus.

Jeremy shook his head. "No, they have to pass this way whatever way they take."

David and Brant looked at each other, the newbies trying to figure out if they've just put their lives in the hands of a bunch of incompetent fools.

Suddenly, there was a double tap on the van walls from Peter. "They're coming."

A sigh of relief floated around the cabin as the van started up and moved off.

Peter managed to slip in behind the second car back, keeping at a steady pace. The buildings quickly fell away as the land around them became scorched and barren. Low, long hills began to rise either side of them as they motored ahead, the lanes becoming filled with trucks and trailers more than cars.

As they stopped at the lights for Sierra Highway, a small station wagon pulled up alongside. The parents in the front were busy in a heated exchange while the kid in the back stared out the window, trying to ignore them. Something caught his attention now, though, and he sat up a little and stared at the van beside him. Peter could see his eyes looking at the fake cabin at the front, his eyes following the line of the van and then seemingly staring at Peter through the window on the side.

Peter's breathing stopped as the boy's eyes opened wider at the realization he was looking at something very unusual. His head disappeared inside as he turned to speak to his parents. The father glanced at the van briefly before returning his gaze to his wife and carrying on their conversation.

The boy looked back through the window again, his eyes now seeing the true nature of the vehicle next to him.

Peter looked at the forward screen, which showed the traffic light still red, willing it to turn before the father looked back around again and noticed the same as his son.

After what felt like an hour, the light turned green, and the traffic began moving once more.

The van and vehicles in front slowed as they approached the single lane slip road onto the N14. It was a sharp turn, and Peter took it. The station wagon continued past, the boy staring back at him.

A little while along the road, it joined the interstate fully and opened out into three lanes of traffic. Peter began maneuvering slowly forward, allowing the cars in front to pull out and away. He kept behind the truck so that the guards wouldn't see a similar vehicle following them, and by the time they passed through a section cut through a hill that crossed the road, he was right behind it.

The hills that remained on their left were a contrast to the open plain that spread out to their right. Peter banged on the wall again to let them know they were ready.

Marcus stepped forward and poked his head around the cover at the front, allowing the wind and dust to enter the tiny cabin. They were about fifty yards away from the truck that was moving smoothly on autopilot. Mike shuffled back and retrieved the radio-controlled car and controller from the side shelf. He slid forward again until he was near the panel in the floor. He turned the car over and flicked its power switch. A small red light appeared, glowing on the faces that were looking down at it, creating an eerie effect in the darkness.

He removed the piece of cork he'd placed over the syringe for safety, lifted up the panel, and handed the small car to Jeremy.

"I need you to lower this down to the floor while I bring it up to speed, then you gently set it down," Mike said to him.

Jeremy nodded and took the car. Mike slid forward until he was as close as he could be to the opening. He switched on the controller, and a small screen flickered into life on top.

He took a deep breath, his face wincing from the throbbing in his ankle, and started moving the left joystick forward. Instantly behind him, the wheels of the car began whirring, their pitch and volume increasing the further he pushed forward.

He looked back. "Okay, lower it down."

David and Brant hovered over them, watching the spectacle and feeling useless, completely out of their depth.

Jeremy lay on his stomach over the hole and began lowering the vehicle toward the floor. He tried to focus on the car as the floor thundered by beneath him like a cheese grater. As he moved car closer to the tarmac, he realized his hands were on the underside of the car. That felt a little too close, so he began moving them to hold the top of the car's roof instead. As his fingers released their grip, a sudden gust from a passing truck whipped the car from his hands.

A sudden wash of panic sprang from him as his fingers gripped nothing but air, and he instinctively lurched forward. Just as the car's front tire smacked into the road, his fingers were able to grasp the car once again.

He paused there a second, his eyes closed and his breathing erratic. He sat back up, bringing the car with it, his chest pumping.

Brant stepped forward and placed a hand on his shoulder. Jeremy looked up and saw Brant's hand out. He handed over the car and moved back to calm down.

Brant moved into position and tried not to notice the stare he was getting from Marcus. He got his hands in place and lowered himself down. Once again, the wheels began to spool up as the car was slowly lowered. When it was an inch from the floor, he looked over at Mike, who nodded. Delicately, he allowed the tires to make contact with the road, feeling a slight tug as it ached to drift backward.

"Faster," Brant said.

Mike moved the joystick further, and Brant could feel the car keeping pace and then wanting to push ahead. He gingerly let it go, ready to pull it up again if needed. It wobbled slightly but then held true. He sat back, his empty hands raised like a gambler showing nothing up his sleeves.

Mike looked down at the screen and began moving the car forward. He looked around the side of the cover to see it emerge from underneath him. He began moving it further forward, under the truck in front and out of sight. His eyes returned to the screen as he switched on the headlights of the car, illuminating the underside of the truck. He stayed staring at the screen for a second, getting his bearings, before moving it forward again. He could see the drive shaft spinning just above the car, the tanks and lines on either side.

As it moved under the cabin, Marcus noticed the road ahead. From the right-hand side, he could see Lake Palmdale coming into view and the road bending around its bottom edge.

"There's a bend in the road coming up," he said.

Mike continued focusing on the screen as he inched the car forward, squinting down, trying to locate the air intake pipe. There it was.

He moved the car closer and pressed another button on the controller that raised the syringe higher and into position. He lined up the needle's point to the pipe so that it was almost touching, then ramped up the speed to push it through.

The needle pressed against the pipe until the car's front wheels started to lift from the floor and become unsteady. Mike backed off and wiped his brow. Everyone was looking at him with breaths held.

He pushed forward again until the tip touched the pipe, but, again, the wheels started to lift before it penetrated.

"Shit," he muttered.

"What is it?" asked Marcus.

"There's not enough power to push the needle in."

Dave looked across. "What about ramming the bloody thing in there rather than gently poking it? Always worked for me!"

"It might work," said Marcus.

"It might snap the needle as well," said Mike.

"Well, we've got to do something. The battery on that thing won't last forever!"

Mike nodded and returned his full focus to the screen. He allowed the car to drift backward a little, creating a run-up.

"Okay, here goes," he said as he pushed the stick forward as far as it would go. The car raced ahead and was just about to make contact when the pipe slid sideways. The truck had started turning around the lake.

The car below continued to shoot forward and out in front of the truck. He quickly lowered the speed and maneuvered it to the side and back underneath, holding his breath to see if it had been spotted by the guards.

The brake light came on as the truck slowed down, but then went off again as it straightened from the turn, regaining speed out of the curve.

Mike wiped his forehead, his fingers beginning to shake on the sticks. Everyone in the van was unaware of what had just happened, so they simply sat there watching Mike look up at them for a second.

He took a deep breath and realigned the car once more.

"Is the road straight?" he asked.

"Yep," replied Marcus.

With the all-clear, a red warning light began to flash on the controller. The battery had been racing flat-out for longer than expected and was starting to feel it. He wasted no time and hit the joystick forward hard once more, and this time its line kept true. He could almost feel the jolt as the needle struck the pipe and miraculously remained intact.

He pressed a button that was taped to the side of the controller to release the gas and sat back.

"It's in," he gasped.

There was relief on some of the faces, but the others continued to allow the fear to show. After a minute, he leaned forward, focusing again on the screen of the remote control. Now he had to try and remove it from the pipe without crashing it under a wheel. He reduced the speed to allow the drag of the road to pull out the needle, but it remained stuck firm. He wiggled the steering column as the throttle was pulled back even more, and suddenly, the car broke free. It swam left to right, and each time it raced past the pipe, Mike could see the shiny metallic glint of the needle point still attached. There was nothing that could be done about that as Mike tried to bring the car back under control to retrieve it. The warning light started to blink furiously now as the battery drained away fast.

"We won't be able to get it back," Mike said in panic, and before anyone had time to reply, he swerved the car off to the side of the road where it scurried up the hill and crash into a rock pile, splintering into pieces.

He slumped back against the side of the van, his head running with sweat.

"It's done."

Chapter 73

Jane sat there, nursing her cold cup of tea with the others around the living room. They had followed Mary back to her house up the street and had been sitting in silence ever since. Desi was starting to fidget when Jane asked, "What part do you think they're up to now?"

They all looked at her, their own minds running through the same scenes and asking the same question.

"Look, Mary," said Desi, ignoring the question and looking down at her cup. "This is nice and all, but do you have anything stronger?"

Expectant eyes were on Mary now as she thought about it. "Well, there's some of Mike's beers in the fridge and his whiskey's in the cabinet down there."

"Perfect."

Desi got up and headed straight for the cabinet while Jane stood and headed for the fridge. Beverley smiled across at Mary. "Would it be okay if I made another tea?" she asked.

Mary returned her smile. "Of course, dear. I'll come with you."

They left Taylor sitting there, caught between the choice of beverage and feeling out of place. His mind had been racing, wondering how Jeremy was coping with it all. He wished he could have traded places with him. He finally stood. "I'll have a beer," he said, following Jane to the kitchen.

Desi returned to the sofa with a twenty-five-year-old bottle of single malt on her lap. She removed the cork and took a deep inhale of the stem, swallowing down the spit that had started to coalesce in her mouth. She was just about to lift it to her lips when the others returned. Mary placed a glass in front of Desi before returning to her seat.

Desi looked at it, then at her, and took a long swig from the bottle anyway.

They sat there now in silence again as they took sips and gulps of their new drinks. Beverley looked at her watch. "The guards should be out by now," she said.

They looked at her, their own minds turning over what came next. Jane closed her eyes; this was Peter's bit.

Chapter 74

With the floor panel replaced, the sound of the road beneath them dulled a little. David looked at his watch as they sat there, waiting.

"How long does that stuff take to work?" he asked.

"Beverley said we should give it three minutes," replied Jeremy.

Those three minutes dragged on forever. Each minute and mile taking them closer to the adult facility and farther away from home.

Finally, Mike shuffled back and knocked on the cab wall, signaling to Peter to move up and connect.

Peter had begun to get a feel for the vehicle, but at the signal, the pedals had suddenly felt as if they were made of sponges. His right foot pressed down a touch and then backed off as he thought he was gaining too fast. He tried again, and once more he backed off. Everyone inside could feel the movements, back and forth.

"What's he doing?" asked Marcus.

"He's just getting the feel of her," replied Mike.

Okay, come on, Pete. You've got one job to do, and it's the smoothest, steadiest job there is.

He tried to think of classes and lectures that were particularly dry, where there wasn't a hint of emotion to be found, to trick his body into calmness. He found one that even he hated and kept that in the back of his mind as he very gently pressed the pedal once more.

The van didn't respond, or at least it didn't feel like it, but after a few seconds, he noticed that the distance was being shortened.

That's it, smooth and steady.

When they were a few feet from the truck, Marcus lifted the covering to open up the front of their modified car. The sight of the truck's rear suddenly there was startling. If this was their picture when driving normally, it would surely result in a crash, so their heartbeats instinctively increased.

The distance continued to shorten until it was close enough for Marcus to lean forward, grab the bar at the back, and guide it in.

From Peter's position, it looked like the two parts should be bumping into each other by now, but he knew that the truck would come into the back of the van a little way before that. He was staring intently at the screens, making sure to align the sides to dock as smoothly as a glove sliding over a hand.

Mike shuffled forward and looked down at the locking mechanism at the back of the truck and tried to picture the reverse key that he had made. He leaned forward to look underneath to see if they matched, but as the van moved closer and its back slid into the space, visibility disappeared, and he had no choice but to wait for the clunk of success or failure.

The doors continued to come in closer and closer, and it struck them all that just the other side of those doors were their children. So close and yet so far.

The movement back stopped suddenly as the lock and key below them made contact. Not a clang of metal on metal, more like a gentle kiss.

Peter felt it through the seat of his pants. He wondered if he would have to accelerate more to get it to fix on or not. If he did, then it would increase the chances of a crash—or at least alert the truck and cause it to go into emergency mode. He decided to wait a few seconds.

From as close as Mike's ears were to the metal key below the van, he could detect the sound of metal scraping on metal, slowly and deliberately as the key slid into position. With his eyes closed, he could almost picture the two parts coming together and the lever being pushed back. In the next second, there was a clunk and click. He sat up beaming a wide smile. "We're on."

Peter felt it too and struggled not to ease off the pedal but to maintain speed. This was the most difficult part, as they were now two independent vehicles joined at the middle as one. Any variation from either would cause both to spin out. He took a deep breath and tried to remain as still as possible.

Chapter 75

From the back of the truck the boys could feel the change too. They all looked up at the sound of metal on metal and felt the click of the key going in.

Their faces ranged from excitement, to panic, to fear.

"This is it!" said Miles.

Donnie shuffled forward and leant toward Chris.

"Don't forget what I told you, rat. I'm still gonna get you."

Chris leaned away from these words as Miles gave Donnie a warning look. Donnie sat back again, trying to control the emotions that were flooding his system. He couldn't wait to get the fuck out of there, to get the fuck away from his shitty family and to his beloved Lucy.

Ed's breathing began to be audible now as his automatic pilot started to fail. His eyes began searching around him as if he was coming to in an unknown place.

Eyes started turning toward him as his breathing increased.

"I can't do it. I can't do it," he began mumbling.

"Can't do what?" asked Miles.

"I can't go back. I can't leave."

"Of course you can, buddy. It's all gonna be fine."

"No," he said, louder now. "I can't."

Miles glanced over at Donnie, a look of panic in his eyes.

Donnie got the message and slid closer to Ed.

"Look, I don't know about you, but I'm getting the fuck out of here, and if anyone gets in the way of that, then…well, they're gonna be very sorry."

Ed's shoulders continued to pulsate with each short and sharp breath. Donnie hit Ed's shoulders, forcing them back so he sat upright. "You fucking hear what I'm saying, freak?"

At these words, Ed looked up, a sudden spike of anger taking over the panic. He stared at Donnie, eyes piercing.

"Ahhhhh!" he screamed, launching himself at Donnie. Donnie fell off the seat to the floor and raised his hands and knees to protect himself from the furious punches that rained down on him from above. Despite his attempts, several blows made contact, flailing his head side to side.

Then, all of a sudden, it stopped. The pounding ceased and was taken over by ringing and a swirling dizziness. Donnie managed to raise his head a little, enough to see Chris holding Ed in the corner, struggling with all he had to keep him contained long enough to calm down.

Donnie sat up, some control returning to his mind, trying to compute what had happened and who had saved him.

"Calm down, just calm the fuck down," Chris said as Ed began to stop struggling and become still again.

After a few seconds Chris sat back, his hands up and ready to tackle him again if needed, but it wasn't. Ed looked down at Donnie and began to cry.

Donnie saw his chance and stood to retaliate, but Miles stepped in front of him, blocking his way.

"Get the fuck out of my way," he yelled.

"No, Donnie, we're gonna be out of here in a few minutes. Let it go."

He wrestled with the thought but finally stepped back. He raised a finger to Ed but said nothing. He sat back down near the doors, away from them all, to nurse his wounds and brood about what had just happened.

Chapter 76

"Okay, that should be it," Mike said looking at the others.

Jeremy nodded and stepped over to the side compartment as he pulled out a roll of tape and two pressurized cans. He stepped into the light to read which can was needed first before returning one for safekeeping.

He handed the tape to Marcus. "Wrap two strips around the bar with a two millimeter gap between them."

"What's that stuff do?" asked David.

"I don't know exactly," he replied. "Beverley explained that it's like a piranha."

They all looked at him with a frown.

"She said to imagine the molecules in the bar all joined and knitted together. This stuff acts like teeth, in that it takes a bite out of the joints and breaks them apart."

They nodded with some understanding.

"So, it eats away at the bar?" asked Brant.

"Yep."

"What stops it from eating away the whole thing?"

"That's the clever part. The stuff in this can has only one set of teeth and when it takes a bite, it can't open up again to take another. Whatever it touches first is cut."

Brant motioned to the other can nestled on the side. "And what about that one?"

"That one has two teeth, one on either end. It clamps onto one surface with one set, and then, when the other surface is introduced, it bites down on that and joins them together."

"So, it's like a glue?"

"A very sophisticated glue. Beverley is a smart lady."

David smiled and nodded. "She sure is."

"Okay, it's done," said Marcus from the front.

Jeremy stepped forward and placed a thin plastic straw on the end of the can's nozzle to produce a localized spray. He was just about to start when Brant grabbed his arm.

"Shouldn't you be wearing gloves if it's that strong?" he asked, looking worried.

Jeremy looked down and replied, "Apparently, the teeth have a very selective diet of only this metal. It shouldn't cut through anything else."

He didn't look as convinced of this as he might have been, and the others looked even less so.

Jeremy thought for a moment. "Do we have any gloves?" he asked.

Everyone else looked around the sparse van and eventually replied in unison, "Nope."

Jeremy rolled his eyes and returned them to the bar. He shook the can and raised the end of the straw to the gap between the tape. He paused with a moment of doubt, screwed his face up in expectation of pain, and pressed the cap.

A slow stream of liquid blew out and onto the bar, and at once, a thin line began to appear between them. As the spray began to slow down, Jeremy removed it and shook it again. A drip landed on the bar below the tape and created a neat circle etched into it.

"Shit," said Jeremy.

"What?"

"I spilled a drop and made a dent."

Marcus came forward to look. "It's okay. When we put it back, we'll turn it around the other way. Just be careful with the rest!"

Jeremy nodded and returned the straw to the gap to continue spraying as close to the wall of the opening as possible to keep the cut thin. When he reached the last part, the weight of the top section of bar fell and crushed the straw with an unusually large clang for the distance it fell.

Jeremy didn't have to say anything; they all knew it was finished.

He tried to slide the bar out of place, but the weight was too much. Marcus and Brant stepped forward to help. Once it was out of the way, there was nothing that now remained between them and their boys.

Chapter 77

From inside the back of the truck, the air pressure changed and a crack in the door was visible. There had been no movement or excessive sounds like cutting, explosions, or helicopters whisking them away, and with disappointing ease, the door swung open.

Across the space, five boys and five men stared at each other, searching for recognition as if they were at the airport terminal watching the arrival gate for that one face they'd been waiting for.

Chris saw it first. He stood up and walked to his father. They held each other tight, their first contact in what felt like forever.

Donnie stood and walked toward his father. A mixture of love and anger flowed through him, and he didn't know how to express either until his dad drew him near and hugged him. He allowed the relief to escape and hugged him back.

William found his father at the back. He had never really hugged him before. David had always insisted on shaking William's hand like an adult, to get him ready to be a man, but the gesture now seemed a little too detached, so he just stood there.

David looked around at the other fathers hugging their children and stepped forward to do the same. It felt unusual and yet comforting, and he wondered why he had never done it before.

Brant walked into the back of the truck and sat next to Ed, who was curled up in the corner.

"Ed," he said softly.

Ed turned at the sound of his name from an unfamiliar voice. His questioning eyes finding its origin.

"Who are you?" he asked.

Brant's eyes remained on his. "I'm your father," he replied. "Your biological father."

A deep furrow formed on Ed's forehead, and his eyes searched for meaning in those words.

"It's a long story, but one I hope will make sense when your mom explains."

Ed looked behind Brant at the others and asked, "Where's my dad?"

"He's driving the van. Come on. Let's get you over."

As the bodies cleared a little, Miles looked down to see his father on the floor. He hobbled over to him with a smile.

"What happened to you?" he asked, joining his father.

Mike pulled him close and breathed in his son's fragrance for the first time in years. His tears flowed at what had been taken away from him for all this time. His mind knew it would be many more years until he had his son in his arms again, and his body wouldn't let him go.

Eventually, Miles pulled his head back. "It's okay, Dad. I'm out now. So, what happened to your leg?"

Mike's waterlogged eyes fell on Miles's with the pain of now having to tell him how he was now free and how he was going to remain so.

"Miles," began Mike. "I had to injure my leg like yours in case the DNA machines would register the damage."

Miles laughed at him. "Why would they need to register the damage in your leg?"

Mike couldn't find the words. Miles looked around at all the fathers who were stood there, and the penny finally dropped.

"No, Dad…no."

"I'm sorry, son. It's the only way."

The other boys looked down at Miles and wondered what he was talking about.

"You can't take my place. It's not fair."

"I know, son, but it's what a father does to keep his child safe."

Chris looked up at Jeremy. "Dad?"

Jeremy nodded. "It's true. The only way to make sure you get out and stay out is for us to replace you."

Stunned looks now fell on the faces of the rest of the boys. They looked at their fathers now, aware of the sacrifice they were prepared to make for them.

Fathers and sons began to embrace again, tighter than before, aware that this was a farewell as well as a hello. Ed looked up at the man he had only just met, stepped forward, held him tight. Brant didn't know what to do at first, but then he allowed his arms to fold around his son and hold him for the first time; his heart recognizing the love that had been missing for so long.

From the cabin of the van, Peter scanned the horizon on the screen to keep the connection between the vehicles stable as the road gently bent around the sparse landscape. He squinted into the dazzling picture of the road ahead now, and his eyes opened wide. He banged on the wall and shouted, "Guys, we've got a problem!"

Chapter 78

The mood around the living room table had begun to ease somewhat, lubricated by a little alcohol. Mary had been telling them about Miles, how he used to enjoy playing in the park behind the house. His favorite was the roundabout, and he would beg to be spun faster and faster until he could barely hold on. Mary couldn't look as Mike grabbed the rail as it passed and flung it forward again and again.

"The playground wasn't quite the same once they removed the roundabout after complaints of it being dangerous."

Desi scoffed. "Fucking state, sticking its nose into places it don't belong."

"They were only trying to keep the kids safe," Mary replied.

"But where does the line end? They try to control every aspect of your life so you become a scared simpleton, too afraid to speak up and challenge them."

The room fell silent until Taylor spoke. "There is something to that," he agreed.

Desi looked up at him, surprised at her ally.

"Have you heard about the changes coming to our currency?" he asked.

There were shakes of the head all round.

"Our banks got rid of paper money a while ago, which seemed okay at the time. Sure, those who worked cash-in-hand or did jobs on the side were furious at now having all their income taxed, and those who sold illegal items had difficulty explaining any additional income, but it was sold as a fair way for everyone to pay their share."

"You don't have to tell me that," Desi said with a knowing nod.

"But the next phase is for the Bank of America to introduce its own cryptocurrency into the market."

"So what?"

"The cryptocurrency will begin to be phased in to replace digital money. It'll be done gradually by offering better rates and generous discounts if used, but this type of currency is programmable."

They all looked a little lost as to the meaning of this, until Beverley got it.

"You mean it can be programmed to be spent on some things and not others?" she said.

"Exactly! If the government thinks you should lose weight, then it won't allow you to buy that burger and fries. It'll decline the payment and only allow your money to be spent on salad."

"What? Get the fuck out of here," said Desi.

"That's not all. If the government wants you to buy more American goods, then it will limit how much foreign goods you can spend your money on, or even worse, if it wants to control the price of stocks on the market, it can increase the sales from these companies by reducing the allowance that people can spend on the others."

"But surely they can't control how you spend your money like that?" asked Mary.

"Really? Why not?" replied Taylor. "They'll do it all in the name of protecting their citizens and being able to control the unpredictable nature and fluctuations in energy prices, food distribution, and improving health. But the outcome will be the same."

"Where did you hear this?" asked Jane.

"It's been talked about for a long time. Hell, the former British chancellor even spoke about it in a speech!"

"But that's not here," she replied.

"If it's there, then it's here."

They sat there feeling even more despondent than before.

"Well, that's fucking cheered us up! Thanks, Taylor," said Desi, wishing she had kept her mouth shut.

He gave an apologetic smile and sat back in his seat.

Jane looked down at her watch, which caused everyone else to do the same. The few minutes that had passed since they'd last looked felt like days.

Chapter 79

Jeremy leaned toward the cab and shouted, "What's up?"

He could hear Peter's voice ring through the wall. "There's a sharp turn coming up. I'm not going to be able to keep it together."

Panic spread around the walls of the van along with those words as they started their rushed farewells.

Marcus pulled his son closer before slapping his back and releasing him. Donnie did the same and felt something thick and soft beneath his father's shirt.

"What's that?" he asked, looking down.

"Ummm, it's nothing."

Donnie lifted up the front of his father's t-shirt enough to see a mule pack wrapped around.

"You're fucking kidding me? You're going in to sell drugs! So, this isn't about getting me out at all. It's about you making money!"

"No son, no. But why not make hay while the sun shines eh?"

"Get away from me." Donnie backed away, the feeling of respect he had only just found for his father eaten away in one gulp by anger.

Marcus stood there alone and pathetic, watching his son move away from him in mind as well as body. He looked down at the floor and shuffled into the truck.

Ed stepped back from Brant, a little embarrassed at the embrace they shared.

"Thank you," he said.

"No problem," replied Brant, his hand out. Ed took it. "We'll talk again soon. You know your mom and dad are pretty incredible people."

Ed smiled and nodded, stepping back into the van.

"Be good," said Jeremy as he held Chris one more time. "And be nice to your sister. She's missed you."

"I will," replied Chris.

Jeremy kissed his forehead, his eyes wet from the pain of saying goodbye to his son once more.

"I'll write," he said as he moved toward the truck.

"In code?" Chris replied with a laugh.

"Thanks, dad," William said.

"It's okay, son. It's my fault to begin with. I hope you can forgive me?"

"Of course. Will Mom be waiting at the house for me?"

"Well, you won't be able to go back to the house…for safety reasons. You'll be staying at the beach house."

William accepted this and smiled. He liked the beach house. David stood there, knowing that the situation he had put his wife into was a pathetic attempt at control and came from a place of anger and need that was deep inside him. The way his son was looking at him now, full of admiration at the sacrifice he was giving churned his stomach and the thought of what his son's face would be like once he was told that his dad had negotiated the house and savings for his freedom, broke his heart.

"Listen, Will, tell your mother to contact me as soon as possible, will you?"

"Of course."

He pulled is son close again, taking a last hug, savoring the thing he had only just found.

Mike's arms still couldn't let his son go. The pain that had been there from the time he saw him lying in the hospital bed, from the court case and sentencing, to the lonely nights thinking about what he could have done differently…it all came flooding out. He was about to lose his son again, with his wife unable to comfort him as before. He was going to be without both for the first time in his life.

Another frantic bang on the walls echoed. "Guys, it's getting close!"

"Mike," called Jeremy.

Mike pulled Miles closer and kissed his cheek. "I'll see you soon, son. I love you."

"I love you too, Dad," Miles cried as his father was helped into the back of the truck.

There was a pause as they stared across the space at each other, a raft of emotions flowing between them, until Chris asked, "So now what?"

"Fuck!" Jeremey let out and flew from his seat. He rushed to the side compartment and pulled out the other spray can to give to him.

"Listen, once the doors are closed, spray this on the bottom section of the bar, then maneuver the top section into place, and it should knit together. If it looks like it needs it, give it another spray around the edges."

"What?"

More bangs on the wall meant they were out of time.

"Trust me," Jeremy said and closed the doors behind him as he backed into the transport truck.

As he did so, the bar came into view. Chris shook the can and sprayed a layer on the surface of the bottom section as instructed, but when he tried to move the top bar into place, it wouldn't budge.

The others watched him struggle before leaping up to help. They each grabbed a section and heaved it upward. Their combined teamwork brought the bar into place, and as it slipped down onto the other section, the line between them started to vanish.

"Holy shit," said William, as if a miracle had just happened before his eyes.

The join wasn't perfect, however, so Chris sprayed some more around the sides. Apart from a slight kink in it, a person wouldn't have been able to tell it was ever broken. He saw a little dent below as he ran his fingers over the tiny hole. He shrugged, sat back into the cabin, and banged on the wall.

"About fucking time," Peter mouthed under his breath as they raced through an intersection.

Slowly, he began raising his foot off the accelerator, feeling their speed slow slightly as the truck in front took the strain. They rushed past what looked like a deserted budget motel, still connected.

Peter looked down at the brake pedal, knowing it was the only option left. The slip road to continue on the N14 formed on their right as the truck in front edged them over the line onto it. He placed his foot on the brake, taking the weight, yet feeling the shape and edges of the rubber underneath. He willed the slightest movement downward, and with a sudden jolt, they were loose. The steering suddenly became heavy in his hands as he swerved and pulled the wheel this way and that to gain control.

The boys inside were thrown into a pile on the floor from one side to the other.

The truck in front had suddenly lost its speed as it took the corner, and Peter could see them crashing into the back of it. He pulled the wheel right, into the entrance of a family support center, knocking the row of dressed dummies that lined the sidewalk beneath the wheels as they came to a skidding halt.

Dust flew past the van as a shirt that had broken free from its dummy floated away. Peter climbed out and ran to the front of the vehicle. He looked inside to hear the moans of bodies disconnecting themselves from each other. He pulled the cover back across the opening, then looked behind him. The truck was continuing its way along the road, oblivious to the close call.

He jumped into the cab and made a U-turn to head back, hoping that he would get there without flashing blue lights behind him.

Chapter 80

The men in the back of the truck barely felt anything apart from the gravity of the turn and a small bump that could easily have been a pothole. They sat there in silence for a minute as the truck rolled on, trying to extend their senses to pick up any feeling of emergency from the vehicle.

The surreal nature of their position was starting to become apparent. They were about to be taken to prison without a crime, hearing, or sentence, and they were doing so purposefully.

Jeremy looked over at Mike. "You doing okay?"

Mike sniffed to hold back his tears and nodded. He looked up and smiled at Jeremy. "We did it."

"Whoa, don't go counting your chickens!" piped up Marcus. "We're not in there yet!"

The smile slipped from Mike's face a little, but it couldn't be removed completely. He still had the smell of his son still drifting around his senses.

Five minutes passed before David asked, "So what happens if that machine over there doesn't recognize any of our DNA?"

Without realizing it, everyone's eyes had been drawn to the small box next to the door. It and the one waiting for them in their cells were the only things that could bring this whole enterprise down, and there was nothing they could do about it except wait to find out.

"David is it?" Marcus asked.

"Yes."

"Well, David, are you sure that you're Will's real father?"

In the dim light, David flushed with anger. "Of course I fucking am."

"Then you have nothing to worry about."

The sudden seed of doubt that had been planted quickly sprouted as David thought back to the early days when he and Beverley first got together. He remembered the excitement and thrill of getting what he wanted and the fun they'd had. But then he recalled how that changed suddenly when he broke her company away from her dream and into a more profitable sector.

She had not left him, not in body at least, but her mind had been fractured by what had happened. It was a few months after that they discovered she was pregnant with William. Was it possible she'd had an affair? That William wasn't really his?

He stared over at Marcus. *You bastard*, he thought.

His mind raced for solutions, for things that would settle his fears, and it presented two for him to hold on to. One was the nature of Beverley. She was kind, loyal, and sensitive, at least back then, so she wouldn't have done that, not that early on. The second was that she had made friends with these people, this misfit band of recent fugitives. If she had any doubts about who William's father was, she would have told them. There was too much at stake not to.

He looked over at Brant and reconciled his worry.

A few minutes later, they felt the truck slow and make a turn, stop again and start to reverse. The tension in the small confines of the truck escalated until it was palpable.

"So, it's just a matter of rolling your finger over that thing now, right?" asked Brant.

Jeremy, Marcus, and Mike all looked at each other.

"Well, there's another thing that could be an issue."

David's and Brant's eyes opened wider.

"The truck has two locks, a manual one and an automatic one. When it docks into the manual key, it needs the guards in the front to hit the button for the automatic lock to be disengaged," explained Mike.

"You mean the guards we knocked out a moment ago?" David said.

The others didn't answer.

"Oh, that's great, just fucking great!" he said as he stood and began pacing the narrow gap in between the seats.

"Do you think your wife would make a mistake in this?" Jeremy asked David.

He stopped walking. "Not intentionally."

"Then once again, we are in her hands."

There was a swerve and a sudden stop in movement, which made David grab the ceiling. The van reversed until there was a clunk of metal.

259

"Well, that's one lock," said Mike.

They waited for the second lock, but nothing happened. Sixty seconds went by, and they could hear the beeping in the cabin from the second lock signal. Marcus raised his arm and banged the back wall as hard as he could.

Everyone stared at him in horror. He just shrugged.

Another few seconds passed before a click was sounded, and an unnatural metal-on-metal scraping sound followed as the slightly uneven bar was pulled up to open the rear doors.

The heat of the day wafted in but was still a relief from the stifling compartment.

Although it was open, none of them moved.

"So, who's going first?" asked Marcus.

Jeremy stood up and walked toward the box. "Gentlemen, it's been a pleasure," he said as he held out his finger and rolled it over the sensor.

There was a gentle beep, and the small gate to the compound opened, leading the way to his cell. He smiled at them all as he walked out and through.

Marcus was next. Another beep, and off he went.

Mike stood and hobbled over to the machine. The initial numbness from the shock of the injury was wearing off, and the pain was becoming very noticeable. He looked down at the machine, held his breath and rolled his finger over. It took a second longer than the other two, but eventually it beeped, and the gate opened. He smiled back and shuffled in.

Brant looked at David, who answered his look with, "After you."

Brant stood up, walked over, and swiped his finger. A beep sounded, and he strode in.

There was only David left. The seed of doubt had continued to grow, despite the reassurances of his mind. He rolled his finger and almost instantly a beep sounded. He smiled. *I knew it.*

***

Within the cabin of the truck, a guard looked over at his colleague who was yawning and stretching in the passenger seat. He leaned over and whacked his arm.

"Hey, what the fuck's that for?"

"You fell asleep again, dick."

"Fuck off. We're here, ain't we?"

They looked at the camera in time to see the back of legs of the last prisoner walking inside the facility.

"Hungry?" asked one.

"I'm fucking starving!"

"There's a McDonalds a little ways back. Let's grab some breakfast."

Chapter 81

As good as the scotch was, Desi found it hard to swallow. She swirled it around the bottle for a while before knocking back another swig. The burn felt good but did nothing to alleviate the excruciating pain of not knowing what was happening. She looked up finally after a thought.

"Mary, I don't suppose you have a police scanner?"

All eyes turned to her for asking such a ridiculous question and then to Mary with the hope that she might.

"I'm afraid not," she replied.

The disappointment was shared.

Desi stood. "Well, I can't take this much longer. I have to know what's going on."

"If you leave, you may miss them coming back," said Mary.

Desi started pacing, caught between the urge to know and the need to stay.

"Look!" Jane almost shouted as she stood and pointed through the window toward the garage.

Everyone jumped as if hit by an electric shock and stared. They just caught the tail end of the van as it pulled into the garage.

There was a mad scramble as they rushed around the table and furniture to get to the door. Desi made it out first. They all went racing down the street, crazily at first until they felt the potential eyes from the neighbors and then slowed a little.

They rounded the door just as Peter flung up the canvas cover to the back to reveal five squinting boys like some magic trick, a miraculous switch from the older versions to the young.

"Mom!" Shouted William as he leapt from the van toward his mother.

"William!" She rushed forward to meet him, flinging her arms around her boy, her breathing stuttering as she caught her breath and the tears of relief flowed.

"Hey, Mom," called Miles as he carefully stepped from the back. Mary rushed over and almost knocked him down.

Miles held on to her, breathing in the familiar scent of her perfume that he had forgotten even existed.

Chris climbed down and ran to his dad. He couldn't speak, so he just let his arms do the talking. Taylor closed his eyes, not quite believing that he was there.

Donnie stepped toward his mother, not knowing exactly how to react. "Hey, Mom."

"Come here," he said, dragging him toward her. She held him close. His mind was still on his father and the anger he felt, but he decided to let it go, for now.

Jane stepped toward the van with Ed still inside. He sat there as if it were a punishment. She climbed up and sat down next to him. The van sagged as Peter climbed in too and sat on the other side.

"Hey, son," Peter said gently.

"Am I?" he answered. "Your son?"

Peter's eyes burst. "You will always be my son, no matter what. I love you."

As reassuring as it was meant to be, the isolation of the cell, the stress of the breakout, and the shock of his father not being his father, broke something inside of Ed, and a solid steel safety curtain dropped to protect whatever was left of his mind.

Ed began rocking back and forth, his eyes darting around for answers in a mind that had suddenly become blank. Peter saw the change and held him tight. Jane began to cry as she leaned in too, wrapping both in her arms.

Desi stepped back and looked at her watch. "Listen, ladies, I don't know about you, but if the guys didn't make it through, then we've only got a short time to get the hell outta here."

They all nodded and began to file through the door and disperse. Mary waited by the door to close up. As Taylor passed, she grabbed his arm. "Thank you, for everything," she said.

Taylor smiled at her. "It took all of us to get this done, Mary. Never forget that."

She smiled and nodded and began lowering the large metal door into place. As it hit the floor, Miles stepped forward through the little door at the side, grabbed the padlock from where it was always kept, and locked it up. Mary looked at him, watching the scene as if no time had passed. Miles joined his mother as she took his hand in hers and helped him hobble toward the house for the last time.

PART 4

Chapter 82

The soft double beeps of the morning alarm began to bounce off the gray stone walls. Mike turned over and slowly began to return to reality. He lay there a while, disorientated, running through old bedrooms in his mind until he got to the last one. *Oh yeah*, he remembered.

He rolled onto his back and stared up at the lights that began to grow above his head. His instant thought was of Mary. He had woken up next to her for so many years that it remained jarring when he realized she wasn't there. He looked over at where she should be and sighed.

He shuffled to the edge of the bunk and climbed down the rungs. He moved over to the toilet and sat down with a cold shiver. The floor was bare and cold beneath his feet, with a texture that reminded him of his own garage floor. He would normally have already been in there by this time of the morning, and he was surprised at how quickly his body clock shifted to accommodate the change. If he was honest, he actually enjoyed the extra time in bed. What he didn't like was that the time was spent alone.

A month ago, he tried to calculate how many extra hours he would have had in bed with Mary had he started an hour later at the garage. When it came out to over a year, he stopped before adding the Saturdays that he often did on top. More than a year. Every second of which would have been spent holding his beloved.

That, added to the years he must now stay apart from her, formed a resolution in him. Once he was out, he would not waste a single second on something that wasn't with the woman he loved—making her smile and laugh and dance and sing. His heart ached for that time to begin.

As he finished up and began to get dressed, he looked at the wall behind him and smiled. There were several pictures stuck to it, the latest one of a young man sitting astride a beautiful black horse, his hat throwing a shadow over his face. To anyone else, he would be unrecognizable, but not to Mike.

He kissed his fingers and placed it over the picture…and on the one next to it of his Mary.

The green light to the back door was already on. The ground floor's time began at lights on. He walked over and hit the button, sliding the door back to allow the warm desert air to blow in. A waft of cigarette smoke blew across his face, and he leaned out a little farther to see his neighbor sat in the doorframe.

"Morning, Nick," he said.

Nick jumped. "Hey, Mike, how you doing?"

"I'm okay."

"Oh, Stevie said thanks, by the way. It was the solenoids after all. She runs sweet as a nut now."

"No problem. You've got to look after the classics!" he replied, his mind returning to Korinna as he spoke.

He stepped out and walked to the end of the short runway and into the small yard beyond. The basketball hoop drooped at an angle—this was where the previous occupier had hung himself. The net and ball had long since vanished. His view of the world only extended to the building ahead and to the side of his own, which was shaped like a cross. He would only stay out here for a few minutes. It wouldn't be long before the rest were awake and came out too. That's when the shouting started, the threats, the wads of burning tissue thrown through the bars. How Miles would have coped in here he didn't know. There were endless hours of emptiness where any self-destructive thoughts could easily find a crack in your defenses and drive you to do something stupid. He certainly found it hard to keep focused, even with his Mary and son waiting for him. He took a breath and knew he had done the right thing, and that thought above all others kept him sane. He just hoped it was enough to make it through the years to follow.

Chapter 83

A soft orange glow filtered through the net curtains to leave a soft, dappled texture on the pale wall across from her. The warm breeze that flowed around the edge of the open window brushed across Mary's face and caused her to stir. She lay at an unusual angle, her body on its side, but with one arm reaching behind her, as if searching for something. As she came to, the hand began to move across the sheet until it realized there was nothing to be found but an empty space. The hand withdrew to join the other in her chest, holding herself as she used to be held in the morning by other arms.

Slowly, she allowed the other senses to awaken, to realize where they were. As her ears came online, she caught the sound of the front porch door squeaking open and gently being closed. She smiled at this as the image of the scene below her was pictured in her mind.

She sat up. Although the bed was large, she found herself on the edge of her side of it, the same side she had slept on for so many years. She shuffled across toward the window and pulled the curtains away to peer out.

Her eyes squinted at the brightness of the morning, at the wide blue sky above her head that stretched away to the horizon. As her eyes lowered over the beige, bland landscape, dotted only with sparse spots of green, she settled on a figure heading out to the barn. She drew her knees up to rest her head on them as the figure disappeared through the door and into the darkness beyond.

A rattle of china outside the door forewarned of the knock and the door opening.

Mary turned her head. "You don't have to keep bringing me morning tea in bed, you know," she said.

"I know, but I want to, so make the most of it!" Her sister placed the tray on a small table in the corner and came to join Mary on the bed.

"How you doing?" she asked.

"I still can't get used to him not being there."

"It's only been a few months; it'll get better."

"I don't want it to get better. I don't want to get used to him not being there."

Her sister shuffled closer and wrapped her arms around her. Mary leaned her head on her shoulder.

Outside the window, Miles appeared, leading a horse into the open.

"Well, I know someone who's having a good time," Mary's sister said.

"Yes, he seems so relaxed and different here."

"Not him, I'm talking about my old Mary-Lou. She's not been exercised this much since she was a foal!"

They both laughed as they continued to watch Miles climb on the horse and get comfortable.

"He's a natural."

Mary nodded, feeling pride well up.

The horse turned left and right as the it settled with its rider. Miles looked up at the window to see his mom and aunt staring back at him. He waved, a beaming smile on his face as they both waved back.

His heels touched behind him, and Mary-Lou trotted forward, nice and steady. He took his time arching around the house until he was out of sight of the window. He checked back to make sure before clicking his heels harder."

"Ya! Come on, girl," he called as Mary-Lou sprang into a gallop, both of their eyes narrow slits as they flew into the wind, the dust blowing away behind them.

Chapter 84

Brant took his time getting up from his bunk. The days passed slowly, so there was no need to rush. Time seemed to move differently in here. The heat of the morning had already begun to grow, and the tiny vent in the back door did nothing to circulate any air. He opened the door whenever the yard came to his level, but rarely went out. He didn't want to be recognized by anyone he may have put in here and wanted no part of the aggression and violence that echoed across the yards. He couldn't understand why these people looked to be so antagonistic in such a place of solitude as this. It was as if the war they carried within themselves needed to be let out somehow or else its destruction would be turned inward.

He climbed halfway down the ladder of his bunk and made his bed. His mind had been so much clearer since being in here, without the workload, without the alcohol, and he found that some of his old military ways had started to return. The neatness of his room and his bed especially. Perhaps it was the small, stark room that reminded him of his quarters, or maybe it was the set routine of waking, eating, and sleeping that brought it all back. Whatever it was, he was pleasantly surprised.

Bed done, he dressed and put away his bedclothes. He looked down at his socks as he scrunched up his toes, then stretched them out. He had grown so accustomed to wearing his boots everywhere, even in his own home in case he was called out for a case, that he never appreciated the feeling of freedom such a thing could give you. *Simple things*, he thought.

As he continued to look at his feet, the delivery door slid open, and an envelope was pushed through. He gave his toes one last curl and stretch before stepping over to retrieve it. He sat down at his desk and opened it up.

On top was a photograph taken from a sailboat. At the bottom of the picture, he could see a hatch that led inside, and above that rose the sails. Behind it, rows of tiny office buildings began to fade in the distance and gave way to an expanse of water that stretched far into the horizon.

Behind the picture were two letters.

Dear Ed,

I hope this letter finds you well and in good spirits and you enjoy the photograph. When you are able, you'll enjoy your time sailing around the lake, becoming more and more like your old self every day. You'll enjoy the clean air, the water on your skin, and the sense of freedom that comes from seeing nothing but a clear horizon before you.

I have also checked on the likely parole time, and it's looking like it should be in just over two years. I know it sounds like a lot, but there is a lot waiting for you out here. I also checked the conditions, and you will be able to submit a letter instead of appearing in person. With your mental health needs, it shouldn't be a problem.

I'm looking forward to that day when I can get to know the real you better.

With love,

Dad

Brant smiled and looked at the image again, getting a sense of the freedom Ed would feel in such a place. He could almost taste the clean, cool air.

He folded it up and replaced it in the envelope, pulling out the second letter. This one was written on the same small notepad as the first, but the handwriting could easily be mistaken for that of a small child. The lines of each word like a wave upon the page.

Dear Ed,

I'm getting better. Thank you for saving me. See you soon.

E

Brant could feel the emotion inside as he read the letter again. It wasn't just the content that made him feel that way; it was the effort and care it would have taken Ed to write it. He was beginning to learn more about his son, a person he hardly knew and yet was a part of him. A part that had begun to fill a hole he didn't know was there.

Chapter 85

"Girls! Get your butts down these stairs. You're gonna miss breakfast!"

Jane walked into the kitchen to find the boys already up and finishing off.

"I swear they're getting later and later on the weekends."

Peter looked over at Ed and both shared a sly smile.

"What have you two been talking about?" she asked.

"Nothing!" replied Peter.

Ed just shrugged his shoulders, looking all innocent.

"Hmmm, you two are trouble."

They smiled again as Peter drained the dregs of his coffee. "Right, you ready to go?"

Ed nodded and rose from the table to take his bowl over to the sink.

"It's okay, honey. You can leave that. I'll be here a while waiting for the girls to finish breakfast."

He smiled at his mother, hugged her, and headed for the door.

"Hope you both have a nice time," Jane said as Peter approached the sink.

"Thanks, we will."

He was about to go when she took his hand. "Try to get him to say something today, just a word."

Peter turned to her. "The doctor said he'll speak when he's ready, that if we try to force it, it could set him back longer."

Jane nodded, knowing all of this, of course; she just didn't want the last words he spoke to be those from the back of the van.

He leaned forward and kissed her. "Enjoy your day with the girls."

"If they ever get up!"

He walked to the door to join Ed, who was waiting there, knowing the rules about not opening the door himself.

"Okay, buddy, let's go."

***

The wind blew across their port side as they motored out of Burnham Harbor and onto the lake; the noise of the outboard engine drowned out all other sounds around them. As they rounded the entrance and continued to head south, the breathtaking sight of Lake Michigan opened up before them.

Peter sat with his hand on the tiller while Ed looked over the cockpit at the view ahead and around him.

"Okay, Ed. I'm gonna turn her into irons."

Ed nodded as Peter moved the tiller away from him, squinting up to check the wind vane at the top of the mast. Once it was between the tail fins, he straightened it out and nodded.

Ed instinctively climbed on the cockpit roof and unfastened the mainsail ties, allowing it to unfurl over the boom. He slid back down and unlocked the halyard line and began pulling the rope as hard and as fast as he could. The mainsail rose higher until he couldn't pull any more. He reached down to grab the winch handle and began cranking it back until he was happy.

He looked back at Peter as if to ask a question.

"Yes, Ed, we can put the headsail up too."

Ed smiled and unlocked the headsail line. The furling genoa at the front of the boat became free and loose and awaited the direction of choice. Ed leaned over to the left of the boat to make sure the line ahead was free, then leaned back to the right to wind the rope around the winch and begin pulling again.

The headsail unfurled like a flag, flapping and luffing in the headwind. Peter turned off the motor and pointed the nose south once more. As the wind caught both sails with the sound of bedsheet being whipped over mattress, they filled out to a beautiful full curve.

Ed looked up at the tell-tales and began tightening the lines until they were all flying sideways. Once happy, he sat down and looked at Peter.

"Great job," Peter said to him.

As they continued to hug the coastline, Peter could see his university buildings coming into view. He felt so lucky to have been granted a position there, especially after his sudden resignation from his previous role. But he explained that he had needed time with his family after the incident with his son was starting to take its toll. They university understood and were also sensitive to the care of his nephew after his sister had taken ill suddenly. Nobody questioned the similarities to pictures of his own son. They simply put it down to family genetics.

He looked over at Ed now, whose focus was intent on the water around them, gazing up at the sails occasionally to make sure they were trimmed to the correct position.

The small Macwester Rowan 22 had been for sale by a faculty member. One look at her, and he knew that it would be the perfect thing for Ed to find something outside of himself to focus on.

The wake of a passing speedboat headed toward them; Peter spotted it as Ed's focus remained farther away. As they rose with it, then dipped into the next wave, water sprayed over the bow and onto Ed's face. He wiped it away with a smile and a look of excitement that, to Peter, was worth everything, including the guilt he felt for the man who was paying the price for it.

Chapter 86

David forced himself to remain in bed until the morning beeps had finished. His mind was already going over the weekly report and how he would reply. Frank had warned him to slow down to one or two letters per week. They had already researched and planned what communication would be monitored and what keywords and phrases to avoid, but the sheer number of letters would raise too many suspicions if he continued writing that many times a week.

He couldn't help it though. From the time he was in school, selling term-paper answers, he had always had an active mind and imagination that was bent on wealth and success. His initial goal of getting out of the slum of his neighborhood had grown into a feverish monster that enjoyed consuming as much as it did in spending the money that it made. But in here, now, was the first time in his life he was hampered in doing the things that drove him, which meant the swirling motivation had nowhere to go but inside.

Frank had sent him a couple of books on how to calm the mind and stay in the moment, but they were mostly full of bullshit, as far as he was concerned. He highly doubted the exaggerated claims of the authors. There were a couple of things, however, that he did think might be useful to try. One of which was to delay the next activity for a few minutes in order to slow down the racing thoughts and notice the "here and now."

As he lay there on the bed, counting down the minute that followed the beeps, all he could focus on was getting the next second over with.

When he got to sixty, he immediately climbed out of bed, sat at the desk, and brought out the most recent notepad. Several full ones were already piled up in the back corner where this one would shortly be housed. He had been thinking about a way to restructure two companies he recently purchased in order to make them a single entity, allowing the pension fund to be reduced and with the excess funneled out—this time, with somebody other than a family member taking the fall.

Once he had the initial idea down, he stopped and looked around at the bare walls surrounding him. He tried to picture the deep mahogany boardroom that he practically lived in, the smell of the polish, the feel of the plush furniture, and the wide windows that overlooked the city. He turned back toward the table and imagined it to be the solid leather-topped desk from his office. These were the things that really allowed him to remain calm, not the breathing and mindfulness exercises, but the remembrance of all that was important and all that was waiting for him when he was free. It didn't matter that he had appointed several directors to take the bulk of the work; his mind was always there.

A guilty pang sprang up from his stomach as he remembered his son and the look on his face in the back of the van; the feeling of pride in himself for doing something selfless. He had tried to keep that feeling alive by writing occasionally, but he was so busy managing work from a distance that it had slipped by the wayside. Along with it went the generosity that had washed over him in the back of the van. When Beverley contacted him as he had asked, he just told her that Will had nothing to worry about—that he would be given a job as soon as he was out and to enjoy his freedom. The compassion he had momentarily felt during the jailbreak had corrected itself. He had no intention of handing over the things that he was paying so dearly for.

A thought suddenly occurred to him, and he flipped over to the next clean page of his pad to write it down before it vanished. He put a short title at the top to remind himself later of what it was about - *Getting the beach house back.*

He smiled to himself as he scribbled away.

Chapter 87

Beverley sat on the beach with a blanket wrapped around her shoulders watching the sunrise. Although she was facing west toward the ocean, the dark blues of the sky were already being washed into lighter shades as the earth turned on its unceasing journey. It was impossible to spot the gradual change of hues as a hint of orange began to stretch over the dunes behind her and into the distance. The sunset was more dramatic in this place, but she rarely had the time to enjoy it as much as she did in the mornings, before William woke.

She checked her watch with a sigh. She looked out to sea one last time and stood, brushed down her dress, and began walking back to the house. The sand felt cool as it pressed up between her toes. As she got to the rocks, she brushed off her soles and slipped on her sandals to continue. The house was just over the dunes and five minutes across the field.

She slid open the patio doors and headed for the kitchen, leaving them open to allow as much of the fresh morning air to flow in as possible. The pot of coffee she'd put on before heading down to the beach was brewing away nicely, the warm roast smell tantalizing her tastebuds and bringing a homey feeling along with it. She poured herself a cup, then turned on the stove and began making breakfast pancakes. The mixture of the two smells seeped out of the kitchen and floated around the rooms of the single-story building, sneaking its way under doors, winding itself around the folds and edges of the duvet...until it reached William's nose.

She had discovered it was the perfect combination to get him up and moving without having to shake him awake or shout through the door. After a few minutes, he appeared at the kitchen doorway, hair tousled. He scraped a chair back at the table and slumped down.

She turned her head. "Morning, honey. Sleep well?"

He yawned. "Yeah, not too bad."

She continued to cook as she spoke to him, "Don't forget to be online on time today for your course review. Miss Burfoot has put herself out to be able to help you, so don't let her down."

She could sense the moaning from behind her. "I don't see why I have to bother; I'm doing alright."

"You have to bother," she said, turning to him, "because you seem to be more interested in going to the beach with your friends instead of finishing your education. You were doing so well before coming here, and I don't want it to go to waste. I had to beg to get you into the Virtual Learning Program, so don't blow it."

"But it's pointless. Dad agreed to give me a job when he's out."

"That's not the point. I don't have to work at the school, but I choose to, for me. You know what he said last time we spoke. You need to finish your education before he even thinks about you working for him."

"Pfff, he owes me."

Beverley stopped all movement, shocked at her son's sassiness. "Where did you get this attitude from William? You've been gifted a second chance, a chance that most people don't get. I didn't risk everything to have you blow it all by hanging out with those girls and getting into trouble. You haven't told them your real name, have you?"

"No! Of course not!"

"Good. It's dangerous for you to be with them so much, in case it slips out."

Although he wanted to retort, he kept quiet.

She didn't know how long he would keep following the rules, even as loosely as he did, before something went wrong. They had the parole hearing in eighteen months, so they had to hold on until then. If he blew it, they would all go down.

She served up the pancakes and sat down opposite him. She smiled across the table, and he smiled back with a cheeky grin and a sparkle in his eyes. She knew he had missed out on a lot and wanted to make up for it, but it had to be within boundaries that would keep them safe.

Chapter 88

Desi hated this place. The pulsating music, the naked gyrating girls, the lecherous men; it was enough to turn her stomach. However, she was impressed with what Marcus had set up here. A perfectly legal All-Nude-All-the-Time dancing extravaganza where men were presented with every form of fantasy and desire right before their eyes, which could do nothing but turn them into sex-hungry slaves whose only organ capable of thought was their dicks.

And then there was the not-so-legal back rooms where the girls could take these men to release the pent-up urges that had been stoked at the front.

It was a perfect system. Charge to create the desire at the front, then charge to relieve it at the back. And unlike the drug trade, there was no growing, packing, or shipping involved. No stock depletion. It was a renewable resource.

Despite the efficiency, she had still made changes since taking over. The girls were treated as people with some ability to make decisions. She brought in several more girls that allowed longer breaks between each client to clean up and re-set. She shook up the men around her and replaced many of them with her own people. The girls would say the atmosphere was a much kinder one. Desi would describe it as professionalism that sought to increase the turnover of money while decreasing the turnover of staff.

As she walked in now and through to the back, the staff's eyes were on her, checking what mood she might be in. Although they hadn't seen it in full yet, she had a reputation for taking no prisoners if she wasn't happy.

She could feel them staring and liked the feeling of power and importance it gave her. When she'd removed Marcus's men from control, they obviously reported back to him through Bob. Marcus had gone ballistic, demanding they be returned and for her not to get involved. It was his business, and she was just a caretaker.

That was a red rag to a bull. She sent a very nice letter back to her "son" in prison, stating that she was taking over every part of the operation, that she was enjoying being in charge so much she had decided she'd keep it all, changing it beyond all recognition and keeping profits for herself, now and in the future.

The thought of her simply taking it all with no ability to do anything about it drove Marcus wild. He bounced off the walls with no way of releasing his frustration, apart from screaming at his neighbors and causing friction. He had been holding the drugs for a while, scouting out the demand and creating links before he would release any, but Desi's actions had reduced him to such a state that he needed some himself to chill out.

She wished she could see the look on his face when he found out the stuff she had packed was nothing more than oregano and flour, not the weed and cocaine he expected.

She went through the back corridors and into a room she had set up for herself as an office, furthest away from the noise of the music. She sat down on the leather chair and poured herself a drink. She raised the glass to her father, who she wished would be looking down at what she had achieved. She then poured another and raised it again.

"Thanks, Marcus, for everything."

***

The freezing temperature of the desert night gave way to the blistering heat of the day. Donnie woke and stretched before rolling over onto his side. There, next to him, wee the delicate curves and outline of Lucy. Her body reminded him of the mountain range that was just outside his window with its soft landscape and delicate surface. He leaned forward and kissed her skin now, feeling the wriggle of acknowledgement beneath his lips. Her body shuffled back, spooning into his as he wrapped his arm around her, safe and secure.

Since being here in Alamosa, he had felt a change, a release. It took a while for the realization that he was actually here to sink in. Away from LA, away from the world he'd known, and here with the girl he loved. At first, it created an anxiety, the kind you feel when you look down at the winning lottery ticket, checking and rechecking that the numbers were correct; hoping the feeling of elation won't suddenly be snatched away from you when you realize the nine was really a six. But Lucy helped with that. She had her own demons to contend with, and together they made it work.

It wasn't quite their dream, of course. It was the plan his mother had created to keep him safe. When he told her he wouldn't go anywhere without Lucy, she wasn't as furious as he'd expected. Perhaps she recognized her own stubbornness inside him. His mother had contacts here and arranged for him to work at La Casa Cannabis, just out of town a fully licensed superstore of weed. They provided him with a fake identity at her request and a small apartment for them both. The money they had saved was kept quiet and added to whenever they could. Their dream was still waiting for them, and they intended to make it there one way or another. The extra amounts of weed he stole from the store and the boys he got selling it at the local school all moved that dream closer.

He had wanted to write to Miles and tell him everything, but he knew it would be too dangerous. He had written just one letter since being out and that was to his father. It was not pleasant and was framed as a parent admonishing a child so as not to raise suspicion; but it was one that he thought was needed. It explained his anger about being brought up the way he had been, the disappointment he felt when he realized Marcus was using the breakout for his own profit, and the fact Donnie wanted nothing more to do with him. He was going far away to find his own path. He laid it all out there.

He hadn't received a reply, and for that he was grateful, but that didn't stop him checking with fear when there was something in the mailbox.

He pulled Lucy closer to him and kissed her neck, burying his head in the folds and curls of her hair, the only place he felt at peace.

Chapter 89

Along the back of Jeremy's desk, spread across the spines of the books, was the town he had created. He had delved back into them upon his arrival, to put his mind in a place that was safe and familiar. If he hadn't, he didn't know how he would have coped with such a massive contrast from the life he knew.

He sat at his desk now and stared at them, allowing his mind to wander the streets and alleyways he knew better than his own neighborhood. Passing along Stickle Drive, under the tall poplars that lined either side of the road, turning down Church Street toward the vicarage. That's where he saw it, the piece of cloth still hanging to the cracked balustrade that had broken off and killed the visiting clergyman from London.

"Yes," Jeremy mouthed as he leaned forward and began writing the scene in his notepad.

He spun around to look at the wall behind him that had maps, characters, and plot points stuck to it. He ran his finger along the path he had just taken in his head to check the angle from the police station to the church.

He returned to his pad and wrote down the details about what would be seen from their window.

From behind him, the delivery door opened, and in slid his lunch. Bending over it, he could identify some kind of potato and meat with the green mush of peas...maybe? Or broccoli? That was one of the things he missed most about being in here, a good meal with a delicious glass of wine. His mind went to that thought now, his nose picking out the invisible hints of berry and chocolate from his favorite malbec, his mouth becoming wet with the thought of a delicate steak falling apart on his tongue, his lungs taking back the mixture of the two swirling around his tastebuds.

He looked down again at the slop that awaited him on the floor and swallowed hard. *It will just have to wait*, he told himself as he picked it up and began eating, trying to keep the flavors and smells of his imagination intact enough to superimpose them onto each forkful that passed his lips.

As he continued to gnaw away at a piece of meat, his mind naturally fell to his family. What would they be doing now, what would they be having for lunch? It would be late afternoon where they were, so lunch for them had been a while ago.

He tried to picture the apartment block where they were, the rooms inside, the layout. He hadn't been sent any pictures, just in case there were any issues and it could be identified. So that just left his imagination, which mostly presented him with the noise and smell he associated with the city they were in.

Taylor would be at work, so that he imagined very much like it had been before. Maddie had been persuaded to come with them, the pull of the bright lights and big city creating an excitement in her that stomped all over the dread of leaving. Chris would be either in the apartment or walking in the park, maybe hanging out in the museums. In his coded letters, he had told Jeremy how he spent a lot of his time wandering around, getting his bearings, appreciating the freedom, and thinking about what he was going to do with the next part of his life.

The parole letter had come through, which gave "Chris" just eight months left to wait before a fuller freedom would be his again and Jeremy would be released. He had decisions to make about where he wanted the direction of his life to go and how he wanted it to look.

The walking helped with the thinking, and from the last letter he received, his son was moving toward joining the military. The idea of serving and being useful to his country, as well as leading a life that was full, excited him. Both Jeremy and Taylor encouraged it, pushing more toward the Navy, and perhaps something in engineering rather than front-line operations.

They didn't know how the stigma of being an ex-convict would be seen by the military. It seemed to be that you were forever paying for your crimes, that the prison sentence you thought was the only cost was just the beginning. God only knew what it would have been like for their son if he had been in this room for so long, isolated from the world and community so much so that he lost his identity.

***

Chris walked north, past the park. His wanderings had taken him to some interesting places and allowed him to discover more of the city than his fathers would probably want. The feeling of isolation he felt in that cell had remained for a long time and in this city of people who never look up, it looked likely to stay. But up here, he was embraced by people who took him in and made him feel welcome and alive. He looked different from them, sure, but they never let that get in the way.

When they'd discovered that he had been in prison for selling drugs, instead of shunning him, they drew him nearer. He felt a comradeship like he'd never had before. Many of their families and friends had joined the military, and by the look of the recruitment offices, it looked like a good idea. They encouraged him and even helped him earn some money before he signed up. It was only selling a small amount of drugs to the guys in suits in the south of the city, certainly not the same level as it was before, and the men he sold to were the ones in charge of the system, so he felt somewhat safe.

Time had eroded a lot of the worries about prison, and when he looked back now, it didn't seem so bad. He couldn't see how the adult version would be any different, so although he felt bad for his dad in there instead of him, he knew he'd be alright.

The New York Times

Prison System Failures Spark Major Investigation

Taylor Price, May 1, 2038

With pressure from the US Secretary of State and calls from our international partners, the president has today opened an investigation into the state of the prison system. The investigation team will be led by recently retired Admiral Sarah Levine, a controversial figure after her shakeup of the support provided for soldiers with mental needs when they've left service. Her appointment has been welcomed by the Department of Justice, who have little choice but to allow it to take place, despite its attempts at blocking it in favor of holding an internal review.

A statement from the Justice Management Division (JMD) that followed the president's announcement today said it "was proud of the 100% reduction rate of murders its facilities have achieved."

When pressed on the increase of suicides from 8% to 99% of the 267 deaths in state prisons, they refused to comment except to reiterate their massive investment in the service and its widespread use of AI interventions.

It is true that the AI interventions stopped the majority of suicide attempts, but the level of support that follow such actions is so poor, it continues to leave mental health scars and depression that further isolates the prisoner once released. The JMD refuses to recognize the independent study of ex-convicts by the Prisoners Lives Matter campaign, which indicates the isolation and level of aggression and violence they experience in their exercise yards (their only source of contact with other human beings) is a direct cause of the staggering depression and suicide rates.

Further to their findings, the report indicates the successful reintegration figures and low reoffending rates reported were not due to the level of service provided but are skewed due to the high rate of suicides after release, the bulk of which come from juvenile inmates who had been transferred in.

The recent high-profile suicide of Marcus Fuller, a resident of California who ran several adult-entertainment and gentlemen's clubs with links to prostitution and drugs, in one of these facilities further stoked the need for a review. It wasn't the death of Mr. Fuller that caused the commotion, however, but the fact that it was supposed to have been Mr. Fuller's son, Donnie, who should have been residing in the cell following his arrest for smuggling drugs across the Mexican border.

So far, the JMD have provided no explanation as to how this could have happened.

Donnie Fuller is still missing.

It is unknown whether the scope of the investigation will include the enormous budgets handed over to private contractors who refit and run these institutions or their links to government senators, but with the completion of this enormous task several years away, it is unlikely that any change in either the funding or system will be affected anytime soon.

Afterword

It was Fyodor Dostoyevsky who wrote, "The degree of civilisation in a society is revealed by entering its prisons" from his classic novel, *The House of the Dead*. He was a Russian novelist, short-story writer, essayist, and journalist whose literary works explored the human condition in the troubled political, social, and spiritual atmospheres of 19th-century Russia. Despite the number of years that has passed since then, the premise of how we treat those who have broken society's laws reflecting on the rest of its citizens, is one that still holds true today.

Winston Churchill said a society's attitude to its prisoners, its "criminals," is the measure of "the stored up strength of a nation" and in first-world countries, you would expect there to be a high level of this strength. However, the treatment of prisoners while in the system is only half of the story. What work is done to teach and rehabilitate prisoners? How are they brought back into their community once released to ensure they become beneficial members of society? Unfortunately, the answer is one that is poorly lacking. If this subject interests you, then I would recommend reading "The new Jim Crow" by Michelle Alexander on the justice system in the US.

In this book, the parents use codes to message the boys inside prison to let them know what's going on. I love codes and hidden messages, so much so that in my previous book, *The Black Path*, I have hidden such messages within its pages. If you can find and decipher the two passcodes and initials, head to my website and enter the codes to reveal a special gift. Good luck!

About the Author

Antony was born in 1973 and raised in Knowle-West, a suburb of Bristol in the UK.

He has had many experiences in life including the Royal Marines, as a behaviour specialist, a managing director, an assistant principal, a photographer, a hypnotherapist, and more. Each area he moves into is influenced by the ones that came before. He has written nonfiction books on behaviour and language based on research and work carried out in schools and has extensive experience with children and behaviour.

He is also a former Taekwondo Champion and coach of the British team and a gold and silver medallist for Team GB in the pentathlon series of Laser-Run. He has been featured in many books and publications and has also won The Prince's Trust Inspiring Leader's award for his work.

Other books include

The Black Path

Behaviour Language Scripts for Teachers

Find out more – www.antony-curtis.com
Follow me on Intstagram at Antony_Curtis_Author
#SoukDaddy

Printed in Great Britain
by Amazon